Earl Ma

Book 19 in the Anarchy Series
By
Griff Hosker

Earl Marsha

Published by Sword Books Ltd 2018

Copyright © Griff Hosker First Edition

France. I was given the task of ensuring that England remained safe and secure while he sought land in the east; he wished land in France.

Before I left Stockton, probably for the last time, I had decided to take a progress around the land I had defended for so many years. I knew that it would be a hard journey for the land would be filled with ghosts. There were few men left now from those who had first followed my banner when I was a young knight following my father, Ridley, to the Tees Valley. Only Sir Harold of Hartburn was left alive. The rest were all dead. Some, like Dick and Wulfric, were buried in my church close by my wife. Others were on foreign fields or along the borders. We had bled and we had died to keep the borders secure.

I now have a grandson, Samuel. His wife had recently given birth to my great-grandson, Thomas, and I would take Samuel with me on my progress. I had much to tell him before I left this earth. He would be earl when his father died. My family would keep this valley safe for all time. Samuel's sister, Ruth, would wish to come. Her husband had died in the recent war and, childless, she had dedicated herself to her brother and his family. She was also devoted to me and I knew that she would want to accompany her grandfather on this pilgrimage to the past. I could not allow her to come. We had defeated the Scots but that did not mean there was no danger. The King had come to an agreement with his sons who had rebelled. There was peace, of a sort, in France, Anjou, Normandy and Aquitaine but the King was doing what he did best. He was establishing his authority. Until his sons were brought to heel he and my son would stay in France. My son had only gone with the King because the King had asked for me first and William knew that I was tired. He and I had grown much closer since the time of Geoffrey of Anjou. The other reason for my progress was to show the people who lived along the borders that despite the recent revolt King Henry ruled this land and his Earl Marshal, Alfraed, would ensure that it continued to do so.

Part One
Shadows from the past

Chapter 1

Stockton

I still kept a handful of the men at arms and archers who had served me and they acted as my bodyguards but I no longer had a squire. I used Sir Samuel, my grandson as my lieutenant and his squires, Thomas and William looked after my horses and my weapons. I was old and if I had to use my weapons again it would be unlikely that I would survive. My reactions were no longer as quick as they had been and in battle that flaw could be fatal. The pain in my head increased each day and I was more and more unsteady on my feet. Brother Peter had warned me that it would be so. I pretended to drink more and let others think that I was drunk.

I still lived in Stockton but when I left I would not return. I sent for Samuel. His father, my son, was in France with King Henry. I had two sons, William and King Henry. Now I was the only one who knew that secret for Henry's mother had taken the secret of our liaison to her grave. Samuel had the look of both William and Henry about him. The castle had an empty feel to it.

"Yes, Earl Marshal?" He looked like me and, for some inexplicable reason, that pleased me. "You wished to see me."

I nodded, "I am going to drag you away from your lovely wife and son." He smiled. "I will not keep you away for long. I wish to travel to the border and let the border knights know that the Warlord of the North still rules this land. This will be a show of power."

"I do not mind. I feel guilty about the time allowed to me to be with my son. My father and the other knights fight for the King in France and I enjoy the peace of the valley. Besides, I would like to ride the borders in a time of peace. I do not think I have ever enjoyed such a time."

"When I have finished the progress, I will leave the north for I have neglected my duties in the south. I intend to ride as far as Norham and then head south. I have to ensure that London is well-governed. London is not like England. It is like a whore in a cheap inn. It will open its legs for any who has coin. The King expects me to watch all of his realm and not just the part which is most precious to me."

I saw, in his face, disappointment. "You will leave the north? But what of Thomas, my son? When will he hear the tales of your battles?"

"When you tell him." He looked crestfallen. "I am old, Samuel. I have outlived all those with whom I shared the trials and tribulations of the struggle to put the crown on King Henry's head. Wulfric, Dick, Edward, all of those knights now lie dead. I have outlived my time. I am just grateful that I can speak to you. That is another reason why I ask you to come with me. This will give us time to speak to each other. I would know your mind and I have things to tell you too."

He seemed to examine my face for signs of deception. I kept a neutral expression on my face. I hoped he would not see through my eyes and into my heart. He gave me a sad smile, "Then I look forward to the journey and hope that it might never end."

The tic inside my head suddenly flared and made me close my eyes. The one thing it would not be would be a long journey. I opened my eyes. "I am taking Sir James with me. I would have you ask Sir Harold if he might wish to come with us. His son, Sir Richard would also be a handy knight to have with us. With your father away, you will need other knights on whom you can rely. There are too many old men now, Sir Tristan, Sir Gilles, Sir John and Sir Philip all spend more time talking about war than fighting. The mantle of Cleveland is a heavy one. You will serve the next King of England and he will need you to lead knights on whom he can rely."

"And we just bring our retinues?"

"Aye but leave enough in the castle to ensure that it is guarded well. This valley is the most precious to me in this whole isle of Britain. I would keep it safe."

When he left to organise the horses and men we would need I went to speak with the steward and housekeeper. I had been putting this off for some time but since Brother Peter had given me his news I had stopped procrastination. As I wandered the castle I looked at each stone and step. I stroked each door as I passed through them for I was not sure if I would ever return. I took detours that were unnecessary just so that I could see every room: the beer and wine cellars, buttery, the guard rooms, the pages' chambers. Every room held a special memory for me. I saw the spot on the cellar floor where we had found the murdered priest on that Christmas so long ago that few would even remember it. I saw the room where Alice had helped the young ladies to make the tapestry of Sir Gilles fighting a dragon. I looked out from the gate where I had faced down more enemies than I had greeted friends. I peered down at the ferry which was our lifeline to the south. I found my steward and housekeeper where I knew that I would find them all along. They were both in the kitchens with the cooks.

My presence in the kitchens was unusual and Alice looked concerned, "Earl? Is aught amiss?"

"No Alice, I would have a word with the two of you. Come to my solar and bring a jug of wine and three goblets. I wish to drink with you and speak."

I could tell that I had taken them unawares. I smiled when they came in to my solar for they had done this hundreds of times before and yet now they looked hesitant and nervous. When Alice had poured the wine, she fingered the necklet I had given her some time ago. It had blue stones and she had been astonished when I had made her the gift.

"Sit, old friends." I raised my goblet, "To old friends."

They smiled and drank. "Old friends." They were both on edge. I had never been the sort of distant lord who just saw the livery and not the person but I had never sat and drunk wine with them.

"I am here to say goodbye. I will be leaving this valley soon and I may not return. I am of an age where I would say goodbye to those I love." They both looked shocked. "Alice, you have a cottage now close to the Ox Bridge. There is an annuity that will keep you comfortable. You have coin enough. Enjoy your life. William, your son John now acts as steward. Enjoy your grandchildren! You have both more than earned a peaceful retirement."

"Where do you go, lord?" William's voice showed his concern.

"Fear not, William, I do not go to war. My days of drawing a sword and facing enemies are long past. I have duties to perform for the King. I am getting old and I know not when I will return." It had been on my lips to be truthful and tell them all but that was unfair of me. They would worry. "We are of an age and know that we do not always have the luxury of a goodbye. I would like to say it now. None of my warriors has been more loyal than you two and my home and family would not be what they are without you. For that, I thank you and know that I respect both of you. There are kings and princes who are not worthy to have your loyalty. I appreciate it."

Alice could not control herself and she wept. William nodded, "You are right, lord. We are all getting old. I have buried three friends this winter last and who knows when the next will die. It has been an honour for us to serve you. You have done all for us. Our families prosper and there is no safer place to live in the whole of England."

I nodded and turned to the still weeping housekeeper, "Come Alice. You should be pleased. You can visit the castle whenever you like but you will not have to serve."

She forced a smile, "Lord, I enjoyed serving you and your family but you are right. Time moves on and we all get older. I am happy that you say I can still visit the castle. Master Thomas is a delightful bairn. Sir Samuel and Lady Ruth were older when they came here. I should like to see Master Thomas grow. If the Good Lord allows it."

We chatted for a while about the people we had known and then they left me. I clasped William's arm but the embrace which Alice and I enjoyed was held for the longest time. I kissed her cheek and she smiled like a young girl. I sat alone and looked out on the river. There had been much unsaid but that was ever the way with old friends. When the goblet was empty I wandered down to the stables. Aiden and his two assistants, Edgar and Edward were just returning from their game keeping duties. They had some rabbits slung over their saddles.

"How are the woods?"

"Teeming with game. With the Earl away no one has hunted them, my lord. You should take Sir Samuel out for a hunt."

I shook my head, "I have duties for the King which will keep me busy. That is why I come to speak with you. I fear that the tasks I have to perform may keep me from my valley for some time. I come to say goodbye."

Unlike Alice, the three knew better than any that life was fragile. We had all been lucky. Aiden nodded. "The best day of my life, lord, was when you and your father bought me as a young slave. You freed me soon enough but even as a slave, my life was good. I thank you. I would not have had such a long life but for you. It has been a joyful life. Even though you have become a powerful man you have never changed. You are still the easy young knight I first met. Many lords change but not you.

You have made me as part of your family. I have enjoyed helping to make the Earl and Sir Samuel into warriors."

"And yet you had no children of your own."

He laughed, "None that I know of. But I had Edgar and Edward and their sons. They suffice. I have helped to train them too. I know that there will be men to follow Sir William and Sir Samuel long after I am gone." I held out my arm and he clasped it, "You take care, my lord. You are a good man and that is rare."

Edgar and Edward, who had been two orphans I had taken under my wing, also clasped my arm. "It is the like of you three who are England. It is not the knights with the armour and the banners. It is not the merchants counting their coins or the priests seeking riches. It is men like you. I have been honoured to fight alongside Englishmen and there is no greater honour."

My goodbyes said, I could put the rest of my affairs in order. William came to write down my instructions. When I was gone I wanted none to question my bequests. I summoned Brother Peter to be a witness. When William had gone and I was alone with the only man who knew of my ailment I asked, "Will I become worse as time goes on?"

"That I cannot say with certainty. I believe it is likely. All that I know is I saw something untoward inside your skull and I know that you have had spells where you lost control of your actions. That may worsen. I do not know for sure. I would be happier if some other knew your ailment."

"No, Brother Peter, I would not burden them. I ride with Sir Harold and my grandson. When we have visited the borders, we will head for London. There I hope to see William Marshal. With the King in France, he needs to know that I will not be able to help him much."

"You will tell the Earl?"

I laughed, "I will tell the Earl that I am old! He will work the rest out for himself."

"Then before you go I will give you a draught. It is something we brought back from the Holy Land. It helps to numb pain and to ensure that you sleep. Do not take too much or it can be fatal." There was a knowing look on his face.

I nodded, "Then I will be careful and measure out each dose. There is not too much pain at the moment. I shall save it for the future."

My last visit was to the streets of my town. It had grown immeasurably since I had first Arrived. The single blacksmith's forge of Alf had now become workshops producing high-quality metal. The tanners provided many cargoes to be sent abroad. I went to visit Alf. He no longer worked. He had suffered an illness that left one side of his body and face frozen as though cursed. It did not change his mind which was as sharp as ever.

His daughter was flustered when I arrived at his home, "My lord! We were not expecting you and…"

"Sarah, it is the Warlord. He comes and goes as he chooses and he has visited me in meaner quarters than this. Fetch some ale from the ale wife." She bobbed her head to me and fled. He smiled, "When her husband was killed it gave me someone to watch over me but his death made her to me a nervous fey thing. Sit, my lord."

I waved a hand at his house. The only finer one was Ethelred's. "You have done well for yourself."

He nodded, "My sons all have fine homes and Sarah will have this when I am gone and that will not be too far in the future."

She returned with the ale. Mary was a good ale wife. Her husband had been one of my men at arms. We were all connected in some way. I raised my goblets, "To those who have gone before."

He nodded, "Aye lord. A good toast."

"I am leaving Stockton, Alf and I do not think to return."

He nodded, "Even if you do then I fear I will not be here. I pee blood these days." He shook his head. "Still I have had a good life."

"You have indeed and I am grateful for all that you have done for my family and for me. The mail, helmets and swords you have made for us have saved us many times."

"Aye, I did good work but you saved us too, lord. I believe we were lucky to have you as a lord."

"Perhaps."

We spoke of the early days and my father. We talked of Wulfstan and the other Varangians. His daughter refilled our goblets three times. I only left when I saw that Alf was in some discomfort. I am sorry lord but…"

"Do not apologise old friend." I helped him to his feet and embraced him. He patted my back with his one good arm. I strolled slowly back to my castle soaking in every stone and cobble on the streets. I examined every face and listened to every voice. All were precious to me.

We left a week later. Sir James de Puiset also came with us. He was the nearest we had to a household knight. I had four knights along with their squires. My four men at arms and four archers were augmented by another twenty men at arms and twenty archers. That was more than enough for what we had to do. We headed for Fissebourne for I wished to take my leave of Sir John. He had also been unwell of late. Too many wounds and a hard life meant he would not stir from his castle again.

Riding north I took a last look around the land which had come to be my home. Thorpe had seen many battles with the Scots and as we headed up through Wulfestun I could not help but glance east, that was where I had rescued Adela and I had slain Tancred de Mamers, the killer of my father. That was more than a lifetime ago. Sir Harold saw my look and said, "When we rode abroad in those days you had your palfrey Scout and I knew nothing about being a knight! I was still an outlaw who had been plucked from the forest by a young knight. We have both travelled a long road."

I smiled, "You read my mind. We have come far. You have grandchildren now and your son is a knight."

"And it is all thanks to you. If you had not come through the forest then Dick and I would have been hanged for poaching."

I studied Harold. He was now grey. He had had few wounds in his life. He was lucky. He had been a good archer but he had become a better knight. With Sir Leofric and Sir John, he was one of the first knights who had served me. "And now I take you and your son away from your family."

"Fear not, my wife has William, my youngest son, and he is a mighty handful!"

His son, Sir Richard, said, "He should be here helping my squire John or my brother, Walther but he is irresponsible."

Walther was a good squire and he would be knighted soon. I remembered my own son, William. He had been wild for a time but the crusades had changed him. "Do not worry. Young men have wild phases. They grow out of them."

Sir James asked, "Do you visit with my uncle, lord?"

I shook my head, "The less I see the Bishop of Durham the better. You must have all the good blood in your family for that man is a snake and I know not how he still has his head." The Bishop of Durham had been involved in a plot against the King and I had been convinced that he would be punished but the wily Bishop had managed to convince the King that he could help to intervene in the matter of Thomas Becket. He had been forgiven.

Sir James laughed, "He thinks just as highly of you, lord!"

My knights laughed. Sir James had burned the bridges with his uncle. He served me and was a loyal bachelor knight. We rode to Fissebourne and stayed the night. I was too old to camp and I had planned our progress using the castles of the north.

Sir John was the knight closest to the Scots although he was still fifty miles from the border. He acted as a lookout for us. "The Scots will not recover, lord, not in my lifetime anyway. The merchants who pass south speak of the reparations the Scots have to pay. With English garrisons in the five largest castles, I think we have finished fighting the Scots."

I was relieved. When I left the north to head south my land would be secure. Samuel and my knights could control it.

Sir James had been a knight of Durham. He was also well-travelled and understood the politics of court. He was the one who raised the other issue, "And rebels? What of those who support the young Henry? King Henry has crowned his son joint king. What if other lords support him?"

The Bishop's nephew was right. Henry, Richard and Geoffrey all sought the crown. I think that was why the King kept his youngest son, John, with him. I sipped the wine, "We remain vigilant. Luckily the knights of the north are loyal."

He was like a dog with a bone. "That is because you are here, lord. When you go…?"

He was right but I put on a brave face, "Until my son returns then you support Sir Samuel. He will be lord of the north until the Earl returns."

"That is a great responsibility, grandfather."

Sir Harold said, "The Earl had such responsibility when he was your age. You have good men around you. Do as your grandfather did and trust them."

When we left to head north I began to worry, not about the situation in the north, but further south. With the King in France along with my son those lords and barons who supported Richard and Young Henry might well seek to make mischief. We rode as far as the Bishop's castle at Berwick and we found the land safe and secure. We were greeted like conquering heroes by the farmers and burghers of the towns. That was the best way to measure peace. They felt safe and secure. We passed the bastion of Norham. Although it was the castle of the Bishop of Durham the constable was a good man. It had fallen before and we had improved it so that it was as impregnable as any castle in England. We called in at Rothbury and then headed over to Brougham Castle and finally Carlisle. There the Constable confirmed the peace and the subjugated nature of the

Scots. It was when we reached Carlisle that the letter sent from the King finally found me. Edward and Edgar had cut across country to deliver it. It came from the King and it asked me to go to Chester to deal with a problem in that area. I did not divulge the contents of the letter to the others. I would wait until I had seen the problem first hand. They also handed me another letter from Sir Leofric. That one I kept even closer to my breast.

We headed south to Chester. I considered letting most of my men return home but, as we headed south down the fertile Lancashire plain, it became obvious that Samuel and the others had no intention of abandoning me.

Chester was problematic. The Earl of Chester, Hugh of Cyfeiliog, had joined the rebellion against the King. Captured with his mercenaries he was now held prisoner by King Henry. I did not care what happened to the Earl; he was a rebel. His absence, however, might encourage the Welsh and they were ever eager to eat into English land. The seal around my neck gave me, as Earl Marshal, total power. I wondered if I would have to use it. My hope was that Maud, the widow of the fourth Earl of Chester was still in the castle. The daughter of Robert of Gloucester she was an old friend. If she was there then I had an opportunity to do that which the King had ordered. Edward had also brought me a letter from Sir Leofric. Having read one I wondered which was the more serious of the two!

I saw her on the gatehouse of the castle. She was greyer but still the woman who had helped me to capture and hold Lincoln Castelo for the Empress. By the time we entered the outer ward she had descended the stairs. She was fond of me. Some of my detractors implied that I had had a relationship with her. That was untrue. She had been a loyal wife to a poor husband and worse Earl. When I dismounted she hugged me and kissed me.

"Earl Marshal! You are here and all will be well."

I smiled, "I do not know about that. I was heading south but King Henry has diverted me here."

"The Welsh?"

"The Welsh!"

We laughed. She turned and saw Samuel, "Goodness me that has to be your grandson! He looks just like you, Earl!"

Samuel stepped forward and bowed, "This is Sir Samuel, William's son."

17

"What a fine-looking young man! You have been lucky with your children, Earl." I said nothing for I knew she was hurt by her own son's disloyalty. "Here am I chattering like a magpie. You have ridden long and hard. Come I will have rooms prepared for you. Your men at arms know their way around the warrior hall." She linked Samuel and me, "Two handsome men on my arms. I am a lucky woman!"

Once in the hall she took command and wine and food was brought as well as bowls of scented water and cloths for us to bathe the dirt of the road from our faces. She had her men put chairs in a circle around her. She smiled but it was a knowing smile, "You chose these men and therefore you can trust them." I nodded. "Good. For once, Earl Marshal, the Welsh are not a threat to us but to each other."

Sir Richard said, "That is good, is it not? The Welsh kill each other and we gain more land."

Sir Harold shook his head, "Richard, listen more and speak less! That way you will not be so embarrassed."

Maud patted Richard's hand, "Watch the Earl Marshal and learn." She turned back to me, "The reason you are here is because of me." She lowered her voice. "I wrote to the King two years ago. Prince Dafydd ab Owain Gwynedd is the most reasonable of the Welsh princes and he sought a wife. The King thought it was a good idea and he is to marry Emme of Anjou, the King's half-sister."

I saw Richard open his mouth but his father shook his head.

"And the other Welsh princes?"

"His brother Cynan died this year but there are two others Rhodri ab Owain Gwynedd and Maelgwn ab Owain Gwynedd. They have raised an army in Anglesey and have laid waste the lands around the Clwyd Valley."

I held up the letter from the King, "And King Henry wants us to ensure that Prince Dafydd ab Owain Gwynedd prevails." I nodded. "Now I see. It seemed to me that there was no reason for this command." I saw that Richard and Samuel were still confused. "The Welsh are good hill fighters but our knights and men at arms are their superior. Our archers are the only ones who can match the Welsh." I turned to Maud. "What forces do I have at my command?"

"Not as many as you might have had. My foolish son took the knights and most of the men at arms with him to France. We have fifty archers and forty men at arms in the garrison."

"Not enough."

"Sir Hugh of Mohald has six household knights, thirty men at arms and thirty archers."

"Still not enough."

"Have the fyrd been called this year and the local barons?"

"No."

"Then we had forty days of service from them. How many are there?"

"There are five hundred which can be called to arms quickly."

I nodded, "Then that might be enough." That would give us fifteen knights, one hundred and four archers, almost a hundred men at arms and five hundred peasants. I had fought the Welsh before and they did not use many knights. "Have the Constable send out the summons. I would meet with Sir Hugh here. If he has the castle at Mohald then he knows the Welsh." She nodded. "Does the Prince bring any men?"

"Aye, Earl Marshal, they are gathered at Denbigh."

"And he is there too?"

"He is. The wedding will take place at St. Asaph and as his brothers have been raiding ever close the prince wishes to be able to send then hence."

I hesitated, "Countess, if I were not here would he defeat his brothers?"

She gave a disarming smile, "You are here and we need not worry!"

I had my answer and I laughed! "You should have been a man Maud for you have the mind of a general. I take it you have scouts?"

"Good ones."

"Then have them sent to find these two Welsh brothers. I would that this was finished sooner rather than later."

My knights went to speak with our men and, after the Countess had given her own orders we sat together speaking. We were old friends. Maud was one of the few left from the civil war. "The King will not hurt your son."

She smiled, "I know. Henry is a good King. Although some find him a little uncouth and others a little blunt I saw him with you when he was a squire. The young man you trained is still in there. He is the work of the Warlord. He will do that which is right."

"Aye and that work is now done. He has his crown."

"Yet you still watch out for him. When others sit and enjoy their old age you still ride this land doing the King's bidding." There was concern in her voice.

"It is not so bad. I have my grandson with me and I get to meet old friends such as you."

"Your grandson does you proud. I meant what I said. He looks the double of you. Now you are greyer but when you were younger you could have passed for twins."

"He is also a fine knight of whom I am inordinately proud. My son William and I were parted for many years. We are now reconciled but Samuel is constantly at my side. When he leaves me in London it will be a hard parting."

She leaned over and took my hands, "Alfraed, speak with William Marshal. You know you can trust him. Let him be the one to hold the reins of power until Henry returns. You have done more than enough. This is not right."

I laughed and squeezed her fingers, "You may be right but I could not stop now, even if I tried. There is something in me that drives me on. It is a compulsion. As much as I wish to stop I cannot."

"Aye, I can see it. You swore an oath to the Empress and even though she is dead it is there. Promise me that you will not fight. You can sit atop your horse and give commands. Let the others fight. They are all younger. Use your most powerful of weapons; use your mind."

Chapter 2

The scouts returned before the five bands of the fyrd were mustered. The two who returned first were typical foresters. Wearing browns and greens and with nut-brown faces, they showed the evidence of life in the open. They knew their business too. This was the borderlands and a mistake here would be fatal.

"My lady the Welsh are gathered close by the fishing port of Conwy. They raid the farms. So far the monastery at St. Asaph has been left untouched but their scouts have been as far as Rhuthun."

"How many men do they have?"

Oswald looked at me, "A thousand at least but few horsemen. The knights and mounted men at arms protect the standard of Rhodri. Maelgwn has with him some wild Irishmen." He shook his head. "They have limed hair and fight half-naked!"

I nodded. I had fought them before. King Henry controlled Ireland but only the parts where we had built castles. In the west and the south, there were many places where the Irish still ruled. They hired themselves to any who would pay them to fight. "My lady, I would have the Welsh watched until this Prince Dafydd ab Owain Gwynedd reaches us."

"A good idea. Oswald, keep us informed as to their movements."

The Countess had good maps and we were studying them when Sir Hugh of Mohald arrived. He was a typical Marcher lord. With his castle on the River Alyn, he guarded the approach to Chester. He was a man used to making his own decisions and his own laws. I liked him as soon as I met him.

He held out his arm, "A real warrior at last! Good to meet you, Warlord. I am honoured." He suddenly realised that he had insulted the Earl of Chester, "My lady I am sorry… I…"

She laughed, "I agree with you, Sir Hugh. This is a real warrior and the last of a dying breed."

I felt the hairs on the back of my neck prickle.

"Aye, I can be a little blunt. So, we make war on the Welsh, my lord?"

"We do but it is to make Prince Dafydd ab Owain Gwynedd more secure."

He nodded, "It buys us peace for a time. Until we have more castles like mine then the Welsh will still raid. Apart from their island of Anglesey, there is precious little farm land for them. What is your plan, Warlord?"

"The fyrd is mustering but I will not attack without the Welsh. I would rather the Welsh bled in their own land than Englishmen on English soil."

"Amen to that. My castle is a good place to muster. They have a hill fort at Denbigh but it would not withstand a sustained attack. From what my scouts have told me the Welsh are moving slowly. Their men are too busy ransacking and looting."

"Then I will send the fyrd and their lords to join you there. Avoid conflict if you can. I would have our presence and intentions kept hidden for as long as possible."

He nodded, "The Prince had best be quick for the fyrd are becoming restless. They like to get back to their farms. A battle will hold them but only if we win." He left and we waited for the Prince.

Prince Dafydd ab Owain Gwynedd arrived in the early evening. He had with him forty knights but none were armed and mounted as well as even Sir Richard. He had four hundred men marching with him and I was pleased to see that half of them were archers. He was younger than I expected and he did not look like a warrior. That was disappointing. We would have to beat his brothers soundly and then the Prince would have a chance of holding on to his kingdom.

"Earl Marshal! When our brother, King Henry, told us that you would be here to lead my armies I knew that we would win! Where are the rest of your men?"

"This is all that I brought. The men of Cheshire are mustered at Mohald."

He frowned, "Ah, Yr Wyddgrug. I am disappointed I expected the army which humbled King William of Scotland."

I sighed, "This will do, Prince. Your brothers are raiding the Clwyd. We will march to Mohald tomorrow and then begin our sweep north along the valley."

"Why no go directly to St. Asaph? That way we could cut off of our enemies."

"And the people of the Clwyd would suffer. This way we pick off their men as we move and ensure that they have to meet us in battle."

He shrugged, "You are the Warlord. I am in your hands. I will be interested to see how you do this!"

I sensed that my knights were becoming angry. They preferred to fight for England. This Welsh prince was not winning any friends with his words. "And I look forward to watching your men defeat their countrymen too."

I bade farewell to the Countess at her gate. I never saw her again. The ones who had endured the civil war were becoming fewer in number. Soon it would be a distant memory. "You take care, Warlord." She frowned, "I think you are not well. Take no risks. You have a family who needs you. You have served England well enough. Serve yourself."

I kissed her cheek, "And do not worry about your son. Henry will punish him by making him wait for his lands. It will do him no harm. And as for my family? Do not fear. I will keep Samuel with me as long as I can!"

The hillsides around Mohald were covered in the hovels which men had erected. The knights who led the fyrd had tents. It looked disorganised. That was the way of the fyrd. The men at arms and archers would be more organised. Ralph of Lincoln led my archers and Guiscard the Gascon my men at arms. William had taken the more experienced men such as Roger of Bath with him to France. I had confidence in my men at arms and archers. All had fought in the Scottish wars.

Sir Hugh had not been idle. "The bulk of their army is at Rhuddlan. They have warbands raiding up and down the Clwyd Valley. As you ordered me we have left them alone. It was hard for they are causing great mischief; especially the Irish!"

"Tomorrow we begin to take this land for the Prince."

I held a counsel of war with the Prince, his lieutenants, Owain and Gruffyd, Sir Hugh and my four knights. I saw the resentment on the faces of Owain and Gruffyd at the presence of Richard and Samuel. I did not care. My two young knights had already done more than the Welsh warriors. "We do not have enough knights to be wasteful. Sir Harold here will lead the knights." I looked pointedly at Owain and Gruffyd, "All of them. They are our reserve. We use them as a threat. We keep one hundred with the baggage. The other four will act as sweepers down the two valley sides. Our attack will be led by Sir Hugh and myself. Along with the Prince we will attack with the men at arms backed by the archers."

Owain said, "You would risk the Prince?"

I smiled, "I risk myself and it is necessary. I want the men we fight to see that Prince Dafydd ab Owain Gwynedd is not afraid to fight and that he is the leader. We will not be in danger. Our standards will make the Prince's brothers think that we have few knights and it will tempt them. When they bring up their main army then the men at arms and the archers will be the shield and the knights will be the lance. They will cut to the heart of the enemy." I waved over my son's squire, Thomas. He had wine. He poured some in my goblet. "Thomas here will carry my standard. We will be behind the archers. Think of us as hunters. The fyrd will stop the game from fleeing up the valley sides and stop us from being attacked on our flanks. The men at arms and archers will drive the game so that it is all gathered in one place. Our attack will be slow and steady. It will grind them down and whittle down their numbers. When Sir Harold leads out knights it will be a final act and should give us a complete victory. Prince Dafydd ab Owain Gwynedd, you need for your brothers' armies to be completely destroyed. Then and only then will you be safe."

We spent some time going over the signals I would use. The rest departed leaving me with my knights and squires. "Samuel, I am sorry that I have taken your most experienced squire but I need someone on who I can completely rely. I think Sir Hugh and his squire will be strong but I am less certain about the Prince!"

Samuel smiled, "I am happy with William and I think that Thomas will be honoured to be the one to carry your standard."

We rose in the dark of night. I wished to be moving by dawn. I went to the horse lines. I no longer rode a warhorse. In fact, the horse I had taken from Stockton's stables was a palfrey. White Star was not a young horse but he was reliable and steadfast. He had been in battles and knew how to conduct himself. His last rider had been Simon. He had been my squire and now lay in a French grave. We headed over the ridge and down the road to the valley bottom. Dawn broke behind us in the east and bathed the mountains in blue light.

Guiscard the Gascon had already arrayed the men at arms. More than half were mounted. Ralph of Lincoln had dismounted the archers and co-opted twenty of the fyrd to act as horse holders. Each archer had his quiver of arrows and two spare bundles on each horse. Our fletchers had been busy. Behind the archers were the Welsh men at arms. When I appeared next to Sir Hugh and the Prince the fyrd on the valley sides began to cheer. My men at arms beat their shields. The Prince preened himself until he managed to hear the words, "Warlord! Warlord!" His face darkened. I could do nothing about the men's choice of chant.

I turned to Thomas, "Signal the advance!"

Guiscard spurred his horse and the three lines of mounted men at arms rode down the valley. Twenty of my archers rode ahead of my captain of men, Guiscard the Gascon. The rest of my archers walked their horses behind the dismounted men at arms. It would be a slow advance. We had covered less than half a mile when, from the valley sides, I heard the clash of steel and wood as the fyrd flushed raiders from cover. I saw my archers dismount, take their bows, nock an arrow and then release their deadly missiles. I heard cries. The mounted men at arms meant I could not see the result of their arrows. I did not need to. I knew the worth of my archers. When they remounted and we continued I knew that we had first blood.

We passed the bodies and I saw that they were Irishmen. With limed hair and tattoos I knew them to be brave but reckless. It would have galled them to run from the fyrd. As the morning passed we started more men from cover and as noon approached we had killed almost a hundred men. None had been taken prisoner and I knew that word would have reached the Prince's brothers.

"Prince, you know your brothers better than I do. How will they fight?"

He shook his head, "I know not for this is the first time I have led my men. Owain and Gruffyd normally lead the army."

I was disappointed and I now knew why the King had sent me. He did not trust his new ally to be victorious. As we closed with Denbigh a larger group of warriors broke cover. These had horses and knights with them. I guessed they had been in Denbigh Castle. Made of wood it might withstand Welsh raiders but not the Warlord. They headed down the slope as the fyrd approached. They were not afraid of the fyrd but they had seen the metal snake in the bottom of the valley and that did frighten them.

Guiscard the Gascon raised his spear and led the one hundred mounted men at arms after the knights and their retinue. Dressed in mail my men at arms were only distinguished from knights by the helmets and surcoats. The twenty knights and their squires who led the Welsh must have thought that the men at arms were their inferiors. They turned their horses to charge them. It was a mistake. The Prince and I had a perfect viewpoint. The twenty archers dismounted and formed two blocks to the side of the mounted men at arms. Guiscard ensured that our men rode in two straight lines. The Welsh appeared more disorganised. They were moving faster for they had the slope with them. Ralph's archers let fly. They did not send volleys. They aimed and took out horses. The Welsh made it easy for them by sending them piecemeal. When the two lines met, one ragged and one resolute, there was a clash of steel and wood. Horses whinnied and knights and squires screamed as they were speared. The archers slung their bows and drew their knives and daggers. They ran after the men at arms. As the men at arms fought the knights, squires and Welsh men at arms, my archers reached up to drag horsemen from saddles and to slit their throats.

The Prince said, "They are knights! What about ransom?"

I laughed, "Men at arms and archers do not receive a ransom. The mail, weapons and horses are more certain methods of making money! You want to win the war and not become richer do you not?" Eight of the Welsh escaped down the valley. I saw that we had not escaped unscathed. Men at arms lay dead. Some men from Stockton would not be returning home.

It was late afternoon when we spied Rhuddlan and the Welsh camp. I called a halt and ordered for a ditch to be dug and stakes to be planted. We would fight the battle the next day. I sent orders for the fyrd to cut down as many stakes as they could.

The Prince said, "Should we give them a chance to negotiate?"

"Beat them first and then negotiate. If they are not beaten they will wait until I am gone and then attack again. I fight for you this once, Prince, and then I leave. I have matters which await me in London!" No one knew the content of the letter from Sir Leofric. I had to get to London as soon as I could. Guiscard set the sentries but I walked the lines with Samuel.

"Why do you do this grandfather? Do you not trust your sentries?"

"Of course, I do. Have you stood a duty yet?"

He looked down, somewhat shamefaced, "Not yet."

"Your father has and I have. They have a great responsibility and the least that the man who ordered it can do is to come speak with them."

I did not know all of the sentries. Only two came from Stockton but they all knew me. I spoke to each of them. Where one looked nervous I cracked a joke. It was not a very good one but they laughed dutifully. It also allowed me to view the battlefield from closer up. It was as I was speaking with Guiscard that the arrow came flying from the west. It was an optimistic arrow for we were in the shadows of the east but it was a good archer. Had I been with another then I might have been hit but Guiscard, almost without thinking, brought up his shield to protect the three of us. The Welsh arrow slammed into the willow boards.

He shook his head, "Warlord, you are too tempting a target. Sir Samuel, take your grandfather back!"

I smiled, "As you wish." We walked into the dark. I heard angry mumblings from the men we passed. They did not like the attempt on my life. I had not done this deliberately but I would exploit it.

Samuel said, "That was close."

"He was a good archer." I shrugged, "I had on my helmet and my arming cap. The Welsh are good archers but we have better arrows. I might not have died. And now we know that there will be vigilant sentries this night. Tomorrow men will seek Welsh archers and when they find them will hurt them."

We returned to my tent and I ate. The Prince and his lieutenants arrived when I had just finished, "How do we fight tomorrow, Warlord?"

"Exactly as we did today. We have two large blocks of men on the flanks. They will be the fyrd. I would have them plant their stakes and just be an obdurate mass of men. The Welsh will have to climb the valley sides to reach them. I hope that they do so for it will make our task easier."

"But that will not defeat my brothers!"

"No, it will just guarantee that we are not defeated. We dismount the men at arms and archers. Our archers can shower the enemy archers while our men at arms advance. When they do not break the enemy lines, they will fall back. They will run. They will flee."

"Flee?"

"I want the Welsh, and especially the Irish, to chase after us and to try to slaughter us. The men at arms will flee to the two sides of the valley and shelter before the fyrd. Then we will send in the knights, squires and twenty selected men at arms. With archers in support, I hope that we will drive through their own knights and capture your brothers. Then we can begin the slaughter."

Owain sneered, "You expect a lot of things to happen, Warlord. What if they do not?"

"In that case, I will try something else!"

I had a pain in my head and it was making it hard for me to concentrate. I took some of Brother Peter's potion. It did not take away the pain but it dulled it. This was the first pain I had had since I had left Stockton. I saw that as a good sign. I had not had to waste the precious potion. I took out Leofric's letter and read it again. It made for disturbing reading.

Warlord,

I hope my messenger finds you quickly.

I was serving with the King and your son when we were ambushed on the road to Le Mans. I must be getting old, Warlord, for I took a wound in my leg. The wound is not the reason for the letter but what happened on the way home. My squire and I rode in disguise. The King is unpopular in parts of France. His son, Henry, has stirred up much animosity. It seemed prudent to avoid close scrutiny.

Thus disguised we were in an inn on the road to Angers when I spied a device I recognised. It was the de Mamers three golden orbs on a red background. It has been many years since I saw it. There were four men and two of them wore the liveried surcoat. I might have just passed that off as a coincidence and left but I heard your name spoken. When they said, 'Earl Marshal'. I pricked up my ears. We were in a darkened corner and I think they thought they were alone. They spoke quietly but I could still hear most of what they said.

They were being sent to England. They are the men who would be your killers, lord. They had been hired by someone, I could not discover who, but one of them, he was called Hubert said that he would do it for nothing. It was a matter of honour. They were about to divulge more when some Gascons came in. There was an altercation. I know not how or why it began. In the mêlée which ensued, Jean, my squire and I, were thrown to the ground and a Gascon's body fell upon us. By the time we had regained our feet two more Gascons had been killed and we were held, albeit briefly, on suspicion of complicity in their deaths. Had it not been for the inn keeper we might have been imprisoned.

By the time we reached the outside, they were long gone. When we spoke with the Gascons we discovered that the four men were being sought for murder. A certain Geoffrey de la Cheppe and his family were slaughtered in their home. Was there not one of the Knights of the Empress with the same name? I heard names but I am not sure what they meant. They could have been other conspirators or potential victims. D'Oilli, Guiscard, and de Mamers were the ones I heard but there were others.

One of the other men was a Templar. I recognised his sign. I am sorry that I have failed you, Warlord. I will continue to search for them. I did not want to write to your son in case the letter was intercepted. I know that William of Kingston will deliver it safely,

Your squire, your knight and your servant,
Leofric of La Flèche

When I finished I folded it up and slipped it into my purse. After we had dealt with the Welsh and left Wales, I would show it to Harold and the others. Until then it would be a distraction. I had seen neither sign of Templars nor men with three golden orbs on a red background. Of course, they would not know where I was. It was more likely that they sought me in Stockton. I had time.

Thomas was diligent. When I finished reading the letter, I had walked out to stand by the fire. "Earl Marshal, should I sharpen your sword?"

"I have not had to draw it in anger since Alf's son Egbert, put a good edge on it. Do your own. You will need a good edge on your sword tomorrow."

"I know, Earl Marshal."

"I am sorry that you have to sit with an old man tomorrow. I fear it will not be an easy task. I do not intend to go into danger but my banner will be a target for our enemies. We have perilous few knights. I am praying that Sir Harold has other knights as stout-hearted as Sir Richard, Sir James and Sir Samuel."

"Surely they must be!"

I lowered my voice, "Sir Hugh and his men can be relied upon. The Welsh? I have fought in a civil war and it is often hard to know which side men are on. We watch for treachery."

He nodded, "I have attended to White Star and his needs. He is the calmest horse I have ever seen."

"A tip Thomas, a steady horse is better than an aggressive horse. When you use a lance, you will find it easier to hit the mark if your horse is steady." I stretched. "And now I will retire. Have the sentry wake me before the last watch is set."

One advantage of being a commander was that you had a tent to yourself. Many generals used a cot on which to sleep. I did not and neither did my sons. The slight benefit of comfort was offset by the guilt at knowing that your men did not have that luxury. I knelt and said my prayers. Adela and the Empress were first and foremost in my thoughts. Then I asked for protection for my sons and grandsons and finally for the people at home. I had kept them safe so that when I died they would all prosper. Long after the Earl Marshal was dead Cleveland would remember the young English knight who had come with his father and made the Tees a safer place.

I then lay on my fur and slept. I could always fall asleep easily. The difference was that now I was older I tended to wake earlier too!

I heard the sentry enter and my eyes were open as he approached. I spoke before he did and I saw him jump. "Good morning! How goes the watch?"

"Our men slew five men who tried to sneak into our camp. Sir Harold ordered them to be placed on spears before our lines so that the enemy could see them."

I chuckled, "Sir Harold knows how to send a message. Find me some food and ale, eh while I make water."

"Of course, Earl Marshal."

Sir Harold walked over.

"I hear there was some trouble in the night."

"Luckily it was one of Sir Hugh's men at arms who was captain of the guard. He woke Sir Hugh and he woke me. There was never any danger." He laughed. "I had to make water anyway and so I stayed awake."

The sentry brought me food and ale. "Hit them hard this morning, Sir Harold. I want them hurting so that they will not dream of fighting us again."

He lowered his voice, "Can we trust this Prince?"

I shrugged, "He is marrying the King's half-sister. So long as he does not cause trouble for a while then I will be happy. My son and the King will soon be back and then my task will be over."

He gave me a searching look, "Yet you took your leave of those at home. Many thought it sounded like a final farewell."

"Just caution. We both know that men can die at unexpected times. Dick was one such. You and I have enjoyed more luck than we might have expected. It was caution which made me speak, nothing more."

He did not look convinced. He had been an outlaw and they had senses which others did not.

After I had eaten and drunk I sent Thomas to fetch the Prince and my leaders to my tent. Our camp was already awake and I could hear the noise of the Welsh preparing for battle. They would have known that their night attack had failed and they would have it confirmed when dawn broke and the heads of their dead were revealed.

"Prince Dafydd I will need you close by me. When our horsemen charge and break through we should win but…"

"But?" The Prince looked worried.

"If every battle went the way it was planned I might be able to guarantee that you will be safe. Keep your bodyguards around you. As for the rest of you, obey Sir Harold! That is my last command."

Thomas brought me my horse and I mounted. I smiled and waved at Samuel. He did not look worried. He had fought alongside me since he had been little more than a page. He had more experience than the Prince or his lieutenants. As the sun came up behind us I saw that the two brothers had arrayed themselves behind four lines of men on foot. On one flank, their right, were their horsemen while the Irish were on their left. When our knights charged much responsibility would lie with the men at arms and archers who would have to endure wild attacks. I nodded to the Prince's standard-bearer and he sounded the horn three times. The men at arms moved forward. When they were two hundred paces from the Welsh the Welsh archers began to send their arrows towards our advancing men. My men at arms were ready and they held their shields above them. Some, not the ones from the valley, showed their inexperience by having the shield too close to their heads. One died when the arrow came through his shield and into his head. When the men at arms were one hundred paces from the Welsh they stopped, ostensibly to dress their lines. The Welsh sent every arrow they had towards my men at arms and then Ralph launched his own arrow storm. It was not aimed at the mailed men at arms but the archers who had no protection. Every arrow found a victim and then Guiscard led my men at arms forward. We had lost men but dressing the lines had filled the gaps. There was a clash of wood and steel when they came together. Now that the Welsh archer threat had been minimized our archers sent their arrows into the men at arms. They did not kill as many as we would have liked but when some of the horsemen had their mounts struck then the Welsh reacted.

31

Their horn sounded twice. The whole of their line attacked. Our men were ready and they fled to the sides of the valley. On each side, three hundred men were standing behind ditches and stakes. The sudden, apparent rout took the Welsh by surprise. The men on foot were slow to react. The horsemen and the Irish reached the men at arms before they had formed lines and men began to die as our own archers' arrows took their toll.

"Now Sir Harold!"

The horn was sounded and our knights, squires and horsemen galloped down the valley. They were not charging formed ranks. The Welsh were rushing to get at the Warlord. By the time they realised their predicament and tried to form ranks it was too late. I saw Sir James, Sir Harold, Sir Richard and Sir Samuel strike with the spears so quickly that their arms were almost a blur. Many of the men they struck had their backs to the horsemen. Others were trampled to death. A Welsh horn sounded. The knights tried to disengage but the Irish had their blood up and they fought on.

It was hard to sit and just watch the battle but my fighting days were done. What was worrying me was the success the Welsh knights were enjoying. Already some of the men at arms who fought for Prince Dafydd were being slaughtered by knights with lances. I was about to ask for the horn to sound when I saw Sir Harold look up. He shouted orders although I could not hear them. Sir Hugh led half of the knights towards the two Welsh Princes on the hill while Sir Harold wheeled the rest around. Sir Harold had first been my squire when his only skill was with a bow and arrow. Now he was a master horseman. He raised his spear and steadied his line. They calmed their horses and then he lowered his spear and they charged up the hill towards the Welsh horsemen.

Even Prince Dafydd ab Owain Gwynedd was impressed, "Your knights have superb control, Earl Marshal."

"It is years of training and Sir Harold has been fighting at my side for almost fifty years. My grandson has fought in two wars. They know their business."

Sir Harold led them to plough into the rear of the Welsh horsemen. Riders were knocked from saddles and the men at arms and archers took heart. They rallied. Suddenly the fyrd spilt through the stakes and the ditches. They were like a tidal wave. They were ill-armed but they saw lords who could be beaten and they all wanted to be part of that.

I turned to the Prince's standard-bearer. He had the horn, "Sound the general attack! Let us end this! ComeThomas, we have been spectators long enough." I drew my sword and spurred White Star towards Sir Hugh and the knights who were battling their way through the Welsh protecting their princes. Guiscard and his men at arms had massacred the Irishmen and they made a huge wedge to drive down from our right.

Thomas and I almost caught up with Sir Hugh and his men. The Welsh defenders were dying to protect their princes. Thomas was a little eager and when the Welshman who had been feigning death suddenly rose and swung his axe, my grandson's squire almost met an early death. When I was younger men said I had the quickest hands they had ever seen. They might have slowed a little but I was still more than quick enough to swing a back-hand blow into the back of the Welsh neck. Thomas looked around in shock, "Thank you, Earl Marshal! I owe you a life!"

"You owe me nothing! Just be more alert."

I reached Sir Hugh's squire. The Prince and his bodyguards were with us. Sir Hugh and the other knights were tiring. Our seven fresh horses and sharpened blades made all the difference. I had no shield but White Star was a clever horse and he twisted and turned like a mountain stream. I had not fought for some time but my body knew what to do. I used the weight of the blade and the sharpened edge to do the damage. I struck at the weak points. I hit to cause damage, not necessarily to kill.

One of the squires of Prince Rhodri ab Owain Gwynedd saw an opportunity for glory and he rode at me. He had an open helmet and scale armour. He galloped at the white-bearded old man and he raised his sword to end the battle and win it for his lord. I watched the sword come down and, just as it was about to strike my helmet I spurred White Star as I jerked her head around. The squire struck space. I brought the flat of my blade around hard and struck him in his unprotected back. His shout was like that of a vixen in the night. He angrily whirled around. He jerked his horse's head so savagely that the bit tore into the animal's mouth and made the horse rear a little. The squire struggled to control it. I brought the flat of my blade hard against the back of the squire's hand. I heard bones break and the sword was dropped.

"Yield, you have lost and I do not want to kill a young man who has so much to learn."

Two of my men at arms were approaching and he nodded. "I yield!"

I sheathed my sword for I could see that the two princes had lowered their standards. "A word of advice, young master, train your horse better and be gentler. You will live longer. You could have died twice this day. You are a squire and I used the flat of my blade."

"There will be no ransom!"

I laughed, "Live young squire and I will forego the ransom. When you reach my age, you see that there are more important things than coin!"

Chapter 3

There had been great slaughter, especially close to the two joint leaders. Sir Hugh had lost three of his knights and he was in an angry mood. He glared at Owain and Gruffydd who had managed to avoid committing their own knights until victory was assured. Prince Dafydd ab Owain Gwynedd basked in the glory of a victory with which he had little influence. He had sat next to me and trotted forward while Thomas and I had charged. I had done as I had been asked but there was a sour taste in my mouth. King Henry had been short-sighted. One day we would have to come back and conquer this land just to keep England safe. For the moment, however, I was Earl Marshal and I was the King's man.

We entered the town and I rode directly to the hall which Rhodri and Maelgwn had used as their stronghold. Prince Dafydd ab Owain Gwynedd would not afford them the title of prince for they had rebelled. He had them bound and brought before me in chains. I was weary and my head hurt. I desperately needed to take some of the draught. It would have to wait until I had passed judgement.

I took the right-hand seat of the two which stood on the raised dais. I did not wait for Prince Dafydd ab Owain Gwynedd. I was flouting convention and insulting the Prince but I cared not.

"Bring forth the rebels!"

The two princes and the twenty knights who had surrendered were brought forward. "You have rebelled against your lawful lord." I was not sure that I had spoken the truth but no one questioned my word and I continued. "Prince Rhodri and Prince Maelgwn, your lands are forfeit. There are reparations to pay to the men of Cheshire and the knights of Sir Hugh. I deem that to be one thousand gold pieces. Until that amount is paid in full you will be held in Chester." I saw Sir Hugh smile and nod. He and the other lords were satisfied. They would be recompensed for their losses and even the fyrd would go home happy. The Welsh dead had been stripped of all that was vaguely valuable. I had also done the two princes a favour. They would be safer in Chester. I feared that Prince Dafydd ab Owain Gwynedd might wish them harm.

I turned my attention to the knights. They had all surrendered. "The ransom for your knights will be set by Sir Hugh and he will hold you at his castle at Mohald." Sir Hugh's smile became even broader. "You will swear allegiance to your new prince and the King he serves, Henry of England." Prince Dafydd flashed me an angry look. Perhaps he did not realise that marrying the half-sister to the King made him subservient to the King of England. I cared not. My pain was worse.

I rose, "And now I will prepare for my journey south. I leave on the morrow. I have done my duty and obeyed my King's instructions. I am done with Wales."

I strode from the hall. My knights and Sir Hugh followed me. Sir Hugh said as we stepped into the fresh air, "Thank you, Earl Marshal! That was a masterful demonstration. What do I do with your share of the ransom?"

I waved a hand at my knights, "Send it to Cleveland with the share of my knights. I give mine to the archers and men at arms and a quarter for the town of Stockton."

He looked surprised, "None for you, Earl Marshal?"

Sir Harold gave him a disappointed look, "This is the Earl Marshal, Sir Hugh. Do not expect the behaviour you see in other lords!"

As we headed back to our camp Sir Samuel said, "Are you unwell, grandfather?"

"Just a little tired. I will lie down in my tent. Make sure that we are ready to leave in the morning. I wish to reach Leek by dark. I would make Leicester in two days."

"What is the rush?"

How could I tell him that Brother Peter had measured my life in months and not years? "I am keeping my knights from their families. The sooner you reach London with your charge the sooner you can return to Stockton."

Once in my tent, I took some of the draught, lay down and fell asleep. It was a troubled sleep for I was haunted by faces from the past. Names and knights I had not thought about for more than forty years filled my dreams: de Mamers, d'Oilli, Guiscard. All of them had been slain by me but not before they had hurt my family. De Mamers had been responsible for the death of my father. In my dream, he pulled down my castle, stone by stone until all that remained was a hall. When I woke it was dark and I could hear men outside laughing and joking.

As I stood a shadow rose from the dark, "You had a troubled sleep, grandfather."

It was Samuel. "So, you are a chamberlain now. You had no need to watch over me. I feel refreshed after sleep. As for being troubled, that is ever the way with old men. It is the young who sleep well for they have clear consciences. When you get to my age you reflect on all your mistakes. Old men spend much of their time regretting actions."

"Not you, surely."

"Aye, Samuel, even me."

We stepped out of the tent and looking down the valley I saw that the sun was setting. Our knights and men were all seated around a communal fire and they cheered when I stepped into the evening air. They were all in good humour. Some had wounds but none had been lost. Even before they received the coin from me they were richer for they knew where the treasure lay on a battlefield. I could smell the horse meat they were cooking. They loved their horses but the ones they ate were the slain ones that had belonged to the Welsh.

Samuel led me to a spot between Sir James and Sir Harold. "I will fetch food and ale."

I smiled, "Not too much food. I have little appetite these days."

Sir Harold flashed me a concerned look, "You are ill?"

"You know better than any, Harold, men of our age eat less."

He nodded and waved his arm towards the Welsh camp. "We did the King's bidding but I enjoyed it not. The Scots are poor enemies but the Welsh are even worse."

Sir James spat a piece of gristle into the fire and then wiped his hands upon the grass, "You cannot choose your allies, Sir Harold. One thing I learned when I served my uncle, the Bishop, was that all men have hidden motives. King Henry could have married his half-sister to any of the princes. He cared not which one so long as Gwynedd was tied to England. Thanks to the Earl Marshal Scotland is safe. It is why the King stays in France." He looked at me. "And you have to maintain order in an England which is still riven with petty jealousies and the rebellion of ungrateful sons."

Sir Harold nodded, "London is the most treacherous part of the Kingdom. When we fought in the civil war they turned their coats so often that I swear they were double-sided." His son laughed. Sir Harold said, "I am serious. The lords of Gloucester were loyal to a man. London? They would smile and stab you in the back. I do not envy the Earl Marshal. There will be danger each time he leaves his castle. We will stay with you until we are sure of your safety."

I knew that I would have to tell my knights of the new threat. That would have to wait until we were on the road. I needed discretion. If this was a larger plot then I did not want my enemies to know that I had been warned.

The road to Leek climbed from the plains of Cheshire. The lord of the manor was a supporter of King Henry and had been loyal during the revolt. Even so, I would not speak of the letter there. We stopped at the River Weaver to water our horses and eat the bread and cheese we had brought. While we were alone and after we had eaten I brought out the letter and handed it around. I said nothing.

No one spoke until all had had the chance to read it.

"Leofric is not given to flights of fancy. This threat is a real one Warlord."

"I know Harold."

"Who is this de Mamers and why would he hate you so?" Sir James had never even heard of the name.

"I had almost forgotten him. He was a treacherous knight in the pay of our enemies. He had been a crusader and he and a band of renegade knights working for de Brus tried to undermine the King's authority. Tancred de Mamers was an evil man and he had with him Richard D'Oilli and Geoffrey Guiscard. They died too. When the King discovered their treachery, he took their lands from them and they fled to France." I shook my head. "It is so long ago that I have forgotten exactly where but they left England and went from my mind. They seem like ghosts from the past."

James hesitated and then said, "I am sorry, lord, but is this not a little long after the event? This sounds like a serious grudge."

"The families gambled and lost everything. The fourth of the killers, William of Jedburgh, came from Scotland and his family lost nothing of value."

"A more important question, grandfather is, why now?" We all looked at Samuel. He was young but he bore a sharp brain. "It strikes me as convenient that King Henry and my father are in France. You put much hope in William Marshal but Sir Hugh thought that he is also in France with young King Henry. With you out of the way who would keep England safe? Wales and Scotland are quiet; that is thanks to you but what of those rebellious lords who supported the princes? It seems to me, young though I am, that these killers have a vested interest in your death. They gain vengeance and also have a chance to seize power while the King is away."

Harold nodded, "Your grandson may be right."

Sir James said, "And you said there were four of them. Who knows if they were the only four. How many others were disenfranchised by King Henry? The Earl of Chester, Hugh of Cyfeiliog, is under arrest. His mother hopes that he might be given his lands back but he does not know. How many others are there in the same position?" He flourished the letter like a sword, "This is dangerous, Warlord. This is the spark that could ignite a second rebellion."

"When I read the name la Cheppe then I became suspicious. He was a French knight who served with Sir Edward and the other Knights of the Empress. I had not seen him for many years. I am guessing the man who was murdered was a descendant." I took back the letter, "But who gains from all of this?"

"You mean if King Henry the Second of England is deposed?" Sir James was the nearest we had to a politician and he saw that which I had not.

"Young King Henry."

"Aye Warlord and he is in France apparently hunting and enjoying the tourney. None would suspect him. If the country was engulfed in war and the King was in France might there not be a clamour for a rightful King of England, one crowned by King Henry himself, to be offered the crown of England?"

I wondered now at King Henry's decision to have his son crowned King of England. It could come back to haunt him.

"Then we need to be vigilant." As we mounted I said, "Sir James, when we reach London I would have you ride to France to find my father. I will not commit this to a letter but I would have you apprise him of the situation. He needs to know of this plot and these killers who are loose."

"Aye, lord. I think it wise."

"We will say that you leave my service to take the cross."

Sir Richard asked, "Is that not a sin? To tell an untruth?"

I smiled, "King Henry promised to take the cross to atone for the murder of Archbishop Becket. He has yet to take the cross. I am sure that someday Sir James will travel east for a pilgrimage."

"Aye, lord, I would!"

"We do not speak of this in public. I trust our men but if they knew then they would not be able to hide their suspicions. This is a complicated web and we need to find all of the strands before we try to take the spider!"

The Earl of Leicester had not only joined the rebellion against King Henry but helped the French to invade England. He was now in captivity having had all of his lands taken from him. My decision to visit Leicester was deliberate. It was now controlled by a loyal Constable, Sir Richard de Hauteil. The King had appointed Sir Richard but I wished to know the mood of the lords of Leicester. Did they support Earl Robert?

The Constable was a Norman. I had fought alongside him in the wars against Blois and France. Although twenty years my junior we had many shared experiences. In light of the letter I could not afford to totally trust him but I would listen to him, at least.

"I thought, Earl Marshal, that when the King regained his crown we would have a land free from dissent."

"He has four sons and there are many lords who seek power. You are Constable of this castle for that very reason." He nodded, "Tell me, have you heard of four knights travelling around this land and remaining hidden? I heard a rumour of four men wanted for killing the relative of an old comrade in Normandy."

He looked around. None were listening and so he lowered his voice. "As you know I am not English. Some of the lords who live hereabouts seem to think I cannot speak English." He shook his head. "They say things they think I will not understand. I remember serving with your Sir Wulfric. I learned my English from him."

I laughed, "Then you have an earthy understanding of our words."

"I do. You know that in the Holy Land they have a cult who take the hashish plant and are called assassins?"

"My son has been on a crusade and he has told me of them. They cannot be in England for they would stand out. We do not have many such swarthy men. My son's scout Masood is from the Holy Land and he often draws stares and comments."

"No, Earl Marshal, the cult has given rise to an order of knights. They have no name but they share a common goal and end. They are hired killers. I heard of them when I was in Italy and then again in Normandy. I had not heard of them in England until lately. They are from all the races of Europe: there are Lombards, Teutons, Swedes, Spaniards, Frenchmen and English. They have one thing in common. They had all lost lands. It makes them hate those in power and those with lands."

"Then they kill in secret?"

"Sometimes but often they take part in a tourney. You know that men are often killed in the mêlée. It can happen by accident. These killers are deliberate and ruthless."

"They have a leader? A symbol?"

"A symbol? I think not. They are secret and they are clever. As for a leader; if they have one he is well hidden. I tell you all of this, Earl Marshal, for I have heard of a band of knights who travel in this land and they do so in secret. They have supporters who offer them shelter. Some knights may indeed fear them but they are present here in England. When you travel the roads, I would not do so at twilight or at night. There have been many men killed on the road which passes through Sherwood. It is blamed on the outlaws." He shook his head, "Outlaws use arrows and not a broadsword. Outlaws travel on foot and do not ride warhorses. They are here and you would be a prime target for them."

"You are a well-travelled man. If you were to say who was behind it then who would it be?"

"Earl Marshal I have, like you, survived a long time. I try to avoid conspiracies and speculation. I do not know and I do not want to know. I can swear that I know nothing. I told you what I did for you are an old comrade and the most respected knight in the land. I would not have you killed because of my lack of vigilance. I will have some of my men at arms escort you as far as Northampton. Once you are south of there then you are amongst a nest of vipers."

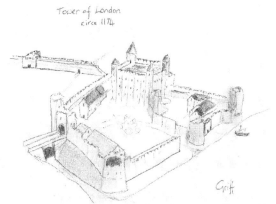

Tower of London
circa 1174

Grif

We saw no trouble on the one hundred and twenty-five miles to London but after I had told my knights my latest news it confirmed their intention to stay with me and for Sir James to take a ship to France. My seal gained us entry to the White Tower. King Henry had improved the castle. Building a tower to guard the entrance of the keep and a warrior hall had been amongst the first. I confess that I did not think he had gone far enough. The south-west bastion tower and gate were a start but I think it needed a moat too. I could do nothing about that. We arrived in the late afternoon. I was tired and my head was hurting more than normal. I was getting through Brother Peter's potion far too quickly. I would have to endure the pain and use less of the remedy. The Constable at Lincoln had confirmed that William Marshal was in France. There would be no one for me to delegate the responsibility. I would have to see it through. Would I live long enough to do so?

I installed our men at arms and archers in the warrior hall and sent for the chancellor, Ralph de Warneville. He was also the Treasurer of York. I had met him once for the Archbishop was known to me. I gave Sir Harold the responsibility of assessing the quality of the garrison and the defences of the Tower. In light of the threat from this new order of knights, we would have to watch for enemies here, in the heart of England.

The Chancellor did not arrive immediately. I did not take offence at that. I guessed it would be caution. He would need to bring the ledgers and accounts for me to peruse. In all honesty that did not concern me. I needed to discover if the plot was widespread. I had to find out just who was loyal and whom I needed to suspect. I sent Guiscard the Gascon and two of his men to visit as many inns of London as they could. They went without surcoats and wore old clothes. They would be my spies. I needed to know the mood of the city and I needed to know if there was gossip about swords for hire. Jean de la Lude and Arne Arneson came from Anjou and Norway. The three of them would pass for mercenaries. I told them to take a couple of days. I wanted a true picture and the three of them would need to assimilate themselves into London. I did not worry about them. They were the best of scouts.

Sir James was eager to set sail for France. He was keenly aware that he might have to travel a long way to find the King and my son. I asked him to wait. "We need to speak with the Chancellor first. I wish to give the King as much information as we can."

The cleric arrived after dark and was escorted by six burly guards. "Earl Marshal, you have arrived not a moment too soon. I fear there is a danger to the King here in his own city."

"Rebellion?"

He shook his head. "Would that it was as simple as that. If there was rebellion in the air then I would have sent for you and written to the King. This is worse. I cannot put my finger on it but there is an air of unease in the city. Many lords are in France. Some fight for the King. Some hide from the King and some are prisoners of the King! Trade has dropped off and taxes are slow to come in. There have been rumours of lords hurt in hunting accidents. Many manors close to London now have no lord."

"That could be a form of rebellion."

"It could but it could also be because the lords who pay the taxes are incarcerated." He leaned forward, "Have you brought all of your knights?"

Shaking my head, I said, "Just four."

He shook his head, "That is not enough."

"It will have to do for that is all that I have brought. I need a list of barons who are known to be loyal to the King. I want no speculation. I need a list which is accurate."

"Then it will be a short list. I will write it before I go."

"Do you have spies?" He hesitated. "Come do not be coy! I know churchmen. I knew Becket!"

He crossed himself, "I have men who keep their ears to the ground if that is what you mean."

"Then have them search for newly arrived knights and men at arms. As you say most are in France or on their estates. I need to know about the new arrivals."

He frowned, "Why?"

"You say there is an air of unease. No one will risk coming to London while there is such an air. Any who come are suspect."

He nodded, "I am glad that you are here."

I nodded, "The list."

He took a quill and parchment and began to write. I knew now that my hope of a sudden visit to abdicate my responsibilities was out of the question. I would end my days in the Tower. It had been some months since Brother Peter told me I had mere months to live. I was living on borrowed time.

The cleric finished. I saw that he had not signed the document. The first three names were known to me. Indeed, the first had been with me when I had captured King William. The others were lesser lords. I did not know them. The first three would be the ones whose help I sought.

Ranulf de Glanvill,
William de Mandeville, 3rd Earl of Essex,
Hervey de Walter, Lord of Parham,
Sir Richard of Peckham,
Sir Geoffrey of Greenwich,
Walther of Leeds

"Were I you, Earl Marshal I would destroy that parchment once you have read it. Failure to do so might result in death for those six men."

After he had gone I wondered at his words. He was Chancellor and yet he was fearful for his life. I sent for my four knights. They had spent the day looking at the security of the tower. It was far from perfect. The arrival of our men, however, had trebled the number of men available to us.

We can improve the defences, lord. The gate which is closest to the city is stone and solid. The gate to the east although weaker is protected by the Tower. There is no gate on the north wall. The river gate has a tower and the south-west bastion tower to protect it. If the gatehouse in the west wall fell then we might struggle to hold the castle."

"Thank you, Harold. Here is my plan. Tomorrow morning, we don plain cloaks. Do not wear your surcoats. Choose four good men to accompany us. Archers would be good. We will walk the streets and discover the mood of the people. Then we shall try to find you a ship, James."

Sir Richard asked, "Why do we walk the streets, Earl Marshal? Is that not dangerous?"

"We will be mailed but I know of no better way to discover the mood of a city. The Archbishop is worried. I wish to discover if he has reason to be worried or if he is just a nervous churchman. It is also some time since I was in the city. There has been much work in the last few years. Let us be as scouts. Your father will tell you the value of a scouting expedition. Instead of discovering where the trees and rivers lie we will see where the roads narrow and can be held. We will find where we might be ambushed or where we might ambush. Make no mistake, Richard. This is war but not one which you have experienced." I saw Samuel nod. I was teaching my grandson another lesson. I had fought in towns and knew that it was a deadly battlefield.

The four archers we took each carried a short sword and a dagger. We crossed the bridge from the tower. At the moment the ditch was almost dry but I had set some of my men to deepening it at low tide. Then we would have water under the bridge to the castle.

. We headed for the area around St. Paul's of the Cross. That was where the markets could be found. We knew we were getting close when we smelled the bread from St Paul's bakehouse. This was the heart of the city. People needed meat, fish and poultry. They needed corn and they needed bread. All of them could be obtained within a hundred and fifty paces of the cathedral. The huge market there was called Cheap. We could buy almost anything we wished there.

My men tried to protect me as we passed through the throngs of folk buying and selling. The fact that they had coin to spend was a good thing. There was prosperity and that would make the people less likely to rebel. It was also a place filled with foreigners. Many were from the foreign ships anchored in the river. They sailed up the river and sold their wares then returned home with the profits and the goods they had bought. I found a stall selling wine from the Vendée. The area of Poitou was very loyal to the King. A visitor from that region would be more sensitive to a change in mood.

"Four beakers of your best red wine, my friend. If it is good enough then I will buy a jug."

He smiled, "Then I will ready you one now for this wine has been kissed by God!"

I handed over the coins and sipped the wine. It was good but a little young for drinking. "Not bad. You must have made a quick voyage or jugged it too soon. I would have left it in the barrel for a little while longer."

He nodded. My words had shown him that I knew my wine. "You are a good judge sir but three months from now and it will be like nectar."

I laughed, "Who knows where we will all be in three months? However, you seem like an honest fellow and I can see you when next you visit if it does not match my expectations."

He looked shiftily at the jug. "I will do you a special price, lord, for I am not sure when I will return here."

"The market is thronged. Is there a better one I do not know?"

"Oh it is good now lord but two years since it had the revolt by the King's sons and I have heard that his eldest son is not happy about his lack of money. If revolution comes again then merchants lose money."

Samuel finished his wine and said, "They have war in France. Does that not affect the markets?"

He shrugged, "Everyone produces wine in France. We make more money here but we will wait until life settles down again. There is an air of danger here, lord. We hear whispers of unrest." He shrugged, "We are not warriors we are but simple merchants. Even the seas are more dangerous. Since the King is preoccupied in France there has been an upsurge in pirates raiding merchant ships. Four of us came together to give ourselves protection."

I handed over the money and gave the jug to Thomas. I did not believe that he was a simple merchant but I could see that there was something which threatened the stability of the crown. I was the lord who had been given the task of protecting the realm and I would do so. I would not be returning to Stockton.

As we went around the various stalls we heard the same message. The market was thriving but it was a case of making hay while the sun shone. All of them saw dark clouds on the horizon. None knew whence the trouble would come but all were concerned and the consensus was that young Henry would be at the root of it all. Alarmingly the rumour of killer knights and men at arms was more widespread. Each was vague and lacked detail but the rumours all had a similar message in them. The rumours were based on fact.

We headed down to the river. The larger ships were on the eastern side of the wooden London Bridge. I noticed that it needed repairs. Like many things, it had been neglected. I saw the ship from the Vendée. That was a possibility but I was looking for an English ship. It took some time but we found one. She was a collier from Hartness. Her captain was a grumpy and melancholic man. "Our coal has not brought the price we hoped, my lord. The forges and weapon-making workshops here in England do not need it. We are heading to Normandy. There they have a great demand for our coal. There is more demand for new weapons and mail there than in England. It is a trickier voyage and we have to be careful in Normandy but there is coin to be made."

"Would you take Sir James here and his squire with you?"

I handed him a coin, "Of course Warlord." He had lowered his voice but I was still shocked.

"You recognised me?"

"When I was a lad we came down from Hartness for the market in Stockton. Aye, Earl, I know you. I am guessing you do not wish your presence known?"

"I would prefer to be anonymous."

"Then your secret is safe with me. William of Kingston is an old friend and shipmate. Your knight and his squire will be safe."

"When do you sail?"

"On the last tide of the day. You have a couple of hours at the most my lord."

I nodded, "Let us return then, Sir James. You need to pack and I need to ensure that you know what to say."

Chapter 4

Once Sir James had boarded the ship I felt much more comfortable. My son and King Henry would know of the threat. It would not be a quick voyage but I trusted both the captain and my knight. That it was not a visible and tangible threat did not worry me. When the princes had revolted we had not taken heed of the warning signs. I hoped that King Henry would this time around. I rode, with a surcoat and armed men, to speak with the three men I could trust. My scouts and spies had still to return with a comprehensive report. I did not mind. I would rather have a full report than gossip and hints. If they came back and told me there were no killer knights in London then I would be happier.

Sir Ranulf was a good knight. The King had rewarded him for his action at the New Castle with a large estate to the north of London. I asked him outright about these killer knights. He looked surprised but not shocked, "I thought them a rumour, Earl Marshal, a legend. I heard of knights disappearing or being found dead but I put it down to outlaws."

"That is what they wish you to think. There is a method to this plan. When they come for me it will be with vengeance in their hearts but there are others that they will kill because it brings their master closer to power."

"And who is their master?"

I shrugged, "If I knew that then the threat would be ended. It could be the French or," I measured my words carefully, "it could be one of the princes."

"Surely not. King Henry is old."

I shook my head, "I am old, Ranulf. The King is of an age with my son. He could live for another thirty years. Would young Henry wait that long? Richard? He is ambitious. Will Geoffrey be satisfied with Brittany? The only one I can see without a motive is John, He has no hopes of anything and four men would have to die before he could attain the throne."

"Or it could be someone who has no desire to rule England but wishes to see us weak."

I had not thought of that and it made sense. "We are all in the dark. Let us try to gather more information and remain vigilant. Have you men you can mobilise in case of danger?"

He nodded, "I lived in the borderlands too long to do other."

"Then I will find us more allies on whom we can rely. I have sent spies out and now I await their return."

We visited the other two lords. Neither were as well prepared as Sir Ranulf but we were both determined to thwart any attempt to take over our country in the absence of our King. What worried me was how far away was the manor of de Mandeville. He would not be able to reach us quickly. De Walter had few men and was ill himself. He was loyal but I doubted his ability to aid us. I told them both that they might need to muster the fyrd.

Guiscard and his men had not yet returned to the Tower. In fact, we might have thought that they had deserted had not a sharp-eyed Thomas, watching from the south-west bastion tower spied the body of Guiscard the Gascon on the mud opposite the castle at low tide. Sir Harold took a boat across the river and returned with his body. He had many cuts on his body. His eyes and genitals had been removed. He had been tortured first and his legs showed signs of having been bound. His friend, Peter Longstride, said, "They weighed him down lord so that he would not be found. I am guessing that Jean and Arne both lie at the bottom of the Thames too."

I was getting old or perhaps my men were not as good as they once were. I had sent three good men to their deaths. Worse, I had alerted the killers that I was on to them. They would go to ground and they would hide. We were now blind and in the dark.

That night it was a sombre hall where we all late. It was Sir Samuel who was not only positive but found a solution to the problem. "Grandfather, we need to do nothing."

"Let them win?"

"They are killers. Who are they to kill?"

Sir Richard said, "Is it important?"

Sir Harold said, "Samuel is correct. Who will they target? The Chancellor? The Archbishop? Those two hold the key to money and the Church."

"We could invite them here and protect them."

Samuel looked at me, "You are forgetting the most important target, Earl Marshal. You. With you out of the way then the Chancellor would be an easy target. If the Chancellor dies you will appoint another. They will come for you."

In a sudden moment of clarity, I saw that he was right. The letter had warned me of this and I had been side-tracked by conspiracy and attempts to seize power. If I was killed then England would be at risk for my son, the King and William Marshal were all in France. This might not even be a plot involving one of the King's children. There were many lords who had claims to the English throne. They would try to kill me.

I smiled, "Then that is good news."

"How so, Warlord?"

"They want a target. I will stop sneaking around and I will ride in broad daylight. I will announce myself so that they can take their chances. We have one advantage over them. We have Ralph of Lincoln and his archers. We use them to be as our guardians. The walls which go around the city are perfect for archers. We ride around the city and make certain that our archers can see us. At the same time, the rest of you can look for that which should not be there. The killers are in hiding but they must come into the streets if they are to kill me. Either that or enter the White Tower and there is but one entrance. Thanks to the King it now has protection. We have a plan. We use me as bait! More wine!"

Samuel was appalled, "You are happy to be the bait?"

"I am old, Samuel, better that I die rather than one of you. So long as we discover the killers then that will be enough but I have no plans to fall to an assassin's sword. They will have to get close enough to me to use a sword. That is all the chance I need."

We spent the rest of the evening planning how we would defend the Tower and how we would draw out the killers. I wondered if they had first gone to Stockton and that explained why Guiscard and the others had not been killed immediately. Had I not left Stockton when I had then there might have been deaths in Stockton. This was better. My people at home were safe. I had Thomas polish and burnish my armour and my helmet. I had not worn my mail mittens for a while but I had them cleaned and attached to my mail. I wanted to be seen and I wanted to be protected.

That night I did not take the draught despite the pain. I prayed to God that if there was to be a death then it would be mine and not one of my knights. I prayed that he would allow me to be the one to end the lives of these killers. Then I slept and I slept sounder than I had in many a month.

When I woke I was refreshed and eager to ride forth. I mounted White Star. Sir Harold had briefed the archers and they had left before dawn. I rode with just my knights and their squires. Thomas carried my banner. This time we did not head for the thronged market. My men had been dumped in the river. The hidden killers would be found well away from there. We rode along the north wall. There was always a watch on the walls. It would not deter a killer but they would not draw attention to themselves. It would be easier if they lodged close to the walls and to the main gate so that they could beat a hasty retreat. There were four such gates: Aldgate, Bishops Gate. Moor Gate and Cripples Gate. I did not rule out Aldgate but I thought it was the least likely for it was close to the Tower. We rode slowly on our progress and I spoke with people that we met. I was not in disguise and the city was filled with people who sought my attention. I was not naïve enough to believe that they were all folk who were King Henry's supporters. We did meet the odd old soldier who had served with me or the Empress and they were given a coin. The majority were those who sought to take advantage of me if they could. We still spoke with those. I used them and tried to discover if knights new to the city had been seen.

We had worked out that they would need a stable for their horses. With that in mind, I ruled out St. Helen's nunnery. Close by was the Warrior's Thumb, an inn with a stable. We stopped there, ostensibly to water our horses but in reality, so that William, Samuel's squire, could check the stables. There were horses but they were poor ones. A knight would have to be desperate to use one.

As we headed towards St Augustine's Monastery Richard began to despair. "Earl Marshal we have ridden for hours and covered but a long mile and a half. At this rate, it would take us a month to discover them."

I nodded, "It probably will. You have other plans, Sir Richard?"

Samuel laughed and I heard an irritated sigh from Sir Harold. "No, Earl Marshal, but time passes."

"And Sir James will not even be at the coast of France yet. He has to ride to find the King and then they can set off home. I expect no help for a month so a month to discover these killers would seem about right, would it not?" He said nothing. "Guiscard, Jean and Arne paid for my impatience with their lives. These men are killers. Do not underestimate them."

We stopped at the gates of the monastery. The friar who greeted us did not allow us to enter. That was not unusual. Friars were ever wary of armed knights. "Would you tell the Abbot that the Earl Marshal is in residence at the Tower? When time allows I would have conference with him there."

"The Abbot is a busy man, my lord. He has many duties and he serves God."

"And he lives in London within the city walls under the protection of the King and his appointed officers." I proffered my seal of office. "I will be here for some time. Perhaps I could visit with the Abbot instead."

He shook his head, "I am sorry, lord I meant no disrespect. Of course, the Abbot will visit with you. A friar will come to the gates when it is convenient."

"Good for I would like to entertain the Abbot."

As we rode away Sir Harold said, "A little suspicious, lord."

"Not necessarily. The recent revolt has made all such men wary. The Chancellor told me that. This is our first expedition and it is yielding me much information."

Samuel was curious, "Information Earl Marshal?"

We had passed some fine houses. "The houses we have passed which have two floors and solid doors are the homes of merchants."

He nodded, "I wondered why we did not inspect them for they have stables too."

"They have walls around the houses but the stables would house one or two horses at the most. Three of our men were killed. All were handy with a sword and a knife. It would have taken at least six men to overcome them. We seek a bigger hall. Did you notice that all of the merchant's houses have at least two men watching the door? They are warriors. They look to be warriors who had been men at arms. When last I was in London this was not so. The merchants are wary despite the busy market."

We were approaching the Guildhall and the house of the Mayor, Richard White, when we passed another of the merchant's houses. This time one of the two men on guard approached me. I vaguely recognised him. He had a slight limp. He smiled and bowed, "Warlord, it is good to see you again."

He hurried on in case I had forgotten him. I called him back, "Alan of Hauxley, I fought alongside you at the Battle of Berwick a couple of years ago."

It was when he spoke that I had recognised him. He had a north-country accent. "As I recall you served the Lord of Morthpath."

He nodded, pleased that I had remembered him, "You showed the Scots that day, lord. Guiscard the Gascon told me that you had returned. London will be safer now."

"You spoke with Guiscard?"

He paused for he heard the edge to my voice, "Aye lord. He was with a giant who looked like a Viking and a little Frenchman." He came closer, "He said he was looking for knights new to the city and I told him that I had seen six such knights. He said he would tell you."

"When was this?"

"Two nights since. I was drinking in the Tabard up by the Moorgate for my dwellings are beyond the wall. He bought me ale and we talked."

"He is dead and was murdered before he could tell me. Where did you see the six knights?"

"I did not know." He crossed himself. "I told him that I had seen the knights seven days ago. I saw them and their squires heading through the Cripplegate. I said that it was strange that they rode such good horses and yet had no servants."

I dismounted and went close, "Have you seen them since?" He shook his head. "And how were they dressed? What livery?"

"That is why I noticed them and spoke of it to Guiscard. None wore a device. Their surcoats were simple brown ones and their shields were similarly painted. I thought it strange for all knights like to carry their mark about them. I wondered if they were knights of some sort of order. Their hair suggested that. They had the full beards and the cropped hair of knights who have served in the Holy Land. They looked to have the same colour as the scout your son Earl William used."

I now saw why Guiscard had been killed but how had Alan of Hauxley avoided their swords. "How were they armed?"

"Mail, long sword and an open helmet with a nasal. Their horses were good ones. They were a mix of warhorse and palfrey." He stroked White Star, "Similar to this one."

"Tell me, Alan of Hauxley, where did Guiscard and the others go after you had told them your information?"

"They said that they would return to the Tower and tell you."

I took a coin from my purse. It was a gold one. "You are in great danger. The men who killed my men at arms are ruthless. Guiscard must have stumbled upon them after they left you. I do not think that Guiscard told them anything. I would ask your master if you could leave his service. There is a place for you in my castle at Stockton."

"I have a wife, children and my wife's parents to watch over. They cannot make the journey."

"Then I pray you to keep a good watch and avoid dark places. There is a great danger."

I mounted and headed toward the Guildhall. I had seen enough and needed to return home but first I would see the mayor. I did not know if I could trust him but I had to let him know that I was now in command of the Tower. If he was an ally that would help and if he was an enemy it would be a warning.

Sir Harold had heard most of what Alan of Hauxley had told me, "Then we know the rough area where they were seen but we have already passed by there."

"Our archers walked the walls. When we return, we will ask them. They may have seen something from above which we missed."

I did not like the mayor. He struck me as a self-serving weasel who was out just to make as much money as he could while he held the office. He was a villain but I did not think he would be a traitor. When he spoke to me he was both fawning and ingratiating. He was not a warrior. I did not doubt that he had slit men's throats but it had not been on the battlefield. After an hour's conversation with him, I felt dirty. We learned nothing that we did not know before. He confirmed the prosperity of the city and reiterated the fear that there might be another revolt. As with the other merchants with whom we had spoken, he did not know whence this threat would come.

We rode back using the reverse of our route. We passed Alan of Hauxley and the monastery. The inn where we had watered our horses was now much busier as trade picked up. People who had been at the Cheap and the East Cheap were on their way home and those who lived beyond the city wall could call for a drink and some food first. It was the middle of the afternoon when we entered the gate at the southwest bastion tower. I was weary but my mind buzzed with insect-like thoughts. I had some of the pieces of the puzzle. Now I had to put them together.

I sent for the archers from the wall. We gathered in the hall for my other men needed to know what we had discovered. I told them how we thought our men had been killed. I saw angry looks. The three men had been popular. "These knights are killers. They will not fight with honour. Be aware of that. Grant, what did the archers see?"

"When you left the inn, a man left and headed west. We lost him in the alleyways. He looked like a warrior." I nodded. Then the knights did have men they were using as servants or spies. I was not surprised. "The monastery has a stable. We could not see into it but there were horses within and a number of them. A groom came out. He had been tending to them."

"Was anyone close to us when we spoke to the two merchant's guards?"

"It was hard to see there, lord for you had moved away from the wall. We cannot protect you from the walls if you are more than a hundred paces from them. There is no clear line of sight."

"Do not worry, Grant, we will now concentrate our attention on the area around the monastery, the Cheap and the inn. I intend to have some of you watch Alan of Hauxley. You will look for others who watch him. Let us see who has the better spies. We will try to get into the monastery grounds." They all nodded. There were few of them but having lost three of their number they were determined. "All of you will wear mail; even the archers. Wear it under your jerkins but we can ill afford to lose more men."

As I walked back to the tower I examined King Henry's new tower which abutted the White Tower. Steps led up to it and the door was at right angles to them. Two men could hold off an army. "Sir Harold, from now on I want two good men on guard here every hour of the day. Make sure they are our men. If there is treachery then it will be here. They may well try to attack us at night when we sleep. The outer defences and walls can be easily breached."

"Aye lord."

I was tired and while my knights organized our defences I went to my chamber. I would not sleep but I would rest my head. Often that alleviated some of the increasing pain I felt. My life had been measured in months; was it now to be measured in weeks or even days? I had helped Maud gain a crown for our son. Now I needed to do one more thing before I died, secure it for him. England was his true crown. Why was he in France? I must have dozed off for I was woken by Thomas.

"Earl Marshal there is a friar at the gate. He has come from the Abbot."

I rose and followed Thomas. My guards had held the friar at the gatehouse by the southwest bastion tower. They were taking no chances. Sir Harold and his son, Richard, were there. The friar did not look happy to have been kept waiting.

"Earl Marshal, the Abbot received your message. He would be pleased to have you dine with him tomorrow evening."

"Good. There will be eight of us."

He frowned, "The Abbot said to invite just yourself."

"And I am telling the Abbot that I will be bringing three household knights and four squires." There was authority in my voice and I saw that the friar would not argue. He nodded.

As we walked back I asked, "What do you think, Harold?"

"I think you were wise to take us. If he had had you alone and been an enemy then you would be dead."

"Yet he is a churchman and if I was killed in his monastery then questions would be asked. Why did they want me alone?" I could not fathom it. We approached the Tower. "Where is Samuel?"

Sir Harold said, "I know not."

I looked at Richard who had a guilty look upon his face. I glared at him, "I am sorry, Earl Marshal but I swore I would not say." I just continued to stare at him and he crumbled, "He and William went into the streets in disguise. He said he would find these knights."

I shook my head, "Young fools! Does no one obey my orders any longer? Thomas, fetch ten archers and men at arms."

We wore our arming hoods and mail ventails. We would have no time to return to don our helmets and get our shields. I would have to use my sword and dagger. The eight men at arms and archers hurried from the warrior hall and I began to run towards the bridge which led to the city. As we passed under the tower I shouted, "Call out the guard and if you hear the sounds of battle then send men to our aid."

Darkness had fallen and the watch was set. The city watch on the walls saw us head for the postern gate. Sir Harold shouted, "Open the gate. It is the Earl Marshal."

The door opened and two of the watch stood there. "Guard this gate. None will be allowed to leave save that I give permission. Understood?"

"Aye, Earl Marshal."

The streets were largely empty. There would be people in inns and taverns but the markets had ended as had the legitimate business of the day. Any men who were abroad at night were beyond the law. The whores and doxies plied their trade but they scurried off the cobbles when they heard the tramp of our feet. We were not trying to move silently. If Samuel heard us then he would know help was at hand and any who planned evil would move from our path. We were nearing the street known as Leadenhall when we heard the clash of steel. We ran.

We turned a corner by Cornhill and saw the backs of five men. I saw that two of them wore spurs. They were knights. A sixth man lay on the ground bleeding. My grandson was tall and I saw his head above those men attacking him. "Stockton!" I gave the battle cry to make the attackers fear us and to give hope to my grandson. Two of the attackers turned and fled. I shouted to John of Oxbridge, "Take four men and get after them!"

I saw William slide to the ground and two men turned to face us. Even in the dark, I could tell that they had swarthy complexions. They should have run but, instead, the two of them charged me. I was taken by surprise and I barely blocked the blow from the first sword with my dagger. As I parried the second sword with my own, Thomas and Richard ran up and skewered the two would be killers with their swords. Even as I pushed them aside I saw my grandson kill the knight with whom he was fighting.

He dropped to his knees. William was lying in a pool of blood. Harry of Norton knelt next to him. Harry helped to heal the men's wounds in battle. Brother Peter had trained him. He began to bind his left arm and said, over his shoulder, "He is lucky, lord. It is a bad cut on his left arm but he will heal. He has a blow to his head but I see his eyes opening."

"Good." I rounded on Samuel, "And what in God's name were you doing? Trying to get yourself killed?"

He looked shamefaced. The wounds to his young squire were his responsibility. "I did not like sitting doing nothing. I thought to look for knights myself."

I pointed to the dead knight, "And you found one! You were lucky we came when we did."

He looked contrite, "I know and I am sorry."

John of Oxbridge returned. He shook his head, "We lost them, Earl Marshal. There was a fist fight outside an inn by the Guildhall and they disappeared into the crowd."

"It is not your fault. Bring these four bodies with us."

Sir Harold said, "And four of you flank the Warlord. He is in danger." I looked at him. "Warlord if two men turn to face twelve then either they are very good or they are dedicated. They went for you. They ignored me, Sir Richard and our squires. You are the target and you are the man they wish dead!"

Chapter 5

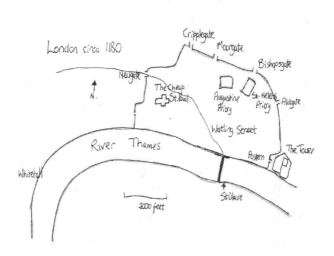

We examined the bodies by the light of brands in the open ground behind the city gate. The knight was, like the other dead men at arms, someone who had been in the Holy Land or hot climes at the very least. They all had good mail, even the men at arms. Sir Harold surmised that they had been sergeants at arms and at least one of them had been a Templar. He had found the symbol of the Templars around his neck. He held the token in his hand.

"See Warlord, we have seen this before."

Richard said, "I cannot read the words. How do you know it is Templar?"

Samuel took it and used his fingers to illustrate as he spoke. "My father has one of these he took from a dead Templar. The two men represent the Templar order. The words are hard to read because this has been borne for many years and some of the letters have been damaged."

"John of Oxbridge take their heads and plant them on spears on the bridge. Let our enemies know that we have taken their killers. Tomorrow I will speak with the Abbot. Until then no one leaves or enters the castle. There will be no exceptions." I looked pointedly at Samuel who nodded.

"And the bodies, Warlord?"

"Fasten them with stones and put them in the river after dark when it is high tide."

Samuel held up a small bag. He opened it and held it to my nose. "What is that?"

"Hashish. Masood, my father's scout uses it occasionally. He chews it. He told me that it makes a man immune to pain. It might explain why those sergeants at arms recklessly attacked us. They thought they were invincible."

We were in a sombre mood when we re-entered the tower. We sat with Samuel to continue to discover what had happened. William was taken to the doctor. "Well? Let us know all!"

Samuel nodded. "We went to the inn. We were looking for a dark-skinned man and we found one."

Sir Harold shook his head, "Then you were meant to find him."

"I can see that now but we thought we were hidden in the shadows."

"These men are good. They would have smelled you."

"Smelled us?"

"You bathed today?"

"Of course."

"Then they smelled the soap you used. They smelled that you wore clean clothes that did not smell of piss or dung. They could have followed you in the dark. Go on."

"We were not completely stupid. When he entered the alleyway close to the Cornhill we did not follow. We thought to find you and tell you."

Sir Harold said, "When you turned then there were five men behind you."

He looked shocked, "How did you know?"

My former squire laughed, "It is many years since I was an outlaw but there are some things you do not forget."

"Why do you think they did not kill you?"

"I think they wanted us alive. The knight who escaped looked to be the leader. I would know him again!" He added eagerly.

"But you drew your swords and fought them."

He nodded, "It seemed the right thing to do."

"And it was. Better a death with a sword in your hand than be tortured like Guiscard, Jean and Arne." I patted the back of his hand. "You have been lucky and learned a valuable lesson." He nodded. I leaned back, "It is me that they seek. Had we more men then I would have every building searched."

Sir Harold shook his head. "This city is like Sherwood to the men we hunt. They know every inch of it. The streets are like warrens. The only way would be to burn the houses and wait for them to flee."

I laughed, "A somewhat drastic approach but it would work. We have more intelligence than we did. Four of their number are dead. We have to have hurt them."

Sir Harold said, "Aye and paid them back for our dead men."

"Tomorrow night, we all keep our eyes and ears open when we are dining with the abbot. He may know something or I might be overly suspicious but he has stables." I looked at Samuel. "Had William not been injured then we might have used the squires to examine them but we only have three now and if the abbot is involved then your excursion tonight will have put them on their guard."

It was late when we retired for I had made certain that all of them, knights and squires knew what we planned. We all had to be of one mind. The next day was one in which we prepared. I would not leave the Tower. Sir James would still be travelling to France. This threat was a bigger one than we had expected. It felt cowardly to sit behind our walls but I had perilously few men. I sent for Samuel so that I could interrogate him more. He could not tell me anything else. That was his lack of experience. He had fought in battles but the murky world of a city like London was beyond him.

After he had finished I said, "Samuel you and your father, along with your sister Ruth are now the only family I have. I would have you safe."

"I am a knight."

"I am not talking about battles and combat. You are the equal of any knight but you are naïve if you think you can take on treacherous snakes like de Mamers on their terms. Promise me you will not be so reckless again." He hesitated, "William could have died because of you."

"I will not be foresworn. I swear that I will not put any man's life in jeopardy but I will not allow you to be killed while I still breathe. I know I have much to learn. Yes, William was hurt, but both of us learned valuable lessons this night."

I sighed. He was of my blood and I had done the same as he when I had been younger. "Tonight, we leave the Tower. Although we are just going to eat I would have you prepare as though for war. Wear mail and gambeson. Have sharpened swords and daggers."

"I will!"

Although we wore mail we dressed in clean surcoats. We would not take helmets and we would leave our shields but we wore arming caps and coifs. If the Abbot thought it rude then so be it. We were groomed and shaved. I wanted the abbot at his ease. I needed to know where he stood. We had walked into a city filled with traps, ambushers and treachery. We had to be ready for anything.

I sent for the Chancellor. He arrived with his guards and looked every bit as worried as he had done the first time we spoke. I told of the deaths of my men and the attacks on Samuel and William. "Then none of us are safe!"

"I fear you are right. I would have you bring your family here to the Tower. It is the most secure building in London. It is not perfect but we can defend it."

"I have no family. I just have retainers and clerks."

"Then bring them and your guards. Until we have aid from France we are vulnerable to attack."

His sergeant at arms, Egbert, nodded, "He is right, my lord. They have more men at arms here and the White Tower can be defended even if the walls fall." He looked at me, "There are plenty of supplies, Earl Marshal?"

"We have enough for three months!"

The Chancellor was convinced. He would be my only extra guest. The Archbishop of Canterbury had taken to his castle at Rochester. That was as strong as the White Tower. I could go to the meal with the abbot confident that I had taken all the steps necessary to keep England safe.

Although our men wanted to come with us I needed them to keep the walls guarded. There was little sign of unrest but it would take but a spark to start a revolt. I had Peter Longstride captain the guard at the city gate. If there was trouble then they would come quickly. This band of knights had come with a purpose and I knew that once I was dead it would be like an avalanche. Were my months, not weeks but days?

Our squires and their horses were not taken to the stables. That interested me. Instead, they were taken to a water trough. The friars had some bags of grain although we had walked such a short journey that it was not necessary. Food and drink were provided for the squires. They had thought of everything. There were platters and goblets for the squires and two ducks had been cooked for them. The Augustine friars lived well. These were not poor friars. They ate and drank as well as any baron. The Abbot greeted me with a smile but the smile was not in his eyes. "Welcome, Earl Marshal. Forgive my friar for his words yesterday. They are very protective of me."

There was something familiar about the abbot but I could not put my finger on it. It was the context that confused me. I had seen someone who looked like him but it was a memory, a shadow from the past and the shadow did not wear the habit of an Augustine abbot.

"Think nothing of it, Abbot…?"

"Call me Geoffrey, Earl Marshal. I am not precious about my title. I am a humble priest who seeks to do God's work."

It was as we sat down and candles were brought to illuminate the table that I saw he had a healthy colour. He looked to be unlike many churchmen. He was muscled and he had not run to fat. If I had seen him in other clothes then I would have said that he was a warrior.

Prayers were said and then the tiny birds' eggs in aspic were brought out. The wine which was poured was of the highest quality and had not been heavily watered. This was not a poor order for there were spices in abundance. I ate one out of politeness.

"You look to be a man who has travelled." He cocked his head. "Forgive me I notice such things. Your skin has been burned by the sun. I do not think that the English sun gave you such a deep tan."

He smiled, "My family left England when my grandfather was killed. My father took the cross and I was born in Outremer. I joined the order in Italy."

I sipped the red wine in my goblet, "A good wine. I have a vineyard in Anjou and this is equally as good. It tastes like it is from the same region."

"I confess that I like my wine. This is from the vineyards close to La Manche in Berry where we have a monastery. I was a canon there before I came here."

The fish was brought in. It was a lake pike. The abbot had spared no expense. He had to have had this fish ready prepared for the feast. There were no lakes close to the city. Had he always planned to invite me to dine or was this for another guest? I was in a suspicious frame of mind. His friars and servants kept our goblets filled but we drank sparingly. We needed our wits about us. I was becoming increasingly suspicious of our host. As the night wore on he seemed to relax more and drink more. I broached the subject of the unrest.

He smiled, "When the King is absent there will always be unrest. We need a King on the throne rather than posturing in France. We do not need France. We have England."

"Yet the King has land in France too: Poitou, Gascony, Brittany, Aquitaine, Normandy, Maine. More of France belongs to King Henry than to King Louis. Is he not right to protect his lands from the voracious French?"

For the first time, the abbot's mask slipped. "Some would argue that the land was stolen from the French." He pushed his wine away and smiled, "I am afraid I have enjoyed too much of this French wine." He laughed, "Perhaps it is twisting my tongue. I am of course a simple priest and politics do not concern me. What I do know, Earl Marshal, is that many more of the poor seek our help. Coin is spent on war when it should go for alms." I nodded as the sweet meats were brought in. Rich butter biscuits which were covered with honeyed nuts were brought in along with figs and goats' cheese.

I found the abbot to be a hypocrite. We had eaten enough in one night to feed the poor of London for a week.

He rubbed his hands as the laden platters were placed in the middle of the table. "This is my indulgence and my vice, Earl Marshal."

Just then Sir Harold rose, "I am afraid I need to make water, Abbot."

He smiled, "Brother Raymond would you take Sir Harold to the garderobe. Ask Roger to bring in the dessert wine.

As he ate I asked, innocently, "Have you heard of a group of knights and sergeants at arms from the Holy Land? They are said to be in the city. Having lived in the Holy Land then you might know them." He looked surprised. The fig with the cheese was halfway to his mouth and he froze. I smiled, "I ask because having grown up there you could have come across them."

"I have not heard of any. They would stand out in this city."

"And yet last night six of them tried to attack my grandson. I have four of their heads on spears outside my gates. You are more than welcome to inspect them. You might recognise them."

He placed the fig and cheese, uneaten on the table. "If I can help I will but there were many warriors in Outremer and I was young."

"Yet your skin shows that you were there recently."

"I think you are mistaken."

I paused and looked at him, "You are a priest, abbot. Do not be foresworn."

He looked flustered and then smiled, "Of course. Now I recall. I am recently returned from Rome and the sun burned brightly there. You have a suspicious mind, Earl Marshal."

"That is how I have lived for so long."

"It is late and I am tired, Earl Marshal. It was good to have this conversation. Now I feel that we understand each other. Tomorrow I will come and speak with you at the Tower. Then I will have a clear head and I will be able to examine the dead men. You may be right. There is a chance that I might know them."

Just then Harold re-entered. He nodded at me. "And I am tired. I look forward to greeting you at the Tower. I cannot promise fare as fine as that which we enjoyed this night but I will send men to the Cheap to see what we can get."

The squires had heeded my instructions and most of the wine was untouched but the two ducks had been devoured. As we mounted Sir Harold leaned over, "I spoke with one of the friars on my way back. Do you know what the abbot's family name is?"

I had an idea but I shook my head, "Not really."

"It is D'Oilli. He is Sir Richard's grandson."

I smacked my right fist into my left palm. "Now I see the web. Have your swords ready and keep your wits about you. I suspect treachery this night. Don your coifs." We did not draw our swords but slid them a little way out of the scabbard. The night was damp and we did not want them to stick. The metal coifs and ventail did not restrict our view as much as a helmet would but we had less protection.

We passed the Cornhill and headed for the convent. The roads seemed empty but we scanned the buildings which were adjacent to us. These killers had shown that they knew how to hide in plain sight.

The town watch had been warned of our departure. I reined in close to them, "Has anyone left since we arrived?"

"Just a wagon with a family. They said they were heading for Tilbury."

"No horsemen?" He shook his head.

"Then continue to be vigilant."

The gate was just eighty paces from the bridge. Sir Harold and I had had the men deepen it so that water now flowed up to the bridge. We would need a larger force of labour if it was to be extended all the way around the walls. As we came out I waved to the men at the gate. There was no sign of the wagon. I should have asked when it left. There was something about it that nagged at the back of my mind.

We had just stepped onto the bridge when White Star whinnied. He never made a sound unless there was danger. I drew my sword and shouted, "Ambush!"

The squires and Sir Richard were confused. Instead of drawing their weapons immediately, they looked for danger. Samuel and Sir Harold had their weapons out as the men clambered out of the ditch where they had been waiting. I spurred White Star towards the nearest killer as John of Oxbridge shouted, "To arms! To arms! Treachery!"

A spear was rammed towards me but I had made White Star begin to move and I jinked out of the way as I brought my sword down across his shoulders. He wore mail but my blade rasped through the links and into his shoulder. Richard and his squire were in trouble. Richard had his sword out but not his squire Walter. Samuel and Thomas galloped towards them. That left Harold and Etheldred, his squire with me. I saw that there were at least ten men. The gates to the city gate towers groaned open. Even as I brought my sword to slice into the helmet of one of the attackers, Ethelred was speared in the leg. Sir Harold went to his aid and sliced left and right. That left me isolated. Three men ran at me. One grabbed White Star's reins while a second thrust his spear at me. I brought my sword down at the third man and our blades rang together. White Star slipped and he began to slide down the bank to the water below. There was a scream as his body crushed the man holding his reins. I kicked my feet free from the stirrups. The other two killers scrambled down the bank towards me.

I heard Sir Harold shout, "I am coming!"

We splashed into the water and, as White Star struggled to his feet, I scrambled away from his thrashing hooves. I still held my sword and I grabbed my dagger. I waded across the ditch. It only came to my knees and I turned so that the men on the walls could protect my back. I heard feet above me as men ran from the castle. The two men who had slipped down the bank came towards me. One was a knight and the other looked to be a squire or a man at arms. Two more men rushed down the bank to get at me. Above us, I saw Sir Harold as he hurried to my aid. His sword came down and struck one in the back but the second whirled and, holding his sword two handed, hacked into the knee of Sir Harold. As my knight fell, the warrior swung himself into the saddle of Sir Harold's horse and galloped down the ditch to the river.

I had to get to my knight. I threw caution to the wind. Instead of waiting for them to attack me, I ran at them. They were both in the water and finding it hard to keep their feet. The flat of a sword clanged off the left side of my mail coif and I lunged with my dagger. I hit the man in the neck. He put his hands to his throat as his breath went from him. He fell at my knees choking on his own blood and a lack of air.

The second warrior swung his sword and hit me in the back. It knocked me from my feet and I landed in the water. Above me, I heard a cry of triumph. "Now is Geoffrey Guiscard avenged. Now the Warlord will die!"

He knew I was old and he anticipated that I would struggle to rise to my feet. He was wrong. I had something to drive me. I had my own friend to avenge. I dived while swinging my sword. His sword came down to strike where my head would have been. Mine bit into his leg above the knee. The force of my blow half severed the leg. His weakened blow hit my back. I landed face down in the bloody, muddy water. I began to choke.

Suddenly hands dragged me to my feet. I looked up and saw that Samuel and Thomas had come to my aid. I brought up some river water and the two of them helped to haul me up to the top of the hill where my men at arms and archers were despatching the last of the enemy. I did not have the breath to shout for them to cease. We needed prisoners. Richard was kneeling next to his father and Harry of Norton was wrapping a bandage around the stump of a thigh.

"Fetch a torch else Sir Harold will die!"

Richard was holding his father's hand, "Do not die, father! This is my fault! I did not have my weapon ready I…"

"Peace. It is not your fault. It was my time." He looked over at me, "I am sorry Warlord, I tried to come to your aid. I am old and I am slow but at least you live. Watch my sons for me. They have much to learn but then so did I. If you could turn a scrawny outlaw into a lord of a manor then Richard and Walter should be child's play."

He did not know that his son Walter lay dead. "You can watch him yourself. Your fighting days are over. Mine are too. We will go back to Stockton and enjoy the salmon in the river."

To my right, I saw the flicker of the torch as it was brought to seal the wound. "It is too late, lord, and you know it. We do not lie to a dying warrior. Fear not, I go to join Dick and Wulfric, Edward and Roger of Lincoln. I …"

His eyes glazed over and he was dead. I roared, into the night, "No!" I should have stayed in Stockton. London might have been lost but Harold, Ethelred, Walter, Jean, Arne and Guiscard would be alive. This city was not worth the lives of the ones who had died. I was not worth their deaths. I sank to my knees and I began to weep silent tears. Most were for the dead; I had lost so many friends and warriors that I had lost count. But I also wept for myself. I was alone. I had outlived all that I cared for All that I had left was my son, William, and his family. Harold was gone and that was the last link with the past. The shadows had come and enveloped my world. Why could I not die and find peace? I began to climb the steep bank.

Just then I had a sudden pain in my head. I could barely stand, "Samuel, get me into the castle for I fear I will faint. The words seemed to come from another and I could barely feel my legs. Was this God answering me? I felt his arms beneath me and I lost the power of my legs. I felt blackness consuming me. Was I dying?

**William
Part Two
A King's war**

Chapter 6

Le Mans France

The King had insisted that I travel to France with him. He could not have the Earl Marshal but he could have his son. Perhaps I was a lucky charm but I did not enjoy the accolade. I wanted to be at home with my wife and my family. My daughter, Ruth, had just lost her husband and she needed me. This was not a war I enjoyed. This was a cagey war. King Henry was using strategy to gain land and power. He was trying to isolate his sons and the King of France. It was a dirty war.

I knew that if my father had been in command then it would have been prosecuted much more forcefully. The war would have been over already. King Henry was trying to show what a clever man he was. He had been accorded accolades and his opinion sought by princes, dukes and even kings. It had gone to his head and he saw himself as a more powerful man than he really was. I knew now, at the age of fifty-two years, that my father was the only really powerful man in the whole of Europe for he was not guided by self-interest. He had the people and the land in his heart. It had taken me many years to realise that. The longer the campaign lasted the more disillusioned I became.

The knights I had taken with me, Sir James of Forcett, Sir Phillip, Sir Padraig, Sir Gilles and Sir Morgan all felt the same. This was more like a game of chess than a war. Neither the King nor his opponent, Louis, seemed willing to take a chance. Sir Leofric was well out of it. I had rarely envied someone a wound but when he had to go back to La Flèche I did. He had left just a day or so ago. It was a lucky wound. Within seven days he would be home and I would still be in France. I would still be with a king who would not bring the enemy to battle but would make us trail up and down the land seeking a better position.

Now, it seemed, we had the opportunity to bring the war or this part of it, to a conclusion. Philip of Flanders had agreed to make peace with King Henry and we had the men whom Henry had left in the north of Normandy available. They were already marching south under the banner of Geoffrey, the Count of Caen. With two hundred banners it would double our army. Despite the small number of knights, I had brought, King Henry regarded my conroi as the most important for I had over a hundred archers as well as a hundred men at arms. They were well led and the most skilled men who had ever followed my banner. I took little credit for that. It was my father who had built them up. I had merely taken them over. All that I was I owed to the Warlord, the Earl Marshal.

We were now heading east towards Chambord. This was a small village just east of Blois but crucially it lay between Bourges and the Loire. King Henry claimed Berry and the French King disputed ownership. If I had been a lawyer it would have been very easy to argue that it was French. The King's grandfather, Henry, had only ever owned the northern part. Stephen of Blois' family, whom my father had fought for many years, had more of a claim than either king. Such arguments were immaterial. Might beat right every time. When the Count of Caen arrived then we would drive south to Bourges and bring this war to a conclusion. Then I could go home.

This was France and King Henry had men who knew the land better than we did. We were not required to scout. My men were the better scouts but I did not complain. Like my father, I resented every lost man at arms and archer. They were all like family to me. Masood, the best scout I had ever met save for Aiden, rode with my archers. He got on well with them. I rode with my two squires, Ralph and Thomas, behind me. Sir Morgan, who had been my squire, rode at my side. The son of a Varangian he had come to us with few polished skills but such natural ability that within months he was already a formidable warrior.

"Earl, will the King's sons revolt any more do you think?"

"Alf, keep your voice down. It is a sore point with the King. He did not actually win the war. He had to make adjustments and come to an accord. That is not King Henry's way. To answer your question, I would have to answer, probably. Geoffrey will soon be married and have Brittany. That will satisfy him; for a while at least. Richard has been given Aquitaine and with his mother incarcerated in Winchester he has his own kingdom. Henry the Younger? He wants England. It is only William Marshal who keeps him on a leash. He busies him with tourneys and hunting. King Henry has given him the Earl as a guard and a mentor. He hopes that William can do for his son what my father did for him; make him a King. I think the revolt is over. And that is why I wonder why the King does not return home!"

"So far we have little to show for our war."

I nodded. "That is why the King has promised to pay us. We have given him the forty-day service to which he is entitled. You will be compensated. The archers and men at arms will receive their money. Any horses lost in the campaign will be made good by the King."

"That is expensive."

"This land is rich. The King did not fight so hard for Scotland, Wales and Ireland. They do not bring in much revenue. When we take Berry, we have a French jewel and the outlay of funds by the King will be justified."

We rode in silence for a while. The land through which we rode was full of vineyards and prosperous farms. This was not England with unpredictable weather and ice for three months of the year. You planted here and it grew. Not only that it grew well. I had been given an estate but when my first wife died I had given it away and gone on Crusade. Stockton and the Tees Valley might not be as rich but it was my home. It had taken the heat of the Holy Land to show me that. I had learned much in that land. I learned the Knights Hospitallers were a worthy group of warrior knights but the Knights Templars were little more than brigands. I had seen lords come from the west and become counts and princes overnight. They rarely ruled well. For me, the crusades had shown me the best and the worst in men. Now that the Franks were losing many of them were fleeing. They were bringing back the worst of the east. I was content with England. This chevauchée on a grand scale did not sit well with me.

One of the King's squires, Philip, rode from the front of the column, "Earl the King would like a word."

I nodded, "Take over, Sir Morgan."

The King was ten years my junior. I had served his father, Geoffrey of Anjou. That and the fact that I was the son of the Warlord seemed to give me a special status. The King had a short temper but I was one of the few who could argue with him. Others dared not do so. His sons argued with him all day. All, that is, save John whom I thoroughly disliked. For all that Henry and Richard argued with their father, they were knights and they were warriors. John was a sulky little prince. I was just happy that he would never be king.

The King was in the middle of a covey of his household knights. When I approached he dismissed them with a wave of his hand. That was his way. His father had enjoyed the company of his household knights. I had been one. He had even preferred their company to that of his wife, the Empress. Henry could be a little more detached. My father had trained him but I knew he had not given him that particular trait. I reined in next to him and he glanced over his shoulder to make certain we could not be overheard.

"Earl, I have a task for you." I nodded. "First I need to take you into my confidence." He explained to me where we were going and what we would do. I was impressed. It was a good plan. It reeked of my father's influence. It combined daring with surprise and yet afforded safety for Anjou and Normandy.

"A good plan sire. It means we can be done with this land inside of a month."

"You have children?"

"Two, sire, a boy and a girl."

"They obey you?"

I was not sure how to answer that. "A difficult question, sire. I have not had cause to order them to do anything yet."

He nodded, "Ah, you are not a king with land to grant." I said nothing. "My sons fight me. I know that their mother puts them up to much of that. The witch is in Winchester and she can rot there. Do you think they will fight each other once I am gone?"

This was another question I could not answer and so I sidestepped it, "You will live a long time, sire."

"My father died young."

"But not your mother."

"I miss her. The advice she gave was sage. I miss your father. To be blunt I would have preferred his company to yours. But his wound…"

I was not offended for I would have preferred to be in England rather than riding through the land of Touraine. "He is old, sire. He should be enjoying his old age in Stockton."

He dismissed the comment with a wave of his hand, "He serves England, as do you." I gave a slight bow and prepared to return to my men. "When we have settled the question of Berry I would have you ride to my son, Richard. I know he admires you and your father."

"And what would I say to him, sire?"

He lowered his voice, "Tell him that he shall have Normandy when I am gone."

I knew that young Henry would not be happy about that. He wished to have England, Normandy and Anjou. He was greedy enough to want Brittany and Aquitaine too but pragmatic enough to know that his two brothers would fight him for them. "He may not believe you, sire."

He turned and gave me a sharp look. "Then persuade him that I speak the truth!" His face softened, "You are well thought of and know how to speak softly. I have not been given that skill. I can be blunt and I can be abrasive. I am too old to change. As soon as the Count of Caen comes and we see how the land lies then you can go."

I sighed, my journey home would be delayed, "And my men and knights, they can return to England?"

He stared at me, "Aye I suppose so but they are good men. I would they were mine."

"They have families, sire. They are Englishmen and this is not their land."

He looked thoughtful for a moment and then shouted, "Oh Earl, one more thing. I have sent a letter to your father. I have asked him to go to Chester to ensure that my sister can marry Prince Dafydd. Then he will sit safely in London and be my representative there. I thought you should know that I have given him the easiest duty I can. I need him fit for the future. He is an important part of my plans for my son John. I would have him do for my son what he did for me: make me ready to rule! Englishmen need a leader they can follow." He looked as though he was going to say something else but thought better of it and with a wave, dismissed me.

As I rode back I think I knew what he had been about to say. He was going to say that he was King and Englishmen fought for their King without question. There might have been a time when I believed that but the death of my wife and the crusades had driven those thoughts from me. Now I knew that which was valuable. I would do the King's bidding for if he owed me favours then the land I ruled would stay mine and stay safe. I was its guardian now that my father had grown old. When I returned to England I would make the Earl Marshal give up his office.

There were others who could be Earl Marshal. I also wondered at the King's words. Had he given up on his son, Henry?

The King stopped at Blois. The Count of Blois, Theobald, was an uneasy ally of King Henry. He would not fight his cousin but he was unhappy about fighting his liege lord the King of France. It was fortunate that Louis was a weak king for that made Theobald an ally rather than a neutral. We had none of his men with us. The Count was in his castle at Chartres sixty miles north. That way he could absolve himself of any problems King Henry might make. I was sent with the main army to make camp at Chambord where we would await the Count of Caen. The Earl of Surrey, Miles de Warenne, commanded the army and, after we have left the King and his men at Blois, he rode with me at his side towards Chambord.

"You know this country, Earl, why God's name has he chosen Chambord? I would rather be at Blois! Living in tents and hovels is not my idea of war."

"There is a huge forest to the south of Chambord. It will allow us to disguise our numbers. The King is cunning, Earl. He has gone to Blois with just two hundred men. The French have spies in the town. They will report his presence."

"Aye, and they will have seen us heading east."

"But not south. I think that our position here is twofold. We are close enough to Blois to block any attempt by the French to invade Anjou but there is a small road through the forest. It leads to Vierzon. That was a castle which belonged to the Counts of Blois and before them the Norman ancestors of King Henry but the French have taken the castle. We take the castle and that will threaten Bourges. We draw the French north to fight us. If they do not then we march south, take Bourges and Berry is ours."

"It sounds simple but a forest does not suit knights."

I smiled, "No but it suits archers. The knights and men at arms travel along the road while the archers are a line of beaters ahead of us. My archers will ensure that any French scouts are eliminated."

"You sound confident about men who are little more than peasants with a bow."

His attitude was that of many nobles and he was wrong, "With respect, my lord, my father and I have discovered that well-trained archers and men at arms can defeat even knights."

"It was your knights defeated King William of Scotland and his household knights."

"But it was our men at arms and archers who ensured that the rest of his army. If you could ask the Scots what they fear they would say our archers."

He smiled, "I think they would say your father first. Since he and Archbishop Thurston defeated their King and the Prince of Cumberland at Northallerton, he has ever been a thorn in their side. He is their nemesis, their bane!"

I smiled, "And before that too!"

The ground around Chambord was flat, there was no castle and if one were to be built then a moat would have to be dug. It suited us for there was wood as well as brush to build the hovels the men would use and there was game in the forest for our archers to hunt.

While the men set up the camp I sent for Masood. "Ride as far as Vierzon. I would know what danger lies twixt here and there. I would also know what the defences are."

He nodded, "It is a pleasant country here but I prefer the hills of your land. A man is closer to God there." Masood was a man of few words. He slung his bow and vaulted onto the back of his horse.

Roger of Bath and Ralph of Wales led my archers and men at arms. As our squires erected our tents I waved them over. "Ralph, you and your archers can go into the woods on the morrow and scout. See if there is danger nearby and hunt while you do so. We will eat well, at least."

"Aye lord."

"Roger, have the men put stakes around our camp and dig a ditch. I am not certain if there will be rain but in this part of the world when the rain comes it can be Biblical!"

"Aye lord."

"How is the men's mood?" I knew that both men would be honest with me.

"To be honest lord they are a little bored. Apart from the ambush on the road to Le Mans, they have had little to do. Even the ambush did not affect them. They do not mind the boredom in England for it means their homes are safer. Here they want the treasure that they know the war will bring. They have had precious little yet.

"The King pays them."

Ralph laughed, "It is not as much as they would get if we were stripping French bodies!"

I understood my men. In the Holy Land, men fought for ideals. In England, they fought for their homes. Here in France, there was no benefit for our men except coin and the chance to slay Frenchmen. "Tell them that the French will have to battle here or lose Berry."

"And then we go home?"

"Aye Roger, and then we go home."

Masood arrived after dark as my men were cooking the three hinds they had hunted. He sniffed appreciatively and looked over to Rhodri of Bala who was cooking, "Do not forget, Welshman, that I am partial to the heart!"

Rhodri grinned, "It is already reserved for you. We awaited your arrival before we cooked it."

He turned to me, "There is nothing between Vierzon and here, my lord. The castle is manned but I would put its garrison at no more than thirty. If they have peasants they can arm it might double the number."

"Good! Enjoy your heart!"

The next day I rode with Thomas of Piercebridge to Blois so that I could report to the King. I met Miles of Caen as I neared the city. He reined in, "How goes it Earl?"

"The land is good for a marching camp and there are few Frenchmen at Vierzon. I go to advise the King that we should strike quickly before they realise where we are."

"Aye, we sat on our backsides waiting for the Count of Flanders to do something. The men become restless. A few deserted and others took to raiding local farms and churches. I had to hang a dozen of them."

"I am luckier with my men."

The Count lowered his voice, "I would not choose some of the barons and their retinue who follow my banner but the King would have numbers." He made to continue his journey and then said, "By the bye, I must have a word with you when you return to the camp. Some news came my way which may be of interest to you."

He had me intrigued but I was duty-bound to speak with the King. He was happy with my news. "We will follow hard on your heels. If we leave the camp in the morning can we reach Vierzon quickly?"

"The mounted men can." He knew that meant the knights and my retinue. Unlike many lords, I had gone to the expense of equipping all my men with horses. In truth, it was not much of an expense. We took more horses from the enemy than we needed. We turned and headed back to our camp.

My squire had been quiet while we had been on the road. "Thomas, is anything amiss?"

He smiled, "Not really Earl but I worry about your father. They say that when you save a man his life is yours to guard forever. Your souls are bound. I know not if that is true but since the battle when I went to the Earl Marshal's aid he has been in my thoughts and dreams."

"He is old, Thomas but, hopefully, he will no longer ride to war. He should have the luxury of enjoying his old age. The King has sent him on a mission to ensure that his half-sister is married. Then he gets to sit in the Tower and do nothing but be the King! The mighty fortress of the Conqueror should be safe enough for him."

"I hope so for I am mighty fond of the old man."

"As are we all."

After I had passed on the message from the King and sent my archers to camp nearer to Vierzon I sought out Miles of Caen. "My lord you have me intrigued. What news did you hear?"

"As you know I have taken a keen interest in the exploits of your father and I seem to recall that one of the knights of the Empress was a knight who lived in the borderlands."

"De la Cheppe; aye he died some years ago."

"His grandson and family were all murdered a month since by a band of outlaws."

"Outlaws killed a lord and his family?"

"You are right to be so sceptical and I do not believe it either. Sir Guy was named after his father and he was a good knight with men he could rely upon. I was squire to his father, Geoffrey. The family was proud of its connection to the Empress and your father. Living on the border they attracted enmity. I am guessing that it was French knights who did the deed to spite your family. Your father has never been defeated by the French and it does not sit well with them."

"Thank you for telling me. I am just glad that my father will soon be safe inside the walls of the Conqueror's tower."

"You should soon be able to join him. King Louis has been outwitted at every turn by King Henry. Even the attempt to suborn his sons did not work."

"Yet neither Henry nor Richard is here to aid their father." Both of us knew that the revolt by Henry's sons was not truly over.

When the King arrived, he swept in like a whirlwind. He was keen to show his sons that he still had the power to take land from the French. He was as unlike my father as it was possible to get and yet my father had been responsible for his training. However, I had been a disappointment to my father and I was of his blood!

Trouble came in the middle of the night. I was woken by Stephen the Grim who was one of our sentries, "Lord, there was a noise over towards the King's tent!"

"Thomas, Ralph, with me!" I grabbed my sword and ran towards the tent. I could hear shouts. It did not sound like a battle but I wondered what had happened. When I reached the tent, I saw a wounded man at arms being tended to by King Henry's doctor.

"You are sure it was Sir Robert Fitzwaller?"

"Yes, Your Majesty! He and his squire came to the horse lines. We told them that none was allowed to leave the camp. They drew swords. Dick was killed by the knight. I managed to get my sword out but the squire stabbed me. Sneaky little bastard!"

Ralph and Thomas joined me. I waved a hand for them to wait.

The King waved an irritated hand. "I am guessing that he will head for the French and tell them that we are here."

"Fitzwaller?"

He nodded, "Indeed Earl and also a traitor it seems. I should have known that there was something amiss when he joined me with just his squire. I thought him trustworthy for he has just returned from the Holy Land."

"If I learned anything in that land, sire, it was that most men's motives for being there were suspect. Perhaps he is a sword for hire and seeks coin from the French."

"Yet he is English! His grandfather had land around Hartness!" The name was vaguely familiar but I could not think why. His name must have been mentioned by my father. "Have the camp roused. He has twenty miles to go. Perhaps your archers will stop him."

"I doubt that your majesty. He is a knight riding from our camp. They would assume he was on some quest for you. The garrison will be forewarned."

The King turned to Sir Basil, one of his household knights, "Well don't just stand there! Have the horn sounded."

I turned to my men, "You two go and rouse our men. We break camp!" The horn for assembly would bring the men running. Time would then be wasted telling them to break camp. King Henry was not my father.

The result was that my men were mounted and ready while the rest of the men were breaking camp. King Henry said, "I will ride with you and your men." He turned in his saddle, "Count, bring the rest of the army as soon as they are ready! Do not be tardy! Thanks to Fitzwaller's treachery we have lost the element of surprise."

The King rode with me. No matter what people said about the King they could never say that he was a coward. With just my men at arms and thirty or so household knights, we galloped through the forest along a road which was little more than a track. I knew that my archers were in the forest but it still took a reckless sort of courage to do what he did. By the time dawn was breaking to our left the trees were thinning. Ralph and some of my archers rode up and we reined in.

King Henry had been brought up, as a squire, serving with the archers and men at arms of my father's retinue. They were easy with each other.

"Ralph, did you see riders?"

"Aye, sire, about an hour since. A knight and his squire came through. He said he was on a mission from you."

"And you did not stop him?"

Ralph spread his arms, "Firstly, sire, our orders were to stop the enemy from approaching our camp. He was riding from the camp and secondly, he was a lord."

The King nodded, "A pity."

"However, sire, I sent Rhodri and Tomas ap Tomas to trail them discreetly." He smiled, "I didn't want them to come to harm if they were on your business."

"Good fellow. If we find them there is a gold coin for you. After them." We rode hard through the early morning. By noon we could see the castle in the distance. We now had a target.

Masood appeared like a wraith, "Masood I have sent our archers to follow the knight we pursue. I am guessing he will head for Bourges. Cut across country and get to the other side of Bourges. I would know if reinforcements are coming."

"That may take days."

I nodded, "Then that will be good news. If you return directly then all will be lost."

"Aye lord." He disappeared.

We moved down the road as fast as we could. We were all mounted and well mounted at that. It was not a Roman Road and in places, there were no stones but it was a firm road made of gravel and pebbles and we made good time. We met Rhodri in a stand of trees just by the River Cher. We could see the castle on the small hill next to the river. "Where is Tomas?"

Rhodri pointed, "He followed the knight and his squire, my lord. They halted close to the gate of the town, shouted something and then rode off. The gates were slammed shut. Tomas followed them."

I turned to King Henry, "My guess is that he would head for Bourges and bring an army."

All the training the King had enjoyed when serving with my father now came to the fore. The King apprised the situation and made a decision. "The army will be here soon. We will wait for them. This little molehill is not worth the effort of besieging. We will leave our men on foot here and push on with our horse. This is not the campaign I would have chosen but it is the one we will have to fight. I may not outnumber the Count of Bourges but I will be mounted and we will have mobility. Come, Earl, let us go and speak with them. Perhaps my temper and your father's reputation may gain us a castle!"

We both took off our helmets and held them in our right hands. Our two squires carried our banners. I saw crossbows rise menacingly from the walls. The bridge over the ditch had been drawn up but it was a dry ditch without stakes. It would not stop us when we attacked.

A knight appeared on the walls. He was not a young man, "Duke Henry, this is the land of the Count du Berry. Why are you here?"

King Henry smiled, "That is not so, castellan, for this land is mine as part of Anjou. I inherited it through my father. I wish to enter my own castle. If you refuse then you disobey your rightful lord and master."

The knight smiled, "Perhaps the Pope will decide otherwise."

I saw that the Frenchman's words had come as a surprise to the King, "And what has the Pope to do with this?"

"When King Louis heard that you had promised Berry as a wedding gift for your son Richard and Alys of France he sent a delegation to Rome to ask the Pope to arbitrate on the matter. Until the Pope has made his decision, Duke, then I am not defying anyone."

Just then the advance elements of the army began to filter from the woods. It was perfect timing. They were the knights who had accompanied Miles de Caen. The King nodded. "Then when I order my men to reduce the walls of this castle and you die there will be no one to mourn. When the Pope has made his decision, it will be too late for you, your soldiers, your families and every person who resides in this castle."

King Henry spoke reasonably. He neither ranted nor raved. It was as though this was inevitable. I saw the castellan look towards the woods. More and more men emerged. The King turned to me and said, loudly, "Earl William, what would your father do in this situation?"

The castellan's attention suddenly reverted to the King and I saw him examine my livery and banner. He had ignored them at first.

I shrugged, "He would not waste much time on it, sire. He would reduce it to kindling and fill the ditch with the dead. Vierzon would become a charnel house."

"You are the son of the Warlord? The Empress' Knight?" I nodded. "Then you are the wolf."

He looked from us to the woods and back. "Your majesty I have but a small castle. You are more than welcome to spend the night as my guest."

"Excellent!" He turned to me and said, "Take the army and keep your swords in the backs of the French. I will join you before the battle begins." I nodded. He turned to his squire, "Fetch my household knights. The rest, go with the Earl."

And so we had our first victory and it was a bloodless one. That day saw the genius that was Henry. My father had trained him well.

Chapter 7

We met Tomas just five miles down the road. It was getting on for dusk because despite our best efforts we could not move any faster. My men were the best mounted and the forced march had weakened some of the poorer mounts.

"My lord they are preparing defences. The knight and his squire reached there an hour since. The squire's horse died just a mile from the walls." He shook his head. My archers and men at arms did not like to see animals used in that way. "I was close enough to see horsemen riding east and northeast."

"Going for help."

"That was my thought, my lord."

"You have done well. Where is a good camp?"

He pointed to the south. "The river is close by my lord and the ground is flat. I reckon it would be flooded if it rained but there is no sign of rain now. To the north of the road is a thin wood."

"Sir Padraig, we make camp here." I turned and saw that most of the army was still a mile or two behind us. "I will go and speak with the Count."

I turned my horse and rode back to the main column. The Count was at the fore. He shook his head. "We have travelled too far on these beasts. If the King asks for a charge then I fear he will be disappointed. We could not manage a trot let alone a gallop."

"They have sent for help. We can camp between the river and the woods. There is water for the horses and wood for stakes."

"You would fight a defensive battle?"

"In this case, yes. They have the luxury of Bourges' walls to which they can retreat if we attack. The walls are stone and built by the Romans. This will not be an easy nut to crack. I would rather make them think that we are weak. As you say, we cannot use our horses for a few days and the King needs to prosecute the attack for the Pope is arbitrating on the matter."

"And he always sides with the French. You are right." He turned in the saddle, "Come on you laggards! The Earl of Cleveland and his men are embarrassing us!"

This was a better-defended camp than the one we had had at Chambord. Here we had double ditches and sharpened embedded stakes. The water from the river was diverted by the use of a small dam to make the land closer to the French boggier. If the King chose a battle using mounted knights it would not hurt us but if I had my way and it was a defensive battle then the archers could use it and be safe from attack.

The Count of Caen sent a rider back to Vierzon to report to the King. I guessed he would spend a comfortable night there. He was a clever man and a night with our enemies might give him more information.

After we had eaten I strode around the defences with my household knights. They all had a good eye for terrain and Tomas had found us a good campsite. We spied the fires of the French. We had no idea of their numbers. They had a better idea of the size of our army thanks to the treacherous Fitzwaller. If the French attacked us then it would tell us that they had superior numbers. My men slept in groups of ten. The organization was of their own choice. They had their own shield and arrow brothers. My father and I liked it as it meant that men slept and fought with warriors they cared about. Each ten had their own leader and each ten answered to one of my captains. It made the delegation of orders and commands much easier. As we went around we spoke to each ten. My young knights and I had fought with these men in Scotland. We had watched men die. That bonded us together. It was the same with my knights. We all remembered Sir Ralph, my daughter Ruth's husband. Each death brought us closer together and taught us a lesson. Most of my men had fought alongside my father and knew the legends that had been Wulfric, Dick and Edward. One or two remembered the knights of the Empress and especially Rolf the Swabian. The fact that we had never been defeated gave them more confidence than any other retinue.

As we approached each fire we heard the banter. That was always a good sign. They rarely grumbled. "You men have enough arrows?"

"Aye, my lord. We do not waste them like some."

"Roger of Bath do you have enough vinegar and honey? We have few healers with us."

"We can deal with anything other than an amputation lord and even then, we could probably save most limbs. All but the head eh, Earl?"

They all laughed.

"And our sentries are vigilant?"

"If they are not then they answer to me."

We headed back to the tent of the Count. I found it sad that the other lords had not walked amongst their men. It was easier to lead men you knew well. I had seen, clearly, that they were in good spirits. The other lords would have to guess. The first sign that they were wrong would be when their men fled the field.

The King had not arrived by the middle watch. My men woke me before dawn as instructed. The Count of Caen also asked to be woken and when he came to speak, deferred to me. "What do we do it they attack?"

"If they see that the King's banner is not here then they will attack., The simple answer is that we defend. We have the knights fight on foot. We have two blocks of men at arms on the flank and the knights in the centre. The archers will fill in behind."

"They are few in number. Most are yours."

"I know and I think that is why the King brought us. We do not have many knights but our archers make up for that."

By dawn, we were in position. Many of the men brought by the Count complained. I smiled as I heard my men at arms threaten them if they did not stop whining. They stopped. We had done the right thing for even as the sun came up the French advanced. How did they know that the King was not with us? Did they have spies in our camp? This was not the time to worry about such matters. This would be a hard-fought battle. I counted at least three hundred lances amongst the French. There could have been more for the walls of the town hid much from us. We had two hundred and fifty. Our King had fifty with him. Their knights advanced across the whole front. They sought to batter us with horse and steel. We all had our own spears but the French lances would help them to strike first. I was glad now that we had embedded stakes. They could get through them but they could not charge in a solid line.

I joined my men at the front. I left the Count of Caen with a reserve of twenty knights. They would counter any breakthrough. Fitzwaller had betrayed us. If he had not gone for help then we might have captured Bourges as we had captured Vierzon and the King would be in a position of power.

I stood between Alf and Padraig. Both were big warriors. The three of us stood a whole head above the rest of our line and I knew that we would draw attention not to mention swords and lances. A horn sounded and the French advanced. They came together. Unless the knights struck us at a walk there would come some point where they would charge and leave the men at arms and crossbows behind. We had but a hundred and twenty archers. It was nowhere near enough but it would have to do.

The French commander knew his business. He kept his knights knee to knee and advancing slowly enough to maintain the integrity of his line. I was not worried. My archers would unleash their hail of arrows when they were two hundred paces from us. Ralph of Lincoln had assured me that with the wind behind we had the range. A few of the horses which advanced had protection for their heads. Some even had caparisons but if my archers' arrows fell amongst the horses they would be hurt.

Behind me, I heard a horn in the distance, as the King and his men approached. It was too late to change our plans now. I locked my shield with those of Padraig and Alf. I had faced horses before and they held no fear for me. The horses would try to turn if they could. The French knights had stakes to negotiate and soon they would have an arrow storm as well. I heard them cheer as they were ordered to the gallop.

"Nock! Draw!" There was a wait of a heartbeat or two and then Ralph of Lincoln roared, "Release!" I felt the air above me move as the arrows made the sky briefly darken. Even as the first flight was in the air the second was on the way and the French were about to have a lesson in why we used bows and not crossbows. The third flight darkened the skies as the first flight struck. I saw horses fall. I saw men hit. Two even fell from their horses. The second and third flights opened more gaps and then the knights in the next ranks had to jump the fallen horses and men. In jumping some fell from their horses. Others collided with men to the side. To someone watching from the rear of the French lines, it would not appear too bad but we saw gaps and there was no longer a solid line.

"Brace!" I leaned my spear against my shield and jammed my foot against the haft.

More arrows dropped and as the range had shortened more men and horses fell. I watched the knight with the blue shield and white cross charge towards me. He appeared to bear a charmed life. I saw an arrow sticking from his mail and his shield had three flights embedded but he came on and he was aiming his lance at me. Thomas held my standard behind me and my father's reputation was enough to draw the spears and lances towards me. The knight had to slow to twist around and negotiate the stakes. He needed to be able to jump the first of the ditches and then skid around the second line of stakes before trying to jump the second ditch. It took the speed from his horse. Many of his companions had fallen but still, they came for the son of the Warlord and his household knights.

The knight had a full-face helmet and I realised that he was struggling to see the obstacles but I knew when he saw me for his lance drew back and he spurred his horse to clear the ditch. I watched him land and then saw the lance as it came for my head. It seemed to come in slow motion. The knight knew his business for he kept it steady. He had won tourneys! I punched my shield towards it and trusted to the placement of my spear. The lance shattered and broke on my shield. My arm was driven back but I held. Then his horse was struck by my spear. I felt it drive into the beast and I let go lest I be dragged with it. The animal veered to my left, away from me, and I saw the knight struggling to keep his saddle. He was unbalanced and the horse falling for I had given it a mortal wound. He failed to keep his saddle and fell towards me. His shield was now a dead weight dragging him to the ground and as a defence, useless.

In one move I drew my sword and stepped from the line. I brought my sword over from behind my right shoulder. It was a sweep and I hit his arm between the elbow and the shoulder. My blade bit deep and grated off bone. I sawed it back and he screamed. The blood spurted and I stepped back into the protection of our line. I glanced down our line and saw that some of the French knights had managed to make inroads. Perhaps the shields had not been locked as tightly or the knights might have been unlucky. Whatever the reason some horsemen had broken our line. We had to stand firm.

A spear came towards Padraig. As he fended it off it veered towards me. I hacked into the spear as Padraig slashed his sword across the knight's horse's throat. The horse reared in its death throes. My household knights all held up our shields for protection. A knight whose horse had been struck by an arrow and was on foot sought to take advantage of our predicament and raced towards us. Sir James had quick reactions. Lowering his shield, he ran at the knight and stuck him bodily. James, who had been a scrawny squire, had grown in size since he had become Lord of Forcett. He was now more like his father Edward. He hit the knight with such force that he knocked him from his feet. Alf used his sword two handed to hit the horse of the knight next to him. He almost took the head of the beast. As the dying horse fell, crushing its rider we reformed our line and brought our shields down once more.

The French knight knocked to the ground by Sir James yelled, "I yield!"

Taking his sword Sir James gestured behind us. "To the rear!" The knight began to trudge and Sir James shouted to his son, who assisted his other squire, William, "Thomas, take this knight to the rear."

There had been a hiatus as the French had reorganised their lines. It gave us time to catch a breath and adjust straps. Wounded knights and men at arms who could no longer fight were taken to the rear and fresh men stepped into their places. Along the flanks, their men at arms were now engaged with ours as the archers continued to whittle down the French. Their crossbows, which had done some damage at first, now had no targets. Crossbows had to have a line of sight to be used. Our archers sent arrows over our heads. Some of the knights with me still had their spears but most had swords in their hands. I took my broken spear and rammed the shaft into the soft earth so that the head faced the French. It would be another obstacle.

Sir James' squire had helped Thomas through the lines and when he returned he shouted, "The King has come! I have seen his standard."

We now had a good reserve. The word spread down the line that the King had come. Knights and men at arms who were not engaged with the battle began banging their shields and chanting King Henry's name. A horn sounded three times and the French knights began to advance once more. They had lost too many horses in their first charge and they came on foot. The knights, with mail, helmets and shields held above them were safe from the arrows my archers continued to rain. The advance would be slower but they would arrive together. They had left their lances behind and came towards us with swords, axes and maces. The stakes and the dead gave us a barrier but the French would only be slowed a little. I saw that the French knights were four ranks deep. We had one rank to receive them with squires behind. If they broke our line then they would shatter our defence.

I shouted, "Brace and prepare to receive swords!"

The French maintained their cohesion right up to the moment where they reached the stakes. I watched one knight run and spring up onto a dead horse. Richard of Stockton did not panic and held up his shield as the French knight came through the air towards him. The French knight mistimed his blow and the flat of the blade hit Sir Richard on his shoulder. Sir Richard's sword drove up between the Frenchman's legs. The body landed with a thud before Sir Richard's squire, Arthur. The squires cheered. Other knights tried the same move. It was a brave one and a risky one. If it succeeded then a hole would be punched in our lines. I had little time to worry about that for the next wave reached us. These had taken the more traditional route of picking their way through the stakes and the dead. Many sought the honour of killing the son of the Warlord. Now I understood what my father had endured these many years. The best of the French sought the Earl!

The two French knights who came for me must have been related for they had similar devices upon their shields. One had an axe and the other a long sword. The axe swung first and I took that on my shield. The sword hacked sideways towards my unprotected middle. My father had fast hands; so did I and I blocked the blow with my sword. As I saw the shield come towards my face I had to step backwards. When I did so I saw that a flying knight had managed to penetrate the line. Knights were fighting with our squires. The battle hung on the edge of a knife.

I stepped forward and punched my own shield toward the knight with the axe. I had to risk being struck by the sword of the other. I could not fight defensively. I was slightly taller than the swordsman and I brought my sword from on high. He could not bring his shield around fast enough and had to block the blow with his sword. Sparks rank but the knight reeled. He had been slightly off balance. My shield had connected with the axeman's shield and he had stepped back. It was time for risk taking and I left the line to punch again before the axeman could recover and begin to swing his weapon. He had to take a long stride back to keep his balance and as he did so I swung my sword backhand at the swordsman. Two things happened at once. First, my sword bit into the side of the swordsman who had seen an opportunity to strike at the unprotected back of the Earl and secondly, one of my archers had had clear sight and sent an arrow into the face of the axeman as he stood.

The risk had paid off but the integrity of our line was gone for the French had broken our line in several places. A wedge of French knights now drove towards our baggage. They were between us and the river. We had to echelon back or risk being flanked. "Sir Gilles! Pull around at right angles! Shield wall!"

With me as the corner, Sir Gilles stepped backwards as did Sir Padraig and their squires. Thomas of Piercebridge held my standard aloft so that all would see that the movement did not mean retreat. Then I heard a horn from the rear. A charge had been signalled. That would be the King who would be attempting to salvage victory from defeat.

Sir Gilles' movement allowed more men through the gap but now they were attacked in the flank. The squires had spears. They lunged and stabbed over the shoulders of Sir Gilles and the others. The French could defend against one attack but not two and knights began to fall. A French knight led his retinue towards me. They came in wedge formation. There were just six of them at the fore but they would still have weight behind them. Thomas rammed the standard into the ground and took a spear so that he and Ralph could hold one over each of my shoulders. As I blocked the blow from the French sword, the two of them jabbed their spears over my shoulder. One scored a hit on the side of the knight's helmet while Ralph's managed to stick his spear in the eye hole of the knight behind. I brought my sword up under the guard of the French knight. The blow to the helmet had distracted him. His own sword was already coming down towards my shield when the tip of my sword began to tear through the mail links of his hauberk. My two squires pulled back their spears for a second blow. Ralph's was still caught in the helmet of the French knight and when it tore free the Frenchman lost his balance and fell backwards. As my sword worked its way into the body of the French knight Ralph and Thomas punched their spears again. The spears kept the French from closing too quickly with us and using their superior numbers.

I heard shouts and cheers from the right as the King and the Count of Caen led our horsemen into the French. Here the stakes helped us for they were facing the French and not our horses. Then there was the sound of the battle being joined. We had our own battle for the French saw their chance to exploit the breach in our line. Padraig was fighting two men as was I. I had the advantage of two squires. He disabled one of his foes but the second managed to smash his mace against Padraig's hand. He dropped his sword. His squire, Henry stepped forward and took on the knight. They fought as a pair. Padraig still had his left hand.

I faced two and one also had a mace. They had seen how Padraig had been hurt and they tried a similar tactic. The knight with the mace swung it backhand at my right hand while the other brought his sword from on high. When I had been training Wulfric had shown me how to use the long Norman shield offensively. I turned it from the vertical to the horizontal. I smashed it towards them and stepped forward. The mace glanced off my shoulder. It hurt but it did not disable me. I punched with the hilt at the helmet of the knight with the mace. Already stunned by my shield he reeled and I was able to swing my sword at his companion. He was slow to bring up his own sword and my blade bit into the mail at his shoulder. Ralph's spear darted out and the knight with the mace was knocked to the ground. Thomas of Piercebridge bravely leapt into the gap and using the spear two handed, he drove it deep into the stomach of the knight. The scream as the spear entered his groin distracted the other knight enough for me to hit him in the face with my shield while I swung my sword at his knee. Chausses are never as strong as a hauberk and there was no gambeson beneath. I broke the mail and shattered the knee. He dropped to the ground.

"Yield or die! I care not which!"

"I yield! I yield!"

Ralph grabbed him and pulled him behind our lines. We had killed those before us and I looked for the next assault. It was then I saw King Henry rear his horse. Its flailing hooves crashed down onto the skull of a brave but hapless knight who was trying to skewer the King's mount. As the knight fell the King slashed left and right. Our dismounted knights who had fallen back now rejoined the fight and I shouted, "Charge!" Thomas waved the standard and we ran at the French. We were still outnumbered but they had lost heavily and our charge decided the matter. They ran and we pursued.

We had little fighting to do for those we caught had often fallen or they were wounded. They yielded. There was little point in dying to a sword in the back! When we had lumbered for half a mile I shouted, "Halt!" The King and his horsemen were still pursuing the French towards Bourges. Enough of the French would make it within the walls to guarantee that we would have to besiege it but the King's arrival had turned defeat into a small victory. We held the field and we had slain far more of them than we had lost.

We herded our prisoners, fifteen of them, back to our lines. A healer was already tending to Sir Padraig. My household knights had suffered minor wounds but we had lost none. Already my archers were searching the field for arrows and relieving the dead of their purses, their treasure and if they were worth it, their weapons. That was what made this a victory. We had not lost the field. They had had superior numbers but we were stubborn and skilled enough to beat them. My father had trained us all well.

Chapter 8

It was dusk when the King and his knights returned. He had lost ten of the men who had set out with him but they brought back eighteen captured knights. He reined in as they neared the battlefield. His surcoat was blood-spattered and I saw that his horse had been wounded. He shook his head, "I delayed too long at Vierzon. I am sorry Earl." This was the first time I had heard the King apologise and I was taken aback. "You and the others held the line well. I am in your debt."

"And now, Sire?"

"Now we can begin the siege. They are trapped inside their castle. The Count of Caen will send men to seal the other side of the castle and then we will construct war machines."

My heart sank. Who knew how long this would take. I was not going home in a hurry.

Most of the knights we had captured were local lords of the manor or were the household knights of the Count of Bourges. We sent a wounded French squire with our demands. Padraig was in no condition to continue and so I wrote a letter for him to take to Sir Leofric. Padraig and his squire could return home and give my wife the letter. It would explain the delay. I had just finished when Masood rode in.

"Well?"

He smiled, "I had a long ride but I found a messenger heading north and east. I followed him. He stopped at a castle on the Loire and I saw two riders sent out. One went north and one went northeast. There was a wood nearby and I camped there. It seemed to me that as the messenger had not returned to Bourges I could wait until he did. If he left alone then I would capture him and persuade him to talk. I had no need to for the next morning knights and their retinue began to arrive. I spied the Count of Orleans and his household knights. He has a royal banner and so I left. I had learned all that I needed to. The King should know that there is a large army heading this way. He will be outnumbered."

Not only would I not get home soon it looked increasingly likely I would not get home at all! The King brooded after I had given him the news. "This is where I need my sons! They have armies! Will they not fight for their inheritance?" It was on the tip of my tongue to say that he had already made it clear that they had all been given all that they would be given. He turned to me. "Go and fetch Richard. He will listen to you. Tell him that Berry will be his. All I want is the army of Aquitaine!"

"He still may not come, sire."

"Make him!"

I shook my head, "Sire he is master of Aquitaine, I am Earl of Cleveland. I cannot force him to do anything."

I could see that the King was becoming desperate. "Henry is of little use and there is nothing left for me to offer him save Normandy and I will be damned if I will give him that. What would the next request be? Would Geoffrey want Anjou? Richard is my only hope. If you cannot persuade him and persuade him quickly then I will have to slink back to Maine with my tail between my legs. If that happens then men will suffer!" He put his arm around me and led me to one side, "William you and your father are the two men on whom I place my complete trust. I have given you Cleveland. If you do this then you can have Yorkshire too."

I shook my head, "I will do it, sire, or try to at least. I do not need Yorkshire. I have no desire for more land. Stockton and the valley of the Tees suit me. If I take my men I will leave you perilously short of men."

He nodded, "Take your knights and an escort of men at arms and archers. You are correct. I will need the others." He put his hand on my arm, "If all else fails tell him that he may have the whole income from Aquitaine and I will allow him to punish the rebel barons."

"Yes, King Henry. I will do my best."

I sought out Padraig, "Yes, lord?"

"Give me the letter. I have a postscript to add. I will take the other knights to Poitiers!" I scribbled a note on the bottom and resealed it. "If I can persuade Richard to come then we may come back through La Flèche. Warn Leofric for his wife will wish to prepare the accommodation."

We left the next morning. I took just ten archers and ten men at arms. I left the rest with their captains. The civil war had meant that the roads and forests teemed with bandits and men at arms whose masters had died. My conroi was large enough to deter all but the most determined of warbands.

As we headed west Sir Morgan asked, "Do you think you can persuade the Prince?"

"The three brothers lost the war, Alf, this could go two ways. He may resent his father so much that he throws me out of his castle as soon as I make the request or he may want to gain favour at the expense of Henry, his older brother. I do not think there will be a middle way. What I do know is that we will be lucky to be home for Christmas this year!"

He nodded, "By then my child will be born. It grieves me that others at my hall at Seamer will see my child before I do!"

"That is the lot of a knight. I fear it will happen again. We bear the cross that is success. We do not lose and so the King will use us before any other. My father has seen more than seventy summers and yet the King still puts him in harm's way."

He nodded and smiled, "Yet despite all of that my life is immeasurably better than it would have been in Miklagård."

I smiled at his use of the archaic name for Constantinopolis. My father told me that my grandfather had done the same. "Then I am pleased that we were able to save you."

Poitiers was a true stronghold. The Dukes of Aquitaine still remembered when the Moors had raided from Spain. It might have been hundreds of years ago but Islam was still a threat. I did not wonder that Richard made it his home. It had a fine aspect and was strong. He was not in residence when I arrived. He was out hunting but such was my reputation and standing that we were admitted and housed. I was even able to bathe!

By the time the Duke returned I felt cleaner and I had prepared my arguments. Richard always surrounded himself with handsome, brave and witty knights. They were all skilled warriors too. He had taken a leaf out of my father's book and made certain that the men he led into battle were his equal. I wondered how he would react to me. I had not seen him since before the rebellion by him and his brothers. While his father had fought him in France I had been helping to defeat William of Scotland.

He beamed when he spied me, "Earl! It is a pity you did not come earlier. We had a fine hunt! A boar and a sow! We eat well tonight!" I know that Richard had his faults but he was also good company. Out of the four brothers, he was the one whose company I enjoyed the most. "And how is your father?" He turned to the knights, "The earl's father is the Earl Marshal of England! My father may be a tight-fisted ungrateful bastard but he knows how to pick a good leader. The hero of Northallerton, Lincoln and now Alnwick!"

"He still does your father's bidding, lord. The last I heard he was helping Prince Dafydd to subdue his brothers!"

"And if he were over here then my father would now be King of France."

"That touches upon my business, lord, and the purpose of my visit."

His face became serious, "Let me wash and change. We will speak after the feast. I am always more agreeable after food and if my father has sent you then I do not doubt I will not enjoy what you have to say!"

I gave a weak smile, "I am just a messenger, lord."

He nodded, "It is a pity that my devious father uses brave warriors in such an underhand way. He knows if he sent any other then I would have them thrown out but the family of the Warlord is ever welcome. I fear you may return to him disappointed."

"Then so be it. I am a man of war and not a politician!"

"Enjoy my castle. We have good wine in Poitou."

I walked with my knights and squires. We visited the town and explored the castle. We each had our own manor and were always seeking to improve them. We saw much that we admired. As we returned to the castle Sir Richard said, "Fine as this town and castle are I would not swop Stockton."

Sir Gilles said, "Nor I Norton. I know not why men leave their own lands to seek their fortune elsewhere."

I smiled as Sir Gilles realised that he had come close to insulting me for I had left Stockton for Normandy when I was his age, "Men leave home for many reasons, Gilles. In my case, it was because I did not want to live in the shadow of my father. How foolish was I? The man casts a shadow which reaches across the western world. You cannot escape his shadow in this world. I still regret those years I spent apart."

Thomas said, quietly, "And yet you are apart again now, lord."

"Would that it was not so. I do the King's bidding. He is not a man to cross." Even as I said it I wondered. My father had treated us both as though we were brothers. If I had refused to come then the King would have been angry but I now realised he would not have harmed me or the valley. My father guaranteed that. It had been a mistake to come to France.

The feast was, as I had expected, of the highest quality. The wine was superb and the entertainment exquisite. Richard had a beautiful voice and he knew how to deliver a song. I might have enjoyed it but I knew that I would have to broach a difficult subject. I did not drink too much. I would not have enjoyed it.

Richard picked up his goblet and said, "Come Earl. I can see that you have had too much on your mind to enjoy the wine and the food. My father has much to answer for. Would that we could exchange parents."

He led me to a balcony which overlooked the inner bailey. There were two seats already there. He had prepared for this meeting.

"I am sorry, lord, but this is not my strength. I am not a man of words. I am a man of action."

"Aye I know and I envy you the time you spent on crusade. That is what I would like to do. I would be a crusader who was not a prince. My great grandfather went as a lord. I would go as a warrior."

"It was an experience. I met my wife there."

"And gained great honour. Men who have returned have told me of your actions. What you did was chivalrous and noble."

"Perhaps."

He sighed and drank deeply, "On then, Earl. Let me hear what my father asks of me." He smiled.

"Prince Richard…"

"That is not my title, Earl. I am the Duke of Aquitaine. A prince implies I might be king and my brother already has that title. This will be all that I rule."

This was not going to be easy. "Your father needs your army. He is at Bourges and the French have sent two armies to fight him. He cannot win without help." He said nothing. "He fights for Berry which is the wedding present for you and Alys."

"Alys? The daughter of the King of France whom my father has used as a concubine these last years? We will never be wed. He can say that Berry is for us but like most things my father says, it is a lie."

There was no anger in his voice, merely sadness. I could understand it.

"He offers you all of the coin from Aquitaine instead of just half."

He laughed, "That is rich. I am Duke of Aquitaine and my father offers me half of the money I am legally entitled to. This gets better and better. What else?"

I spoke quietly, "There is nothing." I took a deep breath, "Lord, if you do not help your father and he loses this battle think of the wedge which will be driven between you and your father."

He emptied his goblet. "And if I help him what will it get me? England is Henry's. I have Aquitaine and Geoffrey has Brittany! The best that I can hope is Anjou and Normandy!"

I liked Richard. Perhaps I should have voiced that which I felt but I was the Warlord's son. "Lord, he favours John. Would you have John be given Normandy and Anjou?"

I watched his face as his demons wrestled inside him. He was a clever man and he could see the endgame. If he did not support his father he would just be left with Aquitaine. He wanted more. He needed the entire treasury of Aquitaine if he was to have a chance to build an army.

"You will be there?" I nodded. "I do not trust my father but the Warlord and his son are never foresworn."

"I will not help you to fight your father."

He smiled, "Nor would I expect you to. If your veins were slashed then you would bleed honour. You cannot do other. I will bring my men and we will come to my father's aid."

I was relieved. I had done my duty. I dared not ask him to go to La Flèche first. I could not risk him changing his mind. I would forego the visit with Leofric. Looking back now I can see that was a mistake but that is with the luxury of hindsight. At the time it seemed the right thing to do. My decision haunted me for years and yet I could not see how I could have changed it.

Richard had a thousand men. His knights numbered less than two hundred but he had well-armed and enthusiastic men at arms. He even had a hundred archers. He confided in me that they were a pale shadow of my own but he was trying to build an army based on my father's. We rode quickly and in the two days I was with him I learned much about Richard the warrior. He was more like his father than his brother Henry. I thought that it was a shame that he was the second son. I hoped as we headed east, that we would be in time. I had brought Masood with me and as we spent the night at the castle of Châteauroux I sent my scout to Bourges to give me an accurate report of the situation. He returned at noon.

"Lord, the two armies face each other but King Henry no longer surrounds Bourges. He has prepared defensive lines where we fought the battle."

"Good, then we are in time."

We heard our arrival being heralded when the cheers rang out from the east. By the time we arrived, it was like a conquering Roman general entering Rome. I knew that Henry would have mixed feelings. There would be relief that his son had come but jealousy and envy that such acclaim was for a potential rival. King Henry knew how to play the part and he greeted Richard like the prodigal son from the Bible. It evoked a monumental cheer from the army. They embraced but I saw no affection in either man's eyes. Then the King turned to me, "Once more I am indebted to your family. Whatever you ask, it is yours!"

I knew the words to say, "Sire, I serve you and I serve England!"

He rubbed his hands together, "Now we have set the French a problem! When it was just me they faced then they thought that they might win quickly. Now that my son has arrived they will be more likely to talk."

Richard shook his head, "I have never heard of a city's walls falling to words. How does this get me Berry as a wedding dowry?"

I knew, from my conversation with Richard that he had no intention of marrying Alys. He was playing a game with his father. This was a world I did not like.

"We have the land between here and Touraine. It is a sizeable piece of land. It is one-third of Berry. We negotiate a little more of the land."

"But you will not get Bourges."

"Not yet, perhaps but if we have Vierzon we can make it a stone castle and that will allow us to build an army large enough to take Bourges." He waved a hand, "Come let us go to my tent. We have much to discuss, my son."

I was dismissed or maybe they just forgot me. Either way, I did not mind. Father and son sought power and land. My father and I just wanted the peace of our home. If there was to be negotiation then that might mean we could get home. I returned to my camp and my knights.

I was needed again the next day when the King and his son went to negotiate with the French. The French delegation was led by the Duc du Berry. Chairs were brought and I saw that there was not only a priest present but a cardinal. He was the Pope's man. I wondered if that was an omen.

Henry took charge of the negotiations immediately, "Berry belongs to me! It is part of the land which my grandfather conquered."

"It is part of France. My lord the lands you rule, Normandy, Anjou, Touraine, Maine, all are part of the land which is France. Your liege lord is Louis." The Duc du Berry spoke with respect in his voice but the force of right behind it.

Henry did not like that. When Duke William had invaded and conquered England it made the family believe that they no longer had any feudal obligations to the King of France. As my father had often told me it was a debatable and contentious point.

Henry spread his hands and smiled, "Then as lord of Berry I will acknowledge King Louis as liege lord of Berry. We need not fight."

It was the Duc du Berry's turn to have a superior look upon his face, "There is, indeed, no need for us to fight, my lord, for this is Cardinal Boniface. He is the Pope's representative."

The papal delegate stepped forward, "King Henry, the Holy Father is most distressed that two such senior kings should go to war over this matter. He orders both kings to cease hostilities until such time as he can make a judgment on the matter."

I saw the King become red in the face. This was an outcome he had not expected. When Pope Adrian had ruled Rome King Henry had had much support for Nicholas Breakspear had been English. Pope Alexander was Italian and he had a rival pope, Callixtus. Both Popes sought favour and the King of France had taken advantage of the situation.

"And when can we expect a decision?"

"The Holy Father has much on his mind. In the fullness of time."

"Then until he decides we hold that which we have taken!" He stood, "Duc du Berry, I will be easy to find for I will be at Vierzon when you wish to speak with me." He mounted his horse and galloped back to our lines.

Richard said, "We have been used, William. My father has what he wants and he has dragged me from my home to do so! I will leave on the morrow."

I realised then that I could leave too. Surely the King would not require me.

The King had wasted no time and even as we rode into camp I saw it being dismantled. He waved us over. Richard did not like the gesture, "We will break camp and invest Verizon. We will sleep in a real bed this night."

"Father I will return to Poitiers in the morning."

"Stay a little longer. We have much to discuss. We have plans to make for your future."

"What future, you have given away the throne of England to my brother." He shook his head. "What remains for me?"

"The Duchy of Normandy!"

It was the one thing which the King could have said which would make Richard reconsider. I did not mind travelling to Vierzon. It was on the road home. In two days of hard riding, we could be in La Flèche! Another ten or twenty days and we could be home in England!

I rode with Richard to Vierzon. Our knights saw to the dismantling of our camp. Duke Richard knew his father well. "It is a lure to make me stay you know. He has no intentions of giving me the Duchy." I could not say anything for I suspected he was right but it was none of my concern. "I will see what delicacy he throws my way. Before I leave I will have it put in writing that I have the revenue from the whole of Aquitaine. Anything else will be more than I had before you came."

When we reached the hall, we saw the disconsolate Constable, his family and the garrison trudging from the castle and the town. The King had wasted no time. Our horses were stabled and we were allocated chambers. Most of the men at arms and archers would have to be housed in the town. Vierzon became an enormous armed camp. All the senior lords were present at the feast that night. King Henry made it seem like a victory celebration but as far as I could see we had a stalemate. The voices were raised and there was a heated discussion. I wondered if it might lead to violence. Suddenly the doors of the hall were thrown open and there stood Sir Leofric, Sir Padraig and Sir James de Puiset. What had happened to my father?

Chapter 9

"What means this intrusion?"

Sir Leofric limped up to the table and spoke quietly, "Sire, Sir James has come from the Earl Marshal with dire tidings. I also have news which may bring disquiet to the King's brow."

Sir Leofric was well known to the King. He nodded, "Come we will retire to the antechamber. Richard, William, you should be a party to this."

Once we were in the room and a guard placed at the door the King said, "Begin!"

"Sire when I travelled back to my home I overheard some knights speaking of a plot to harm the Earl Marshal." I kept control of my face and my feelings. "I discovered that they had murdered the family of one of my father's old comrades, la Cheppe."

I nodded and spoke, "The Count of Caen mentioned that to me. He said they were crusaders."

"Aye, they were. I sent a letter to the Earl. Then three days since Sir James here arrived from London." He gestured for Sir James to continue.

"Sire, London is like a tinderbox. There is unrest in the city and your Chancellor struggles to maintain order. The Earl Marshal has uncovered a plot to overthrow your majesty."

The King glanced sideways at his son, "And who would replace me?"

Sir James hesitated, "The Earl Marshal did not wish this to be committed to paper but he believed it might be your eldest son, Henry."

"But he has the title!"

Richard laughed, "And that is patently not enough for my brother!"

"This is not amusing Richard." The King turned his gaze to Sir James, "This London threat is real?"

"The Earl Marshal believed it so. Your Chancellor was fearful of travelling about the city and had hired himself armed guards to keep him safe."

The King rubbed his beard, "London is full of the worst of men. It is like a cesspit into which all that is venal and vile sinks. They are ever self-serving. They were the ones anointed Stephen rather than my mother."

I could see that Richard had his own views on this. "It seems to me that there is an obvious solution to this. Go to Henry and put him under lock and key. Then there will be no revolt!"

King Henry shook his head, "Make him a martyr? We did that with Becket. No, we must be more subtle. I will go to my son. I will dissemble. He will not know that which I know. William Marshal is a true knight. I will discover what he knows. The Earl Marshal is getting old and he may be wrong. It might not be my son. It could be the French."

I spoke, "That makes sense sire for from what Sir Leofric said we know that these rogue knights were seen in France first."

"You could be right Earl. You fought in the Holy Land. Can you conjure a reason for this influx of killers?"

"It makes perfect sense to me. When I was in the Holy Land there were two kinds of knights. There were those who sought to atone or to help pilgrims; I sought to help pilgrims as did the Knights Hospitallers. Then there were the other knights who sought kingdoms and dukedoms. Many lived outside the law. They could get away with it there. When there was a kingdom of Jerusalem which had power then there was law. Since Nur al-din has come to power then the Kingdom of Jerusalem is hard-pressed to hold the city. These knights are no fools. They will know that Outremer will fall. There are not enough good men there to hold it. The rats will leave that sinking ship. I could see how they would attempt to take over England. They see divisions." Both Richard and the King gave me angry glances. "There is no point in denying that the revolt last year would have given knights such as this hope. Tha Assassin cult works by eliminating the head of their enemies. That is why they seek my father's life. He is, while you are in France, the head of state. With him gone and London in their hands then your finances would dry up. I believe that you are right about the French influence. They weaken you in England and then attack you here."

Richard said, "I am a good knight! I will go to the Holy Land and defeat this Nur al-din."

Henry barked, "You will not! England needs every good knight. I need swords like yours. I will go to speak to my son. I will keep the army together. I will keep your men, Richard." His son made to speak, "You will go with the Earl to London. The Earl Marshal is old but you are not. Exercise your power in that land. Let me see that Richard, Duke of Aquitaine could be king. If I discover that your brother is behind this then I will take the crown from him myself. My grandfather kept a threat to his crown incarcerated his whole life. I can do the same."

He was tempting Richard with the promise of the crown. If his other son proved to be treacherous then King Henry would be ruthless.

Richard took the bait and nodded eagerly, "Aye lord, I will go with the Earl."

I spoke quickly for I did not wish to lose one of my men. "And we will need all of my men to aid my father."

"Of course."

We moved as quickly as was humanly possible but it was still not fast enough for me. We travelled slowly. I was too good a horseman to thrash my horse to death and there were many servants with the Duke of Aquitaine. I did all that I could to speed our journey by sending a rider to La Flèche to have ships ready for us.

When we reached Sir Leofric's manor I was disappointed to see that there were few masts on the river. His constable, Jean of Angers, apologised to us. "I am sorry that I could not get the ships here, lord. Captain William is at sea. I have asked for ships to be gathered at Angers. The man I sent requested English ships."

Duke Richard grunted, "They will feel my boot up their backsides if they do not move quickly enough for us!"

Padraig was healing well and that was good for I was sure that I would need every knight I could if I was to do that which King Henry had asked and save London. We rested but one night and I begrudged that delay.

On our journey to Angers I discovered more of the plot. Sir James told me of my father's visit to the Cheap. As the events were related I could see my father and his clever brain. He always had a good ear and eye. Age may have slowed his sword arm but not his mind. He was as sharp as ever.

Duke Richard became quite animated when he heard of the pirates. "The sea twixt England and Normandy should be the safest patch of water in the world for we control both sides! If I were King then I would have ships which I owned patrolling and destroying these pirates!"

I smiled, "My lord, ships cost money. Where would the coin be found?"

He gave me a look of surprise. "Why, the people, of course! Should they not pay for the protection of their land?"

I heard in his voice the imperious tone of his grandfather and father. Both Henrys had believed in their divine right to rule and to tax. "Sadly, my lord, the people have had many years of unrest. We in the borderlands are used to raids from enemies. The civil war was different. It showed the worst of behaviour from those who should have protected them. Barons took coin from people because they could. There was no recourse to law. Your grandmother and my father were fighting for the crown as was Stephen the Usurper. I am afraid that particular chest has been opened and it will take many years to win back the trust of the people." I felt guilt then for I had abandoned the fight to enjoy life at the Duke of Anjou's court and then the crusades. My father had borne that burden and it had been largely alone.

"Win back?"

I sighed. He did not understand. He thought that the King was owed coin and duty by divine right. I was not the one to educate him. I had a valley to protect. The task of making Henry's sons into rulers would have to fall to another. I would not do as my father had done and sacrifice his life and his family to the Plantagenet dynasty. That would have to be a task for another.

"Let us first save London, lord and worry about that later."

Sir James rode next to me as we neared Anjou, "Your father is weary, lord. He does not know how or when to stop. He should have stayed in Stockton. I know not why he follows the King's dictates so readily. He has done enough. When we fought the Welsh, he was in danger yet he never thought of himself. And there is something else. He is not well."

I nodded, "Fear not, Sir James, when we reach England I will impress upon Duke Richard the need for my father to step back. Perhaps the Duke will take the reins of power."

Sir James was a clever man. As the nephew of the Bishop of Durham, he understood politics far better than I did. "That would be dangerous for all, lord. His elder brother, Henry, has been crowned King of England. He might see it as a usurpation of power."

He was right and there was an irony that the first King Henry did not have enough sons and the second had too many!

We had enough ships for the men but not the horses. We were forced to leave them at the castle of Angers. Our horses would be sent back to La Flèche but Duke Richard's would be retained for his return. The captains told us that they would be heading for Southampton. I did not question their judgement but Duke Richard did. "Why? I wish to get to the White Tower in London as soon as we can!"

Captain Walter shook his head. His grey hairs and leathered skin bespoke years of experience. "My lord we can be at Southampton a day earlier than the Thames. It can take two or three days to sail up the river to the Tower. You can be there in half a day by horse."

I put my hand on Richard's arm. "My lord, these men know their business. Let us heed their advice." He agreed.

I kept Sir James with me as well as half of my archers and men at arms. The rest I spread amongst the other ships. Duke Richard kept all of his household knights with him. I thought it a mistake but it was his to make.

The journey to the sea was as swift as the skilled captains could make it. I sailed with Captain Walter. I think he preferred that to Duke Richard who seemed to think that he was an expert in all things!

"I know your father's captain, William of Kingston. He is a good seaman. He is loyal to your father."

"They are loyal to each other. It is a trait of my father's. He cares for all from the meanest to the greatest. He is beloved in Stockton."

"He is beloved in England, lord." He looked around to see if any could overhear. "If people chose their king then it would be the Warlord."

"That sounds like heresy, captain. Surely God chooses our King."

"Perhaps."

"You hope for a swift voyage? I am anxious to get to my father's side."

"I would hope so but we travel in company. That inevitably slows a voyage down." He waved a hand astern at the other seven ships which followed us. Most were small; there were but two large ones. "Still the number of ships we have and the weaponry available gives me confidence that we shall avoid the pirates. There are many of them these days and they make this patch of water ever dangerous. They do not mind tackling one ship sailing alone but a fleet like this will deter them."

His words were prescient!

When trouble came we were in the middle of the Channel. We were halfway across the sea which separated Normandy from England. We were as far away from land as we would ever be on the voyage. We were leading. Captain Walter was the better captain. I guessed that Duke Richard was fuming to be in our wake. It was coming to noon when the lookout shouted down, "Captain, a ship is being attacked by pirates. It looks like the *'Rose of Hythe'*!"

The captain looked at me. There was a question in his eyes. I nodded, "We cannot leave an English ship to the pirates. Head for them."

"Alone?"

I laughed, "I cannot see Duke Richard being tardy. Besides they may flee when we reach them."

He shook his head, "They have huge crews, lord. We are well ahead of the others. They may only see us and regard us as the main course of this feast. *'Rose of Hythe'* is smaller than we!"

"We will see. Roger of Bath, have the men stand to!"

"Aye lord. Come, you idlers. We have enjoyed ourselves long enough. Now is the time for knife work!"

I turned to Ralph, "Fetch my sword."

"Will you need your mail, lord?"

"I think not."

Sir James joined me. He had been at the bow watching the three ships as they battled. "Whoever is on that ship is making a brave fight of it. They are holding off the pirates."

"Then let us hope the captain can bring us close enough before they succumb." While the men armed themselves, I went to the bow and pulled myself up onto the forestay. I braced myself against the gunwale. Shading my eyes against the sun I saw that the *'Rose of Hythe'* rode higher in the water than her attackers. That may have given them an early advantage. If you could keep men from boarding your ship then even a crew which was outnumbered stood a chance. Once they boarded you then your days were numbered. The *'Rose of Hythe'* had a larger sail and mast than the two pirates. The captain had not furled it and the wind was dragging the three ships northwards. The two pirates must have used oars for their sails were furled. We were now less than half a mile from them and I could see that there were men on the *'Rose of Hythe'* who wore mail coifs and held longswords. They were knights or men at arms. That explained how they had survived for so long. It could not last, however. I saw one pirate reach the stern and although he was cut down to fall into the sea three others managed to use his death to board the vessel.

Our captain was a good seaman and he approached from the west so that we could board the pirate on that side. I turned and shouted, "To me! James, you take half the men and help the crew. We will tackle this pirate."

"Aye lord."

"Masood get into the rigging and use your bow."

"Yes my lord."

"Ralph of Wales, thin them out for me!"

Even though we were still two hundred paces from them because we had the wind we were in range. "Barbed arrows! These do not wear mail."

My archers had both kinds of arrows in their quivers. There were the knight killers: bodkin tipped arrows which could penetrate mail. They also had barbed arrows. These tended to fly further and they caused terrible wounds to a man who did not wear mail. The arrow could not be pulled out and the only way to remove it was to push it through the body.

"Nock! Draw!" I heard the yew as it creaked. "Loose!" The goose tipped missiles soared high and then plummeted on to the steering board of the nearest pirate ship. There were screams and shouts as the arrows found their marks. I ignored my archers. They knew their business. I held on to the forestay with my left hand and my sword in my right. The pirates on board the *'Rose of Hythe'* had seen us and I saw an immediate effect. They began to pull back to their own ship. The second pirate ship had no such worries and they renewed their efforts. Thomas of Piercebridge shouted, "My lord the Duke is heading for the other vessel!"

"Good! Ready!"

The pirate ship was less than ten feet from me. Our captain had taken in some of the sail. It would mean we bumped into the pirate rather than crashing into it. We rode higher in the water and I saw that Ralph's arrows had decimated the men at the stern. The survivors had gathered around their mast.

As our ship neared I judged the time right. "Jump!" I leapt the gap. The wind and the movement of our ship meant I landed clear of the gunwale on the half-naked body of a pirate. He looked to be Frisian. I had no time to ponder further for the pirates had decided to charge us.

The wounded, dying and dead had bled out and blood mixed with the seawater to make a pink puddle on the bleached white wooden deck.

I heard Sir James shout, "With me! Stockton!" He leapt fearlessly aboard the *'Rose of Hythe'*.

The leader of the pirates looked like some sort of Viking. He had two axes, one in each hand. They were a sort of throwing axe. He wore an old-fashioned helmet with a nasal and had a vest made of mail. He roared at me in what I took to be Frisian and he and his men ran across the slippery and increasingly blood-soaked deck. I barely had time to draw my dagger before he was upon me. I crossed my hands to block the blows. My sword blocked his right-handed axe for I took that to be the more powerful blow and my dagger his left. I barely held them for he was frighteningly strong. He was as tall as me and when I saw him draw his head back I knew what he intended. He would head butt me. I had no helmet and it would be an early end to the contest.

Masood had taught me how to wrestle. He was not a large man but I had seen him throw Ralph of Bowness to the ground. My opponent was stronger and I used his own strength against him. I feinted right and when he pushed against me and brought his head back I swivelled. He began to lose his balance and I rammed my dagger towards his cheek. It went in one side and out of the other. When I tore it out blood spurted. As he screamed in rage, blood and teeth were spat out. Ralph and Thomas lunged with their swords at the two men who flanked the Frisian chief. He swung his axe at my head with his right hand. I blocked it with my dagger and swung my sword hard against his side. His mail stopped the blow from penetrating the mail but it was hard enough to crack a rib. I used Masood's foot trick and hooked my right leg behind his left and pushed. His bleeding face and ribs must have distracted him for he tumbled backwards over the bodies of two of his oathsworn. I brought my sword across his neck and severed his head.

In most cases, such an action would end a battle and men would surrender. These warriors hearkened back to an earlier age and the rest of the crew threw themselves at us. None of these had mail. Most did not even have a helmet and their short swords were no match for our steel blades. One of them brought his sword down towards Thomas of Piercebridge's head. Thomas held his own sword up and could not believe it when the Frisian's sword bent! Ralph's sword went through the Frisian. After that it was butchery. We now outnumbered them and we relentlessly worked our way through them. They all died. It was a waste although as pirates they would probably have been hanged anyway.

I heard Masood shout, "Earl, they are fleeing!"

I hurried to the stern and clambered up onto the deck of *'Rose of Hythe'*. I saw a huddle of men being guarded by Sir James and Roger of Bath. They looked to be four men at arms and they had been the defenders. The second pirate ship was sailing east under oars. Her scuppers ran with blood.

I saw Duke Richard furiously waving his fist at them. He shouted over, "The bastards ran before we could kill more of them! I barely made it back! I lost two knights!"

I waved and, cupping my hands shouted, "We will see to this crew and follow you."

I saw the captain having his wounds dressed at the steering board. He tried to rise, "Stay there. Did you lose many men?"

"Four of the crew but that was four too many. Had it not been for our passengers then we would have all been killed. I owe them much. They fought ferociously."

I wondered why Sir James and the others were guarding them. The rest of the deck looked like a charnel house. It had been a bloody battle. I saw at least ten dead men at arms and more than twenty pirates.

"Can you make it to Southampton with your passengers?"

"Aye lord, but they wished to be landed at Tilbury."

"I will have the pirates thrown overboard and then you can sail with us to Southampton."

"But they wish to go to Tilbury."

I smiled to soften my words, "Captain I will make that decision." I wandered over to the men. I saw that they were all tanned. Their mail and surcoats showed that they had had a hard life. The kettle helmets they wore were popular in Outremer. I began to see why Sir James had them watched. "Why are they guarded, Sir James?"

In answer, Sir James held up a chain and there was a metal disk attached. It was the sign of the Templars. "If I have done wrong, lord I will apologise but I think that these are swords for hire."

I unsheathed my sword and used it to raise the head of the sergeant at arms, "Who are you?"

He smiled and I saw the lie in his eyes even before he had uttered a word. "We are just warriors returned from the crusades. We have had enough of war and we return to our home, England."

He made a mistake for his accent was French. He spoke good English but I knew that he lied. "You are a Templar?"

He shrugged, "I won that at dice."

I pricked his throat with the tip of my sword. A tendril of blood trickled down his neck. "I went on crusades, do not lie to me. A Templar rarely gambles and he would never give this up. Either you slew a Templar and took it or you were a Templar. I reached under his coif and took out the cross I knew hung there. "Swear on this cross and I might believe you."

The smile left his face and he shook his head, "I am a Templar, what of it?"

"Had you said so straight away then I would have said nothing but you lied. Templars lie, I know that but there has to be a reason for this lie. You owe us your lives. I will have the truth or I will feed you to the fishes."

"And if I tell the truth will I live?"

I was the product of my father and his men. I would not lie even to one I suspected of being a traitor. "That depends upon your words but I will know the truth when I hear it."

He suddenly seemed to see my surcoat for the first time. "You are the son of the Warlord!"

"I am Earl William of Stockton."

"I served with your father when he was a knight of the Empress. He was a good warrior."

"He is a good warrior."

I saw the debate which raged in the man's head. Sir James said, "I think that you have all been hired to come to England and stir up mischief in London." Perhaps the memory of my father had shaken the sergeant but whatever the reason he gave a sharp, surprised look at Sir James who pushed home his advantage. "I think you serve a knight, D'Oilli? Guiscard? De Mamers?" The shocked look on the face of the sergeant gave me the answer but I asked anyway. "De Mamers is your leader?"

"Lord Hubert de Mamers will have my tongue torn out if he discovers this."

"He will not learn it from me. What were your instructions?" He hesitated, "Come. I know there is an army of hired swords in London and that they mean harm to the King. My father is there and I will do anything to prevent injury to him." Masood had joined us. "You recognise my scout? You know he comes from the Holy Land?" He nodded. "And you know how skilled they are with knives. Tell me all or he will peel your skin from your body piece by piece, layer by layer."

"Do not let the savage near us, I will tell you and then you can give me a warrior's death." I nodded and waved the captain closer so that he could hear. "We were to meet at Tilbury and we would be taken from there to Windsor. We were told that others would join us. The Tower would be taken and with Windsor in our hands then London would fall."

I nodded. His words rang true, "Captain these men's lives are in your hands. For what they have admitted I could have then hanged here and now but you say they saved your ship."

He nodded. "I am indebted to them and would have them live."

"Then take them to Anjou and put them ashore."

"I will do so."

"And you will swear never to come to England on pain of death. You know that I mean it."

"Aye lord."

I turned to Roger of Bath. "Throw the pirates overboard and then rejoin us. God speed Captain and you, sergeant, had better protect this crew for their captain has just saved your life."

Chapter 10

I had much to ponder as we spent the next two days fighting the winds north. This was a bigger threat than my father had assumed. The greatest and most loyal of King Henry's knights were in France fighting to hold on to his father's empire. There was just my father left in England. I had delayed too long! If I had come immediately I heard the news then I might be in England now. Who knew what mischief was abroad. The two castles of Windsor and the Tower guarded the two ends of London. From what the sergeant at arms had said they already controlled the Tower. How? If they had an army at Tilbury and another at Windsor then my father was in serious trouble.

I had to confide my fears to Sir James. He nodded, "Your father was in control of the Tower when I left, lord. He is a canny leader. I cannot see him losing his grip on the city." He hesitated, "Not unless he is betrayed."

Of course, Sir James had been away from my father for a long time. Anything could have happened. Who was there left to trust?

The coast of England was never more welcome than that cold morning when the Isle of Wight loomed up on our larboard side. This would be but the first part of our journey home. We had hours to go before we reached Southampton and then we had to find horses. The last part of the journey would be a very long ride to London. We would not be there for another day or two at least.

The winds which had failed to cooperate all the way north continued to be an annoyance. We did not reach Southampton until late in the afternoon. We would not be able to leave until the morning. Southampton Castle was a royal residence. The constable, John of Winchester, could not do enough for Duke Richard. I had not told the King's son of my news. I wished us to be alone with him when I did so. He dismissed all of the knights so that I could speak openly for my face and demeanour told him of the import of my words.

When I had told him what I had discovered he was stunned. I had rarely seen him lost for words. "I can see a greater conspiracy here than a simple attempt to murder the Earl Marshal.." He rubbed his red beard. "I had thought my brother was at the back of this treachery."

"He still might be. Holding London might be the first stage in a coup which is greater in scale than any of us imagined."

Richard was a shrewd general. "And, of course, we do not know who lies between us and London. If I was this Hubert de Mamers I would have men watching all of the ports."

"I had wished to ride this night but that will be too dangerous. I have good scouts. I will send Masood and some of my archers out before dawn to scout the road north."

"You know Earl I envy you your men. You took that one ship with a single knight backed by your men at arms and archers. I tried with a covey of household knights and lost knights and men at arms. When this mischief is over then you must tell me how you do it."

"To do that, Duke Richard, you must ask my father for he taught me all that I know as he taught your father and your grandfather too. Geoffrey of Anjou was a callow and reckless youth until my father showed him how to lead. When he is gone England will lose part of her soul."

He crossed himself and said, "Amen to that."

When we spoke with the constable we realised that the danger was not just in London. There was unrest in Hampshire. Even with a royal castle close by there were still many incidents of disorder. Travellers had been attacked. Trade had suffered. Ships were waiting in Southampton for cargoes which did not arrive. King Henry had not understood the seriousness of the threat to the crown. Young King Henry should have stayed in England. I could not understand that shallow young man. For all his faults Duke Richard appeared to have the welfare of his homeland as a priority. His elder brother had been given England but because he had not been given all of the coin he wished he had absolved himself of responsibility to spend the time jousting and hunting. King Henry had made a grave error of judgement in having his son crowned.

I sent Masood and four archers out before dawn. We had eighty miles to go and, under normal circumstances, that would take two days. These were not normal circumstances. We would acquire new horses at Farenberg. Ralph of Wales was with my scouts. If the road was clear then he would ensure that there were sufficient horses waiting for us.

The unrest was evident as we thundered through the land. Even though our names were known people were wary. The revolt by the King's sons had done irrevocable damage to England. It would take another generation to repair. Gibbets in every town showed that there were men who would commit serious crimes for they thought they could escape justice. The castles we passed were poorly garrisoned. Some were empty save for a token handful of men. The barons and their men were either in France with the King or on crusade. I kept seeing myself, many years earlier. I had done that and I had left my father to try to hold together this broken land. He had done so and more. He had reclaimed the crown for Henry. Even now, as we hurried north, he was still trying to heal the fragile realm.

We reached Farenberg safely and that was where our luck deserted us. There were just twenty horses to be had and none were as good as the ones we would be leaving. There was no castle in Farenberg and the lord was on crusade. The reeve was apologetic especially when Duke Richard began to rage. This was no time for histrionics. I spoke calmly to soothe the situation, "Duke, we take twenty horses. The rest wait here and join us tomorrow. Whatever the danger to London and my father we will be at his side within the day."

"Very well, Earl. I will heed your advice but we had best leave quickly." Duke Richard wanted to take all of his household knights.

I shook my head, "With respect Duke, we need to take a mixture of men. We leave our squires here." He nodded. "We need Masood and some of my archers."

"No, Earl. We do not need your scout. We need knights if we are to aid your father. Your scout can do nothing in London and your men at arms are not the equals of my household knights. You may bring four archers for I have seen their skills."

I knew that he was wrong but he would not be swayed. He was the King's son. I took Ralph, Tomas, Grant and Henry Warbow along with Sir James. I hoped that the thirteen knights who rode with Duke Richard knew their business. After ale, bread and cheese we mounted. I left Roger of Bath to command my men. The knights whom Duke Richard had left could do as they wished.

With so few archers I could only allow my men to ride thirty paces ahead of us. It would be enough to spring a trap and that was all. Masood and his nose would have detected trouble long before it could harm us.

It was ironical that the ambush, when it came, was close to the old Saxon burgh of Kingeston; it was the place where the kings of Wessex had hunted. We were just twelve miles from London. While the Duke and his knights were already relishing the prospect of a comfortable bed my senses were tingling. Dusk was approaching. Already the sky was darkening in the east. Kingeston had no lord of the manor. He had died in Ireland and King Henry had yet to appoint another. The oversight was a disaster. We had just passed through the wooden walled burgh and were heading for Mortlake when we were attacked. Even though my archers had prepared themselves for an attack the mercenaries who burst from behind the farm and wood took them by surprise. Grant's leg was hacked in two and his horse mortally wounded before he could pull his bow from his back.

Ralph shouted, "Ambush!" before he led the other two away from the men who ran at them. I drew my sword and hefted my shield up. As well as the twelve men on foot who attacked us another ten galloped from behind us. It was a clever trap. The knights at the rear of our column had not heard the hooves which trailed us. The two at the rear paid for that oversight with their lives.

My helmet still hung from my saddle and I had no time to grab it. I knew that Ralph and his archers had not fled. They were giving themselves room to use their bows and to avenge Grant. The only one on whom I could truly rely was Sir James. He would watch my back. I galloped towards the men at arms. One was standing over Grant to take his head when my poor palfrey reached him. I brought my sword down across his back. He wore mail but my height, the force of my swing and my sword shattered the links and tore through his gambeson to slice across his back. Even as the sword from the second mercenary hacked at my shield I was standing in my stirrups to swing across my horse's head. My sword struck the side of the man's helmet and knocked him to the ground. I heard the clash of steel close by me as an arrow whizzed before me to hit a mercenary who wielded an axe in the chest.

Sir James had two men who were trying to get at him. I whirled the labouring horse and spurred him. He did not leap, he lumbered but Sir James had skills. He fended off one man with his sword as he ducked beneath the spear which lunged at his head. Duke Richard and his knights were busily engaged with the mounted men but we still had nine men to deal with. The thrum of three arrows diminished the threat by a third. I leaned from my saddle to sweep my sword across the back of the man attacking Sir James' shield side. I broke his spine with the blow. The man at arms whom I had knocked to the ground now rose and ran towards me. Two more mercenaries fell to my archers' arrows. In the gloom of dusk, I saw that the man I had struck was bleeding but he was determined for vengeance. He held his sword in two hands with his shield about his back. Had I been riding a decent horse then it would have been simplicity itself to despatch the man but my horse was old and slow. I tried to jerk the animal's head away from the swinging sword but I failed. I heard its scream as the sword struck the side of its head. Kicking my feet from the stirrups I felt myself falling. I knew how to fall. Sir Edward had taught me that. As I hit the ground I rolled. I hit the road with my shield and that cushioned the blow but I was given no time to recover as the mercenary raced to finish me off. I lay like a tortoise on its back. I did the only thing I could do, I swung my sword blindly at his leg. It was a race of blades. I saw his coming down. I tried to raise my left arm but I knew that it would be too late. Then my sword hacked into the tendons at the back of his legs. His own sword was a handspan from my head. His leg buckled and he fell to the side. The sword struck my chest but it was a weak blow. I rolled over and rammed my sword under his chin and into his skull.

I saw that my archers and Sir James had ended the threat of the men on foot but Duke Richard and his last four knights were surrounded.

"Help the Duke!"

I ran towards the mounted knights. My left shoulder ached from where I had fallen but I would worry about that later on. I saw Sir Bohun felled by a mighty axe blow from a knight. Richard was fighting like a man who had lost all reason. He laid about him recklessly. Perhaps his ferocity saved him.

Sir James thundered his weary horse into the middle of the mêlée. The Bishop of Durham's nephew did not lack courage. I was a few steps behind and one of the knights saw me and rode at me. The knight was riding a destrier and they were trained to ride over men on foot. Even though my left arm was aching I pulled it back and punched at the horse's head as it neared me. The blow hurt me but it also saved me. I was knocked to the side and beyond the sweeping sword of the knight. I kept my feet and as the knight turned to come back at me I ran towards his left side. He was using his left hand to pull around his horse's head and I swung at his unprotected leg. The knight had good chausse but even so, I managed to break the mail and draw blood.

At that moment one of the mercenary knights shouted, "Fall back!" His call was too late for one of his knights who fell with two arrows embedded in him. Our mounts were not good enough to pursue. We had to let them go.

"Ralph, gather the horses. Tomas, search the bodies. Henry Warbow see to Grant!"

Duke Richard was incandescent with rage, "Bastards! I will have them hung drawn and quartered! The best of knights now lie dead! My brother will pay!"

"My lord, you do not know that it is your brother. It may be but let us use our heads. We will put our dead on the horses and ride to London. We will be there after the watch has been set and will need to ride further east and approach the castle from that direction."

He seemed to calm himself. "Your archers did well." It was as close as he would come to an apology!

One of his knights, Sir Robert, pointed to a dead man and said, "I know this knight. I met him in Rouen six months since. He is Sir Godfrey de Waller."

"De Waller!"

"You know him, Earl?"

"No, Duke, but I know the family. Guillaume de Waller was a treacherous snake whom I met in the Holy Land. This is another connection with Outremer and further proof of the danger we face. They have scoured the cesspits of Outremer to gather the worst of knights and their men. I pray that we are in time."

Tomas found more evidence of Templar involvement. Two of the men at arms had been Templar sergeants. All had coins about them. Most were from France but there were German coins too. This was a complicated conspiracy. I mounted the warhorse from the knight which belonged to the last knight Ralph had killed. We headed for London. Had we reached there before the watch was set then we might have crossed London Bridge and entered through the city. As it was we would need to ride to Sudweca. There we would be able to gather intelligence about the city and by heading further east we might be able to take a boat to take us to the Tower.

South of the river was a dangerous area at the best of times but in these uncertain times, it was even more so. Where we had once been a strong retinue of armed warriors we were now a handful of battered men most of whom rode poor horses. As we neared Sudweca I discussed with the Duke our plans. I say our plans but they were mine. I knew what we would have to do and I would not allow him to dissuade me. His last decision to bring knights instead of archers had almost proved fatal. Archers would have fared better in the dark.

"I will leave Ralph and my archers at the bridge. When Roger brings the rest of the men he can cross the bridge. We will head down the river a further half mile. There are ferries there and we will hire one."

It seemed a simple idea and I could not see a flaw in the plan. Had I had scouts I could have sent ahead I might have known of the problems which awaited us. We rode east and north after the sun had set. There were few people about and that was worrying. When we neared the southern end of the old wooden bridge which spanned the river we halted. Something did not feel right. St. Mary Overley's Priory lay close to the bridge and leaving our horses with our men Duke Richard and I went to the door. We banged upon it but no one came. I was loath to shout. I contemplated climbing the wall but realised it was too high. I needed my men! We banged again.

Next to me, Duke Richard began to fume, "I am a prince of the realm. What mean these monks to keep us waiting?"

"They know not who we are lord. We will try one more time."

This time the banging brought a response, "Who is it? We are peaceful friars! Go away!"

The Duke was about to shout when I held up my hand and said, "I am Earl William of Stockton and I have with me Duke Richard of Aquitaine. I pray you to open the gate for we come on the King's business."

I heard bolts sliding back and the door groaned open. Two friars stood there. "Come in quickly! It is not safe!"

Once inside the gate was barred again. "What is the meaning of this!" Duke Richard did not like being ordered about.

"Have you not heard the news, my lord? The city is taken and the Tower is cut off. Anarchy reigns!"

Duke Richard was visibly stunned. We had expected trouble but not on this scale. I asked, "When did this happen?"

"Two or three days since. Certainly, the gates were barred two days ago."

"Who holds the Tower and who holds the city?"

"Your father holds the Tower but some say he was wounded and the defence is in the hands of his grandson Sir Samuel. As for the city that is under the control of a band of knights. They are led by a crusader. He wears the white surcoat with a red cross."

Just then the abbot came out. He looked terrified, "My lord I beg that you forgive us. We knew not what the Augustine friars were up to."

I shook my head, "Abbot we know nothing of these events. We have travelled hard from France and only recently arrived in Southampton. What do you mean? Speak plainly."

"The Abbot of the Augustine Friars, Abbot D'Oilli, let the knights in through the Moorgate. Many of the garrison of the castle were killed."

Were we too late? "Listen to me. I have more men arriving and we will go to the aid of my father. We need a boat to cross the river."

He nodded, "There is an inn on the north side of the river. It is called the Falconer's Glove. The innkeeper is a loyal man. He is Welsh. His name is Rhodri. His brewhouse is just down the river and when the city fell he fled with his family. He is staying in the brewhouse. He has a boat."

"Thank you, abbot. Keep your doors barred. I fear it will take steel and blood to retake the city." Once outside we rejoined our men. "There has been a change of plan. The city has fallen. We will go to the brewhouse down the river. Ralph you and Tomas will wait there with the horses. When dawn breaks secrete yourselves by the bridge and await our men."

"Aye lord."

Our noses led us to the brewhouse. It lay next to a wharf and I saw the wherry tied up. I was tempted just to take it but something made me trust the Abbot's words. If he said we could trust this innkeeper then so would I. This time our knocking brought an immediate response. When Rhodri appeared, he was wearing a round helmet and held a sword. He was ready to fight us. It was dark and there was no way that he would have recognised us. "Who are you? I want nothing to do with rebels!"

I smiled, "Then that is music to my ears. I am Earl William of Stockton and this is Duke Richard of Aquitaine. We would have you ferry us to the Tower and then give shelter to two of our men."

He sheathed his sword, "Aye, lord and right willing I am but we must do it by night. If those murderers realise what I am doing then my family will not be safe."

"The two men I am leaving with you are good warriors and we have more men arriving tomorrow."

"Then let us go, lord. You can leave the horses in the brewhouse."

As we peered across the river I saw, close to the gates the embers of a fire and I could smell smoke. Were we in time or had we come too late?

The wherry accommodated us comfortably and we rowed across for the wind was against us. That would help Rhodri when he returned. "We will have to head upstream first." He pointed to two blackened stumps. "They tried to attack the castle with two ships. The men on the walls fought hard. The ships were burned. Once we have passed them, then we can use the current." He headed for the wharf which lay close to the walls. There was a postern gate there. It was called the river gate.

"I will have to leave quickly, lord, will you be able to enter?"

Duke Richard said, "If not then heads will roll!"

I knew that we had been seen as we approached as I detected movement. I leapt on to the wharf. Sir James grabbed the rope and held the wherry against the wharf. I called up, "It is the Earl of Stockton and Duke Richard. Admit us!"

A head appeared through the crenulations. There was a fresh scar across one cheek.

"Aye lord. And we are right glad to see you!"

I breathed a sigh of relief. It was John of Oxbridge!

Samuel
Part Three
The Legacy of the Earl Marshal

Chapter 11

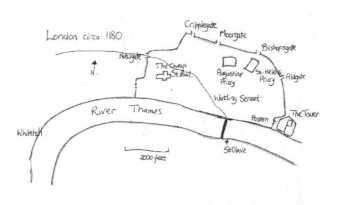

London

As we helped my grandfather into the Tower I wondered at the disaster which had just struck us. Not only had Sir Harold and his squire died so had Richard's squire, his brother Walter. How could things have gone so badly and so quickly? The abbot was a conspirator; that was clearly obvious. The guards at the gate had guilt all over their faces as we passed through. Peter Longstride could not meet my angry gaze. They had not done their duty. My grandfather was a dead weight and had Thomas not helped me then I would have struggled to bear him. There were many questions to be asked but now was not the time.

"John of Oxbridge, fetch inside all of the horses and bodies. None enter without I give permission. Until the Earl Marshal is healed then I command." I desperately wanted to arrest the abbot and bring him to the Tower for questioning but I did not have enough men.

"Aye lord, I am sorry. I do not know how those killers hid so close to the walls. Was it witchcraft?"

"No John; they were clever men. They outwitted the Warlord. One escaped but he shall not escape me. That I swear."

The doctor came to my grandfather's chamber. He examined him but could find no reason for his ailment. Then he felt the Warlord's skull. "There is a wound here. Is it an old one?"

"He suffered one in the battle last year. Why? Could that be it?"

"Perhaps. I will send a man to watch him."

"No!" I know that I sounded angry. I was but not with the healer. "He is my grandfather and I will sit with him until he wakes."

After the doctor had gone I began to take off my grandfather's mail. I took off the arming cap first and then the chausses. Finally, I removed the hauberk. I had done it when I had been a squire. I folded the mail. I doubted that he would wear it again. I would forbid it. I took off his padded gambeson. In his shift, he looked so thin. I covered him with a fur and then went to fetch wine. I lifted his head and poured some into his mouth. He swallowed and I was relieved. I had begun to wonder if he was dead already. I went to fold the gambeson and a small jug fell from it on to the fur. I lifted it and, removing the stopper, sniffed it. This was medicine. Why was he taking it?

My squire, William, timidly entered the room, "Do you need anything, lord?"

I shook my head. "I will stay here until he wakes. Go around the sentries and make certain that they are alert. There is treachery about." He nodded and handed me a platter of bread and cheese along with a jug of ale. "I could not eat, William, but I thank you."

The night passed slowly. The walls and the gate were secure. We had food, water and beer. The Chancellor and his family as well as the other officials were within the walls of the castle. I was not sure that we had enough men to defend the walls but the White Tower was a different matter. We just had to hold one door. Even as the thought came into my head I felt my heart sink. Who would be coming? Sir James might be in France but the message my grandfather had sent had warned of danger and not the disaster this had become. I had to put myself in my grandfather's position. What would he do it he was still able to command? D'Oilli was part of the conspiracy. He had lured us to his priory so that we could be ambushed as we left. We had been outnumbered by our attackers. Was that the full extent of our foes? Ranulf de Glanvill and the Earl of Essex both had manors close to the city and were loyal. My grandfather had said so. I would send a rider to summon them. Then I realised that sending a messenger might be the same as signing the man's death warrant. Our three best men had been murdered. Who would I send?

It was dawn when my grandfather stirred. He gave me a wan smile, "My chamberlain once more."

I held up the jug of medicine, "Grandfather what is this?"

He said nothing but took it from me, "Now tell me what has happened and omit nothing."

I was not sure how much he remembered of the ambush and so I went through it all. I also told him what I planned to do. He smiled and patted my hand. Spying the bread and the ale he used my arm to pull himself up. "I am starving." He swallowed down half of the beaker of ale and then tore a piece of bread. He smeared butter upon it and cut a healthy chunk of cheese. He chewed but he watched me while he did so. "I am guessing that this was for you and you were too worried about an old man to eat."

I nodded, "Grandfather what is the medicine for and why did you fall over? There was no wound. The doctor is mystified."

I saw him sigh. He wiped his hands on a napkin and then turned to face me, "Samuel, I am dying. Brother Peter gave me months to live. I have outlasted his prediction already. I thought I was dead until I opened my eyes and saw you. I have said goodbye to Stockton and I now have one last task to perform. I will save London for the King."

"Save yourself! London does not matter! The King does not matter!"

"Listen to me, Samuel, you are wrong. The King is England and we are honour bound to save it and him. Your plan is a good one. We will send men on the morrow to summon help. Let the Abbot think I am dead. When we strike we will show no mercy."

"Strike who? When? How?"

"There is a conspiracy here of Templars, border knights who have lost land and those who did not find what they sought in the Holy Land. There are family connections and I should have seen them. Now that I think back I recognised the Abbot as a d'Oilli. The city is in danger but we must hold this bastion first."

"How can you think of others when you are dying?"

"We all die. Poor Harold is dead. Wulfric, Edward, my wife, Wulfstan, my father, the Empress, all have gone. I am the last and I am ready to meet my maker for I have done nothing of which I am ashamed. I would that your father was here but that is not meant to be. I have the next best thing, you. You must learn to be me. Your son Thomas will learn from you and then it will be as though I have never died. Now help me to my feet. I need to make water and then we must prepare our defences."

"Defences?"

"You have good instincts, Samuel. There is a conspiracy afoot and we are perilously few in number. Let us assume that we will be attacked. If we are not then we have lost nothing. Always be ready for the worst. If the worst does not happen then you are better off!"

My grandfather seemed to have a new lease of life and yet I knew that it was an illusion. He was dying. I was watching the end of an era. I swore that I would not leave his side. The ale and the food seemed to have invigorated him. Or perhaps he was putting on an act for me. Sir Richard had been busy while I had watched my grandfather. He greeted us in the Great Hall, "Warlord, it is good to see you up and about. There is something going on in the city. The watch no longer controls the gate by St Peter's."

My grandfather nodded, "I need two volunteers." He saw my face. "Samuel, learn a lesson here. Our men have sworn to fight for us. If we sit here and wait for the enemy to come then we will lose. We have too few men.

I saw Davy of Ingleby raise his hand as did Walter Wulfestun. "We will go, Warlord. We will be careful for we have three dead friends we wish to avenge. What is it that you would have us do?"

"Ranulf de Glanvill and the Earl of Essex both have halls beyond the walls towards Westminster. I need you to fetch them here. We need help." They nodded. I took out the map of the land around London and pointed out where they needed to go. They studied it. I watched my grandfather scribble something on a piece of parchment and then seal it with wax. "How will you do it? By horse?"

"No lord, that would mark us too quickly. We will pretend that we desert and head for an inn in the town. The Falconer's Glove lies just within the walls and on the river. We will drink and complain that the Warlord is not the man he was and that we wish to return north to Stockton."

I was shocked but my grandfather appeared delighted, "You are the best of fellows, that might work." He handed them a purse. "This has silver coins. Gold would draw attention to you but this might grease your way through this web of deceit. Tell the lords to approach from the north and not through the city. I fear the abbot is but the tip of this conspiracy."

As they prepared to leave my grandfather showed that he while he might be ill, dying perhaps, but he had not lost his mind. John of Oxbridge, Samuel, Sir Richard, have our archers send arrows after them as they flee. Let us aid their story."

I felt humbled by the two men at arms. They had seen the butchered bodies of their compatriots and yet they were willing to do this for my grandfather. Would I ever be able to enjoy such loyalty? The rest of our handful of archers and men at arms played their part superbly. As the two slipped out of the postern gate and hurtled down the ditch they shouted and jeered. Davy of Ingleby turned and raised his fist. And then they were through the open gate and into the city. Ominously no one tried to stop them. Where was the town watch?

When they had gone my grandfather turned to Richard, "And now we bury your father and your brother. They were brave men and they should be buried in Hartburn but that cannot be." He turned to Harry, "Have Sir Harold's body and that of his son and squire brought here. We will bury them on this mound." The mound he spoke of was in the inner ward and protected by both the Tower and the inner wall. They would lie undisturbed.

Two priests came out with the bodies and, leaving the garrison to guard the walls, the archers and men at arms of Stockton came to say farewell to Sir Harold. The priest spoke the Latin and my grandfather's first squire was laid in the ground with his sword and his shield. My grandfather waited until the soil had been placed above the body and the priests had left. None save the knights and squires had understood the Latin. My grandfather would say the words which we would remember.

"Harold you came to me as little more than a boy. You began life as an outlaw and ended it as the mentor to a King. Your journey was truly wondrous. You were the most loyal and brave of men. Your blood and your spirit will be in Richard your son but I miss the man that you were. There are shield brothers and there are friends. You were both." He knelt and said quietly, so that I could barely hear him, "Wait but a little while and I will join you." He stood and raised his sword. We all did the same, "Sir Harold of Hartburn! A true warrior! We honour you in death! Sir

Harold!" We all roared his name. The words seemed to echo around the castle. Birds took flight and I saw the sentries on the walls watching us. "Thank you, my friends. Now we go back to the walls but we will not forget our shield brother." When they had all gone he turned to Sir Richard, "You can do this?"

"I am my father's son. I will honour him and my brother by defeating these men who so treacherously laid them low!"

The three of us, the warlord, Sir Richard and myself then walked the walls. We both had a lesson that day in how to defend. My grandfather carefully placed each archer and man at arms. There was a method to his plan. He mixed the uncertain garrison with our best men. We had knots of five men spread around the walls and on the towers. He went through each call of the horn. He made it quite clear what we would do. He said the same to each five. "You five are responsible for this section. You sleep in turn and eat together. When the enemy comes, and come they will, then you will fight as one. Make no mistake we fight for England. Know that I will come if you need me."

The effect was staggering. I saw their eyes as they fell under the sway of the legend that was the Warlord. I had grown up with him but it was only that day that I saw how he did it. Each of the men felt that they were one of my grandfather's oathsworn. They would die for him. I learned more in that one day than I had learned in my preparation to become a knight. I felt privileged. I also felt guilt for I was the only one who knew of his illness. There was hope in men's eyes but I did not feel it for I knew that he would never see Stockton again.

By the time the sun began to set I could see that he was exhausted. I took charge. "Sir Richard, take command. My grandfather needs rest."

"Aye Sir Samuel. You are right and nothing untoward will occur on my watch, Warlord."

"I am fine, Samuel."

"We will go to the hall. You will sit and put your feet up. You will eat and you will take your medicine." He nodded. "And then you will sleep."

He put his hand on my shoulder, "Soon I will sleep the eternal sleep. Do not be in a hurry to be apart. I would enjoy each moment I can with you, my only grandson!"

I watched him wearily sit and I sent William for food and ale. He sipped the ale and ignored the food. "Your father and I were estranged for years but since he brought your mother, Ruth and yourself to England

I have never felt as close to him. When I am gone you must be as a rock for him."

"Brother Peter might be wrong. You have lasted longer than he said!"

He smiled and tapped his chest, "It matters not what Brother Peter believes it is what I believe. Now listen to me, Samuel. If I am taken earlier than I would like then it will be up to you to save this city for the King. Use your strength. We have strong walls and the finest of archers. Do not waste men. When you feel the outer wall must fall, then pull back to the tower and the second wall. The castle is cleverly designed. There is but one way to attack and that is from the city. Do not surrender. Help will come. I know not when but we are well provisioned and you must give the heart to those who lack it. They will not be the men we brought south. They will be the garrison. You can make them men."

We spent hours talking of the men my grandfather had fought alongside. He held them all in high esteem and seemed to think that he had done little to deserve his reputation. How could he be so selfless and serve a king who used him? I could not fathom his loyalty. I made him take his medicine during the second watch and he fell asleep in the chair. I covered him with a fur and then went to relieve Sir Richard.

"How goes it?"

"There is no sign of our men and I take that to be a good thing. The gates have been closed. Perhaps that is good too."

"I will watch for an hour or so. Ger some sleep."

"Are you certain? You were up all night."

I thought of my grandfather's words, "I will be fine. I have William with me for company!"

I did as my grandfather had done and walked the walls. I stopped at the gate which led to the city. Peter Pig Man was there with Tam the archer and three of the garrison. "How goes it, Peter?"

He smiled, "Quiet, lord although not as quiet as it would be at the farm in Thornaby."

William said, "What about the pigs, Peter?"

"When they wake they are noisy enough sir but when I walked in the night to check for foxes you could hear your own heartbeat it was so quiet." He pointed to the city. "We have been listening to the town watch. They are like nettled hens, lord. The battle the other day has them rattled. Still, so long as they are talking we know there is no danger."

One of the garrison said, "I do not understand, lord. What does Peter mean?"

"You live in the city surely you know of the undercurrent? There is danger in the streets."

"Aye lord, it has been like this for weeks."

"It is like the embers of a fire. The ash looks white but beneath the white is an orange glow. It could burst into flames at any time. Peter means that if they are talking about the problems then there is no immediate danger. If there was to be a sudden attack then they would be silent. There would be a lord there making certain that they are quiet." I saw realisation fill his face. "I will watch for a while. William, go and check on my grandfather and fetch us a jug of ale."

When he had gone a comfortable silence fell over the men who watched with me in the turret above the gate. I could hear the murmur of conversation from the gate into the city. Peter was right. It was the buzz of words which was reassuringly peaceful. We shared the jug of ale. I smiled at Peter and Tam's reaction to it. They preferred the ale brewed by St John's well. They were partial to their own. As I turned to lay down the horn I saw the first lightening of the sky in the east. Soon it would be dawn. By the time we could see dawn almost upon us the relief had come.

"Before you turn in, Peter, I would have you and your men come with me to the city. Let us speak with the town watch."

"Aye, lord." Four of them picked up their shields and spears. Tam strung his bow. None of us wore helmets but we pulled up our coifs and descended to the gate. There were two guards there. They were from the garrison. They were dozing. It was allowed for they would have been woken by any attempt to force the gate. When they heard the jingle of our mail they hurriedly stood. "Yes, my lord?"

"I am taking a walk to the city gate. Close this one behind me and only open it when I speak. The watchword will be 'Lady Ruth'."

"Aye lord."

The bar was lifted and the gate pulled open. The sun suddenly flared behind us and bathed the old city wall in light. I heard the bell sound from the church of St. Olave. It signalled the opening of the gates. By the time we reached London's walls, the gate had creaked open. The town watch greeted us. Unlike my men, they did not wear mail. They had leather caps and short swords and spears. Their shields were small round ones. They were there to deal with brigands and bandits, not armed knights.

"Good morning, my lord. I am Captain Robert of the city watch. How is the Earl Marshal?"

"He is recovered." I gestured behind me with my hand. Although the bodies had been removed the grass still had blackened patches of grass which showed where horses and men had fallen. "And the city? It is quiet?"

The captain of the watch rubbed his grey flecked beard, "Uneasy lord rather than quiet. The mayor has left to seek help from Windsor."

There was something unsaid. "Richard White did not come to us?"

The captain looked embarrassed, "I would have expected him to, lord, but he said you had taken too many losses already. He feared if more knights came then the city would fall."

"And you, captain, what do you think?"

"I think that so long as the Earl Marshal lives then there is hope. I am reassured by your words and know this lord, we are loyal Englishmen and we will defend this gate against all who would do us harm. We will watch this gate for you."

I clasped his arm, "Thank you, captain, that is all that I needed to know."

We headed back to our gate, "Lady Ruth."

We crossed the grass to the tower. Peter led his men to the warrior hall. "William, go and wake Sir Richard and I will wake my grandfather."

He was still asleep in the chair with the cloak about him. He looked so still that, for a moment I thought him dead. My heart began to race. As I neared him the jingle of my mail and my scabbard stirred him and he opened his eyes. "Samuel." He smiled, "Tell me you have not watched all night again!"

"I will sleep soon enough, grandfather," I told him what I had learned.

"I do not trust this Richard White. The Abbot is treacherous and I believe the mayor is too. Why not send to Ranulf de Glanvill? You get some sleep and Sir Richard and I will watch." He stood and put his hand on my shoulder. "I can see that the future is safe in your hands Samuel. You have a young body but, in your body, races the blood of our family. Your great grandfather would be proud of you. King Harold's housecarl would approve of the way you have turned out."

With such fulsome praise, I left him to collapse on to my bed. I barely had time to take off my mail before I was asleep. Sir Richard's younger squire, Harry, woke me from a deep and dreamless sleep, "My lord come quickly. The Earl Marshal has sent for you."

"What is the hour?"

"It is the fifth hour of the day. There is a battle within the city."

I began to dress. A bleary-eyed William hurried to help me dress. I swallowed a half beaker of flattened and stale ale before rushing out of the chamber, the Tower and across the grass to the gate and the walls adjacent to the city. I saw others running to the walls and, from the east came the sounds of battle. Speculation was pointless. As we climbed the walls I saw my grandfather and Sir Richard.

When I reached him the Earl Marshal said, "The city is under attack, Samuel, and we must sit here and watch. Until Sir Ranulf and the Earl of Essex reach us then we are helpless and can only watch."

The city wall which lay just paces away was lower than the wall of the castle and we were able to see the streets. There was pandemonium in the streets and chaos reigned. There were flashing blades and the sounds of battle. Sir Richard pointed to the river. "See Sir Samuel, those who have boats are fleeing. They are the loyal men of London. I fear the city has fallen."

Just then a knot of men appeared through the gates. I recognised one as the captain. Two of his six men were wounded and I saw them battling. "Sir Richard, come with me. Those are loyal men and we must aid them."

"But the gate!"

"My grandson is right. Go and help. Archers, cover our men!"

"Aye, Earl Marshal."

I unsheathed my sword and ran down the stairs. "Open the gate!" I saw that two men had followed Sir Richard and our squires. We were perilously thin on the ground.

As the gate groaned open I saw that one of the wounded men had fallen. There were two knights and twelve men at arms battling to kill the captain and his watch. When they saw the gate open they renewed their efforts and the knight shouted over his shoulder. "The gate opens! We have them!"

I did not hesitate. I ran at the nearest knight. Even as I swung my sword I shouted, "Captain, get your men inside!"

The knight had a helmet and shield and I just had a sword. He must have thought that he had me and he began to swing his sword towards me. I used my speed to defeat him. Even as I closed with him I swung my own sword and raised my mailed left hand. I grabbed his sword hand and hit his shield at the same time. I had the advantage that I had the slope with me and I took him by surprise. I pushed him to the ground. I retained my feet and I used two hands to raise my sword. I would end his life. Even as I brought down my sword he managed to pull his shield over his body. I heard Aelric shout, "Loose!" The sound of arrows over my head was reassuring. I hit the shield with all the force I had. The shield cracked and the tip of my sword struck the knight on the helmet.

"Samuel, they are safe! Get back inside!"

I saw that two of the men at arms who had been with the knight lay dead while the others sheltered beneath their shields. The five who had come out with me all survived. "Back!" I saw arrows falling on the men who were attempting to leave the city and take advantage of our open gate. Five lay writhing or dead. When our gate slammed shut behind us then I knew that we were alone and we were under siege!

Chapter 12

I saw the captain and his men hurrying with their wounded towards the White Tower. Harry was with them. The small postern gate which led into the city was slammed shut and the walls were manned with enemy soldiers. They were not manned for long. The Earl Marshal shouted, "Aelric, clear those walls for me!"

"Aye, Earl Marshal!" Aelric turned to the ten archers he had with him. "You heard the Warlord. Choose your targets. I want not an arrow wasted."

My grandfather's captain of archers, Dick, had trained them well and each archer drew back and sought flesh. We were close enough so that the kettle and open-faced helmets were no protection. The barbed arrows tore wicked wounds in their flesh. Shields came up but even they proved ineffective. The arrows had such force that they drove through the willow boards. The defenders hid behind the crenulations and sheltered in the two gate towers which had arrow slits.

My grandfather beamed at Aelric. "I will leave you here to watch the gate. Sir Richard and Samuel come with me. We have other gates to watch." We headed from the gatehouse along the north wall. To the south lay the south-west bastion tower and the river. There was little chance of an enemy attacking it for the river surrounded it on two sides. There were just eight men on the north wall. There was a deep ditch and the wall was high. If the enemy, whoever they were, attacked with war machines then we might be in trouble but I knew how long it took to build rams and stone-throwers.

As we approached the city wall which joined ours to the northeast my grandfather stopped. "For once I am pleased that the city walls are in disrepair. He pointed at the break in the wall. There was a ten-pace gap. The postern gate which lay close by had been taken away for kindling and the old Roman wall robbed for stones. A small tower stood at the junction of the east and north towers. I saw four of our archers there.

From their vantage point, they could discourage any attack on the gate. "Keep a good watch, Peter!"

"Aye Earl. They sent two scouts to see if we watched." He pointed and I saw, in the bottom of the ditch, the body of a man at arms. From the sun-bleached surcoat and the tanned hand, I knew him to be from the Holy Land.

"Earl Marshal why have so many men come from the Holy Land? What do they seek here?"

"They seek the same here as they did in Outremer. Land and power. King Henry's absence and the revolt by his sons have encouraged them. I thought when Stephen the Usurper died that this land would be safe in my lifetime. I fear, Samuel, that you will have to continue to watch this land when your father and I are long gone."

Now that I knew of his fate his words were like a knife to my heart. We went through the gate and passed the Tower. Here the wall and the Tower came together. There was a guard room below the roof of the extended tower and it butted out from the curtain wall. It was higher than the wall. An enemy who tried to scale this would need a wooden tower which was so high that it would take many trees to build. None were close by. We reached the Well Tower and I saw that my grandfather had manned it with more archers. The men at arms guarded the walls and the archers used the tower. There was another tower at the river gate and it too had archers. There were also men at arms and John of Oxbridge commanded them.

"John, we need you to sleep in this tower. This gate is one that an enemy could use. If you see any ships approaching, no matter how small then let us know!"

"Aye, Earl Marshal." He pointed to the river filled ditch to the side. "That is a danger too, Earl. If they came at night they could take the gate."

I looked over. The ditch was wide enough for a boat. A wall connected the river gate tower to the White Tower but there was nothing to stop an enemy from taking the gate. We could not afford to lose the men guarding the gate. I saw a solution. "John, give me six men. We will make it safe." I saw my grandfather smile as I hurried down the stairs. He had not asked me what I intended.

"Should I go with him, Earl Marshal?"

"No, Sir Richard, stay with me. Besides my grandson knows what he is about. He has my blood in his veins."

My squire and my men left through the postern gate by the tower. Here there were another four men at arms. "You four come with me and fetch axes." There was a stand of trees on the small mound which lay in the open area of the outer ward. I took off my sword and coif. "We will cut down these trees. I want you to sharpen the points and embed them in the ditch by the wall. William, get a fire lit. We will fire harden them."

When the axes came we worked in relays to hew down the trees, rake off the foliage and cut down the branches. We piled the small branches and leaves for kindling; who knew when we might need it. The larger trunks were cut in two. We soon worked up a healthy sweat. I had just supervised the first three logs being placed at an angle in the ditch when Harry found me, "Lord, the Earl Marshal wishes a word."

"William, David, continue the work. I want a wall of stakes to deter anyone coming through the gap. Cut down those wild brambles and place them between the stakes."

"Aye lord."

My grandfather was in the great hall with the captain of the town watch. One of the doctors was tending to the warrior. He had a wound to the top of his leg. "Captain Robert has some grave news for us, Samuel."

The captain winced as the bandage was tightened, "Treachery, my lord. The Abbot of St Augustine's Priory dismissed the men from the Moorgate and the men who attacked us were allowed in. There were more than two hundred of them and they were led by knights. We stood no chance. I barely had time to warn those who could to flee south before we were overwhelmed. My son and nephew both died."

"I am sorry, Captain." I turned to my grandfather. "So it begins. I have made the ditch a barrier which will slow down an enemy. It will not stop a determined foe."

"I have already sent Sir Richard to give the new signals to the men on the west and north-west walls. If we are breached then they will head for the northeast tower. I have put ten archers on the top of this tower so that we can protect them."

"And now we wait for our men to bring help." In my heart, I feared that they had met the same fate as the other three who had been butchered.

My grandfather smiled, "Let us hope that they have not met the same fate as the others eh? My main hope is with Sir James."

"The seas twixt here and Anjou are wide and filled with danger."

He sighed, "My life has ever been thus. When I fought alongside the Empress and her brother we rarely had enough men. We lurched from one crisis to another and yet we had stout hearts. Let us trust in the men I have trained and your father. He will not abandon us."

Just then there was a faint call from the walls, "They come!" As we hurried from the halls we heard, "The north wall is under attack!" A horn sounded. The men I had left to work on the stakes would return to their posts.

"William fetch my shield and helmet. This will be hot work." I looked at my grandfather as he rose. I would have told him to stay but I would have been wasting my breath.

We headed up the stairs to the top of the Tower. I was amazed that my grandfather could still manage that at his age. William caught up with us as we stepped out on to the fighting platform. I saw the ten archers there. They each had two quivers. The quivers held the two types of arrow that they would need. Atheling was in command. He was now grey but while he might not be as strong he had forgotten more about archery than most men knew. He nodded as we stepped into the light. We went to the north battlements. We had a fine view of our walls and the land which lay beyond it. The enemy warriors were arrayed on the north side of the ditch. They must have known that we would be thinly stretched.

"Samuel, go and look at the city wall. I would know if they would try to attack on two sides at once."

I nodded and, taking my helmet and shield from William, ran around to the fighting platform on the west side of the Tower. We now had archers at just five places: The Tower, the Water Gate, the northeast tower, the south-west bastion tower and the main gate. If there was just one threat we could draw archers from the other two. When I reached the west wall, I saw that they were using crossbows from inside the gate. We could not withdraw those archers. I went to the south wall. Although I was further away from John of Oxbridge and his men I could see them. A pair of small ships packed with men were rowing down the river from London Bridge. They were attacking from the river. They intended to divide our forces.

By the time I reached my grandfather the enemy attack had begun. They had ladders carried by men without mail. Surrounding them came men carry shields to protect them. There were crossbows waiting to advance behind the shields. Further back were men at arms and knights. They were beyond bow range.

"Well?"

"They are attacking at the Water Gate and the main gate."

The Earl Marshal turned to Atheling, "It is up to you, my friend, to keep them at bay."

"We will do our best Earl Marshal."

"Come, Samuel, let us join Sir Richard on the battlements." He smiled, "I have not been idle. I have had spears and darts brought from the armoury."

We entered the gloom of the tower and descended to the fighting platform on the north wall. Sir Richard had organised the twenty men we had at our disposal. It was not enough. My grandfather drew his sword. As a crossbow bolt slammed into the wall above his head he smiled and said, "William if you would be so good as to fetch me a shield. I should hate to be hit with a crossbow bolt. Poor Dick would turn in his grave."

I sensed a movement to my left and I instinctively flicked up my shield. A bolt slammed into it. "Atheling! The crossbows!"

"Aye lord." There was a pause, "Loose!" Our archers hated the men who used crossbows. They called them the devil's machines. Although it would allow the men with the ladders to advance closer they began to thin the men with the crossbows. An archer could send arrows many times faster than a man with a crossbow and the crossbowmen fell. The men with the ladders were at the bottom of the ditch by the time the crossbows fell silent. William brought back the shield.

"Come, there are darts by the walls. They are not as good as arrows but they will have to do." The armoury in the Tower had many types of weapons and Sir Richard had found these steel-tipped darts. I had never used one but I knew that they were effective when thrown from a wall. I laid down my shield and picked up four of them. Atheling and his archers had now begun to hit the men carrying the ladders. The steep ditch made it hard to keep in close formation. I pulled back my arm and threw a dart. It might have been luck or perhaps my aim was guided by God. I know not but my dart pinned a hand to the ladder. The man shouted and used his other hand to pull away the dart. The front of the ladder dipped and I threw a second dart. Others were hurling their darts too. The men carrying the ladders were forced to wait until the men with the shields could give them shelter.

I had two darts left and the men were now at the bottom of the wall. I threw a dart at the foot of one of the men with a shield. I hit him and he fell backwards. I saw an upturned face and I hurled my last dart at it. It entered the man's eye and he dropped the ladder to pull the offending missile out. The same story was repeated all the way down the line. Even so, we were so few that they were like pinpricks. Even worse they were now hidden from the men on the Tower who sent their arrows towards the knights and men at arms who began to advance.

I picked up my shield and drew my sword. My grandfather smiled, "Let us see what an old wolf and a young cub can do."

I heard the first of the ladders as it slammed against the wall. I would stay with my grandfather. Sir Richard, Harry and William went to a point halfway along. The four archers at the northeast tower had a clear line of sight and their arrows were picking off the men with the ladders closest to them. It would be in the centre where we were in the greatest danger and my grandfather and I held that spot.

Two of the Tower's garrison stood with us. Neither wore mail but they held spears. They would be of more use than our swords. Holding mu shield before me I peered over the crenulations. We needed stones here. That was my oversight and I cursed myself. I had been so pleased that I had thought of a way to stop ships landing that I had forgotten an attack over the walls.

My grandfather had fought in more sieges than I had. He said to the two men, quietly, "Wait until the first man at arms is almost at the top. Attack from both sides at once. He can only protect from one shield."

I saw that there were six men already on the ladder. It bowed and creaked for the men climbing wore mail.

"Patience. Make a good clean strike at the same time."

I could see that the man at arms who was climbing had to hold on to the ladder with his sword arm. His shield was held over his kettle helmet. I watched my grandfather's face as he gauged the moment to perfection. The man was almost at the top when the Earl Marshal shouted, "Now!" The shout made the man look up at exactly the same moment that the two men struck. One spear went through the man's cheek while the other drove into his shoulder. He gave a cry and dropped his shield before tumbling backwards. The men had placed the ladder at a good angle for climbing and now it worked against them. The falling warrior hit the third man in the line ascending the ladder. The weight of them was too much and with a sharp crack, the ladder broke. The ones closest to the ground just had a hard fall but the four falling bodies hit them hard. Only one of the men was able to stand and, as he staggered away, an arrow struck him in the back.

My grandfather nodded his satisfaction. "That is one ladder! Now to the next one."

The other men had not had the success which we had. I saw that a knight had managed to gain a foothold on the fighting platform, "Samuel, deal with him. We will see to the next ladder."

I ran down towards the knight. He hacked at one of the garrison and his sword tore him open. I saw him turn and shout to the men ascending, "Hurry! We have them!" Another sentry ran at him from the other side. With contemptuous ease, the knight backhanded him with his sword. The blade sliced into his arm. The knight had a helmet with a nasal. I saw that he had a full beard; a Templar beard. I recognised the knight as the one who had escaped when Sir Harold had fallen. As the knight raised his sword to end the sentry's life I kicked the spear which had fallen to the fighting platform. It flew into the air and smacked the knight's shield. It distracted him and he turned

He advanced towards me, "Move! There is just a boy here to face me! We have the castle."

I did not rise to the bait. I knew that I had a youthful face. It was not looks which counted but skill. This would be a true test of those skills. The battlements were to my right and that restricted the blows I could strike. I had to swing from above or risk hitting the stone. He had no such inhibition. He suddenly launched himself at me. He brought his sword up from below. He was trying to get underneath my shield. I slid my shield down to cover my knee and the sword hit it hard, jarring my arm. I feinted with my sword to gauge his reaction. He just smiled. "I have fought the Seljuk Turks and they have the fastest hands of any. Whatever you do will just delay the inevitable. You will die!"

My father and grandfather had taught me that such posturing was a waste of breath. It was actions which decided battles. I realised that I was slightly taller than he was. I feinted with my shield and then suddenly leapt off my right leg into the air. As I did so I brought down my sword. I took him by surprise. He had not expected the move. He had to block the blow with his sword and the force of my landing was so heavy that he stepped back. He tripped over the unconscious sentry and tumbled backwards. Putting my sword down I quickly picked up the spear I had thrown at him and went to the battlements. The man at arms' face was level with the crenulation and I drove the spear down through his open mouth. He could not scream for I had ripped out his throat and his body fell taking the next two men with him. I had bought time.

The knight roared and lunged at me. One handed I hurled the spear at him. He easily blocked it with his shield but it allowed me to pick up my sword. I stood with my back to the stone so that I had some protection. He would have nothing but a drop from the fighting platform behind him. I saw, to the south, smoke rising from the river. I could not conceive why and I would have to wait for the answer. This battle was poised on the edge of a blade.

"Sneaky little bastard, aren't you?"

I concentrated and made myself become cold and calm. He had lost his temper. He had been within touching distance of victory and I had snatched it from him. I waited for the blow I knew would come. He pulled his arm back and swung with all the force he had. I dropped to my left knee and put my shoulder behind my shield. Instead of swinging my sword, I jabbed it hard at his knee. Like my father and the Earl Marshal, I had a point to my sword and it drove into a mail link ripping it apart. It slid into the flesh just below his knee cap. I twisted my blade as his sword struck my shield like a hammer. I felt myself falling but I continued to push my sword through to the back of his leg. It was the knight who saved me for in his pain he tore his left leg from my sword. I crashed down on the fighting platform. The tearing of his leg ripped his tendons and he could not support his weight. His back was over the edge of the fighting platform and I watched him as he tumbled into space. Below us was the roof of the bakehouse and I heard his metalled body smash into it. Slates fell and he rolled from it to crash onto the cobbles.

I heard a shout from William, "Lord, the ladder!"

He and my grandfather were trying to dislodge men from the ladder close to them and the rest of the defenders close by me were dead or wounded. My left arm was numb and I had to use my sword to push me upright. I sheathed it and picked up the helmet from a dead sentry and when I reached the battlements I threw it into the face of the sergeant who stared up at me. It struck his face hard and I saw blood spurt from his nose. Picking up a discarded spear I pulled my arm back and rammed the spear into the bloody face of the sergeant. His hands came up to protect himself and that doomed him. He fell backwards from the ladder and his motion made the ladder slide to the left.

Just then I heard Atheling shout, "I see Davy of Ingleby! He has men with him!"

I could see nothing for there were knights before me but when I heard the horn I knew that at least one of my men had found help. The horn and the falling ladders persuaded our attackers that they had failed and they streamed towards Aldgate. I looked to my right and saw that my grandfather, Sir Richard and our squires lived still but ten of the garrison and some of our men at arms lay dead or wounded. I hoped that my men had brought plenty of reinforcements. We needed them. Even as the enemy fled our archers on the Tower and in the gate tower, sent flight after flight towards them. Two fell but others were wounded.

My grandfather took off his helmet and embraced me, "Well done Samuel. You handled that knight well for he knew his business."

Sir Richard shouted, "There are just twenty or so horsemen, Earl Marshal. I expected more!"

I looked over and saw eight knights with their squires along with Davy of Ingleby and some men at arms.

My grandfather said, "No matter, they saved the day. The enemy thought as you did Richard. We have more men to face their next attack."

He looked weary and pale. His surcoat was bloodied but then so were ours but I noticed blood dripping from his left arm. "You are wounded!"

He smiled, "It is nothing."

"Healers! The Earl Marshal is wounded!"

All thoughts of the reinforcements left me as Richard and I half carried my grandfather back towards the Tower. The healers met us just inside the door.

"It is nothing!"

"Let me be the judge of that, Earl Marshal. Take off his mail!" The doctor took charge.

Other healers passed us to go to the fighting platform. We needed every man we could save. The reinforcements would just allow us to fight another day. They would not enable us to win the battle. As we stripped his mail I saw that the links were broken on the upper left arm. The padding there was not as thick as on the chest and back. The sword had cut deeply. The doctor quickly tied a cord around the upper arm above the wound to stop the bleeding. He worked quickly but calmly. He used vinegar to clear the blood and cleanse the wound. He peered at it to make certain that there was no cloth in the wound. Then he applied honey to slow the bleeding and help the healing. Finally, he began to stitch my grandfather's pale arm. It must have hurt but he endured it stoically. When the doctor had finished the doctor tied a bandage around it and then loosened the cord. It was then that my grandfather winced.

John of Oxbridge arrived. He saw the blood and the doctor. He looked concerned, "The Earl?"

I am fine, John. What was the smoke?"

He grinned, partly relieved that my grandfather still lived and partly at his news, "One advantage of fighting from a stone tower is that you can use fire. Our archers sent fire arrows into the ships. Two sank. Some scrambled ashore while others were forced to cling to the last ship. They will not try that again."

"Well done! Give your men extra ale tonight. They deserve it."

"And you need to rest!" The doctor shook his head. "Take him to his chamber, Sir Samuel. I will have broth brought. He needs food, wine and rest." He glared at the Earl Marshal. "You will take no further part in this battle!"

My grandfather just smiled, "We shall see."

Davy led the men he had brought around to the river gate. We heard their horses on the cobbles. "Sir Richard go and see Davy and Sir Ranulf. William, find out how many men we have to face the next assault."

Although he was in pain my grandfather smiled as he leaned on me. "Perhaps this was meant to be."

"What do you mean?" We entered the dark of the stairs which led down to the chamber. I had to watch my footing for the spiralling staircase was not easy to negotiate.

"Your father is not here else he would have taken command. Sir Harold died or he would have been the one to give orders. You are learning to wear my mantle."

I laughed and my laugh echoed in the stairway, "You are still in command, grandfather. It is you who make all the decisions."

We entered the corridor where our rooms lay. "When I was your age my father was still alive. He was Lord of Norton and I thought as you did that he made all the decisions. Now, looking back through the tunnel of time, I see that it is not so. He watched me but in the heat of the battle, it was I who made the vital decisions. It was so with you. The key battle was with the knight who gained the fighting platform. You took him on alone knowing that you would defeat him and that turned the battle in our favour. Sir Ranulf's arrival merely ended the battle a little earlier." We had reached his room. Already two servants were preparing his bed and I saw one of the doctor's assistants with a draught. "You go and speak with Sir Ranulf. I will do as the doctor commanded for I am content that you command." He stared into my eyes, "You and not Sir Ranulf." I nodded. He smiled, "I see God's hand in all of this. It is good. It is meant to be. Remember these lessons and teach them to your son."

My grandfather constantly surprised me. I would do as he said. When I entered the great hall Sir Ranulf was there talking with Sir Richard. His household knights were there also. Davy of Ingleby stood in the door. I went to him. "Where is Walter Wulfestun?"

Davy shook his head, "In truth, I know not. We had decided that I would see Sir Ranulf and Walter the Earl. We separated when we left the Falconer's Glove. We thought it for the best and so it was. There were many men armed with swords in the city and by agreeing with their sentiments I made my way through to the Newgate. I slipped through when a conroi of knights and sergeants left to head west along the river. Their security was lax, lord. The knights in the city number more than our garrison many times over." I nodded. "And another thing, lord, they are not all from hotter climes. I saw knights from Scotland and Wales. I heard knights with foreign voices. None had good mail. These are desperate men, lord. They will fight and die hard."

"You have done well now rest."

He nodded, "Do not worry, lord, Walter is a good man. He had further to go to find Earl Mandeville." He lowered his voice. "Sir Ranulf did not bring all of his men. He left behind half of his knights and most of his men at arms and crossbows."

As I turned to speak with the baron I wondered if this was treachery, prudence or politics. "Sir Ranulf thank you for your timely arrival. It is good that the enemy did not know how few men you brought or they may have fought on."

He coloured, "I had to leave my home protected, Sir Samuel. Where is the Earl Marshal?"

"He rests and has delegated the defence to me until he rises. He has asked me to be his lieutenant. I command." I did not allow him the opportunity to question my decision. "This is more than just a little unrest, my lord. These men who have taken over the city mean to take command of this land."

His eyes narrowed, "Rebellion?"

"Worse for these are hired men. Someone is trying to buy the crown."

"Or ensure that it stays on their head."

"You mean young King Henry?"

"It is no secret that he is unhappy with his father. He has the coin and his absence gives him the opportunity to deny any involvement if this fails."

"Until help comes then it is down to us and Earl Mandeville. We have sent to him too. Until he arrives we can only defend. With more men, we might have relieved the suffering of the loyal people of the city. Our men have fought for two days. I would have you and your men take over the watch so that we can rest and eat."

"We have ridden hard."

"And we have bled. I am loath to disturb the Earl Marshal's rest to have him give the order."

This was like combat with swords. I had made the strike and he had blocked the blow. I had raised my sword. He had a decision to make and he made the right one. He sheathed his sword. "You are right, Sir Samuel and it will allow us to see the enemy lines." He turned and spoke to his knights "Come, let us examine our new citadel!"

I turned to William, "Have the servants fetch food and ale for all. Tell the baker I want the ovens producing as much bread as they can. The Earl Marshal ensured that we had enough flour. If bread and ale are all that we have then so be it."

Sir Richard said, "There is plenty of salted pork, Sir Samuel. We will not starve."

"That depends upon how long it is before help comes. If the Earl brings as few men then we have to squat like a toad behind our walls. Who knows what mischief there is yet to come? Davy of Ingleby said that these hired swords are numbered in their hundreds. They are mercenaries come from many lands. There are Scots and other foreigners. I know this bodes well for the land of our valley but London is teetering on the edge of a precipice. We are trapped and know not what goes on in the outside world."

William said, "Sit, lord, and I will fetch food and ale."

"Thank you and when you have eaten put an edge on my sword for we shall need it."

Sir Richard and I took off our coifs and unfastened the mail mittens. I would have loved to take off my mail but I knew that until more help came then we would have to be ready to fight at a moment's notice. William brought the ale, bread and meat. We devoured both. As I chewed I reflected on what I had learned when walking the walls and speaking with my men. No ships had come up the river. That meant they were being stopped downstream. I was not totally familiar with this river but my grandfather had told me that Tilbury was a good place to strangle trade on the river. That meant there were enemies in the city to the west and the river to the east. As the Mayor had fled west I wondered if there were enemies there too. Then I recalled Davy's words: '*a conroi of knights and sergeants left to head west along the river.*' Why would knights head west when we still remained in the east?

I looked up and saw Sir Richard watching me. He gave me a sad smile, "My father and brother died in battle Sir Samuel but was it well done?"

"Well done?"

"Is this city worth fighting for? Is it worth the lives of good men like my father, his squire and my brother? Is it worth the lives of men at arms like Arne, Guiscard and Jean?"

"To speak truly this cesspit of corruption and self-serving lords is not worth the life of one man but it is the capital of our King and if this falls then England might tumble after it. My grandfather told me that the war he fought for sixteen years against Stephen the Usurper could have been avoided if London had remained loyal to Empress Matilda. I would not have another sixteen years of anarchy when I could have stopped it so the answer is that it was well done. Your father has two sons who live and they have his blood. If I fell then I know that Thomas would be raised to be a knight of the north by my father. If a man seeks a long life he does not choose to be a knight. He chooses the church!"

Sir Richard smiled, "That helps, Sir Samuel. I would not want my father's death to have been in vain and I will seek a wife when I return home."

"As my sister discovered when Sir Ralph was killed you need to seize what happiness you can when it is there before you. Do not waste time! It is more precious than gold." He nodded.

I yawned for I was tired. "Before you sleep have the night watch collect as many stones as they can. They can take them from the ruined Roman wall to the north and east of the castle. Have them moved around the walls. Put them at regular intervals along the fighting platform. The next time they use ladders we will give them a surprise."

"Aye Sir Samuel."

I did not manage to get to my chamber until the sun had set. There was much which demanded my attention. I made certain that my grandfather was well and then, after asking to be woken in an hour, I slept.

Chapter 13

The night passed peacefully. Although my men and I were tired we relieved Sir Ranulf and his men at midnight. The dead still lay beyond the walls where they had fallen. We heard the sounds of rats and foxes feasting on flesh. Aelric and Atheling had risked venturing forth to fetch in undamaged arrows. Even damaged arrows, so long as the heads remained, could be reused. My men could all fletch. The city was quiet and I wondered what it meant. We now knew that there were two other bands of men intent on mischief. They hardly constituted an army and yet they were a danger and a very real threat to the realm.

My grandfather joined me in the middle watch. "You should be asleep and resting."

He nodded, "The wound ached and woke me. I lay there looking into the blackness. I shall have as much sleep as I wish soon enough. I thought I would join my grandson who has grown so much since we left Stockton that I can barely recognise him." His put his good hand on my shoulder. I was not sure if it was to help his balance or was for affection. "I wonder if this is what I was like when Wulfstan watched me change from a youth to a man to a leader. I would love to speak with him and my father now. I would ask them if they were proud of me."

I could not believe the words I was hearing, "Of course they would be proud of you! You are the greatest knight in England. You saved England for the King!"

He nodded, "And yet I would speak with them and see that they approve. That is why I wish your father was here for I would be able to tell him that I am immeasurably proud of all that he has achieved." He patted my shoulder, "But you, I can tell. While I am alive I can say that you will be a knight as great if not greater than I. You will be greater when you mould your son into another leader who can protect our land and our king."

I looked at him. I could see his eyes in the light from the brazier which burned in the centre of the tower. "But what if it is a bad King?"

"King Henry is a good king. I trained him myself and I could not be prouder of him if he was my own son."

"But what of his son, Henry? He has shown little signs of being a good king and he may well be the cause of this latest trouble. Am I honour bound to follow him?"

I saw the pain in my grandfather's eyes. He had not thought of that as a problem. He gave me a sad smile, "That will be a decision which you have to make. When King Harold was killed my father and my namesake left England for they could not countenance serving a Norman. My father came back to England to die and I chose to serve King Henry. If there is a bad King of England then you will know what you have to do but I confess that I do not envy you. Times have been hard enough when I was supporting the rightful King of England. I am not sure if I would have lived as long supporting a bad one."

With that depressing thought in my head, we continued the watch. Dawn broke behind us and we could hear hammering in the city. John of Oxbridge had just come to report from the river gate and he said, "War machines, my lord. That must be what they are building."

"Where would they get the wood?"

My grandfather pointed upriver, "Boats. They cannot sail them and half the work of a ram is done if they use the hull of a ship. All that they need are wheels and there will be wagons and carts aplenty."

John of Oxbridge nodded, "Aye, Earl Marshal, you are right. Most of the small boats were taken south of the river but we have seen, from the river gate, many more which remain. There are small ferries which would be perfect. I will go around and warn the others, Earl. I will relight my fire. Burning coals can soon set fire to a wooden ram." He hurried off to inform the rest of our men to be on their guard. We had lost men in the battle and there were fewer of them now.

"He is a good man, grandfather."

"They all are. Men like Wulfric and Ralph of Bowness trained them well. I will miss them."

He stared east to watch our men as they went about their business. He was saying goodbye to all of them. "How is your head?"

He smiled, "The same, there is pain and when I sleep I know not if I will wake but so far the Good Lord has spared me. Perhaps I still have a task to perform. When it is done he will take me. I am content. I would rather it was I who was taken and not you or your father."

I turned to my squire, "William, go and rouse Sir Richard and his squire."

"Aye lord."

As dawn broke we could see that they had moved the ram they were constructing to the Aldgate. It was five hundred paces north of our position. They would be beyond the range of our bows. I knew my grandfather was willing me to say something but I could not think what. I was too busy trying to work out how to destroy a ram. The gate was a double gate. They would have to break one and then move under the fighting platform to the second. So far there were no murder holes. We could add more wood to the first gate and that would slow them. Of course, that would only buy us the time and what would we use the time for? Then it came to me. John of Oxbridge had already suggested it. We could use fire. We might damage the stone of the gatehouse but better that than allow the castle to fall.

I turned, "We should use two more of these braziers and have kindling prepared."

He frowned, "Not oil? Water perhaps?"

"We are too far from the Tower for that. It would be a long way to carry and they might not be hot enough. Fire guarantees that the ram will burn. If we bar the first gate then it will take them longer to break and we will have more opportunity to burn them." When he smiled I shook my head, "You had thought of that already! Why did you not tell me?"

"Because you and your father are the future and I am the past. I knew the thoughts were there. You just needed to work it out for yourself. You have good instincts, trust them. And now I will return to my chamber. I shall rest a little safer in the knowledge that you know what you are about."

"Aye, Earl Marshal." When Sir Richard, William and Harry reached us I turned to the sergeant at arms, "Sound stand to."

"Aye lord."

"Sir Richard, I will take command here, you go to the south-west bastion tower. I am going to gamble and place all of our archers in these towers."

"That will work. Come, Harry. My father and brother will have vengeance this day!"

While they rushed to the walls I said to William, "Fetch another two braziers here and have kindling collected. We have plenty from when we felled the trees to make the stakes. You four come with me." We hurried back to the pile of timber we had felled to make stakes. There were still five or six tree trunks. They had been neither straight enough nor long enough for stakes but they would be perfect as braces for the gate. "Fetch them to the city gate."

When I retched the gate, there were two of the garrison waiting there. "Open the inner gate."

As they did so Aelric and Atheling joined me, "Lord what would you have us do?" Behind them, I saw Sir Ranulf and his knights rushing to the walls.

"I am going to gamble. I want all of the archers in the south-west bastion tower and the Gate Tower. John of Oxbridge thinks that they will use the boats to build a ram. They will not attack from the river. If they try to take the north wall again then we have a short distance to move."

"Aye, lord that would work."

Sir Ranulf reached us. He frowned at the presence of the archers. He was my elder and had far more experience than I did but I would not apologise for doing what both my grandfather and father would do in the same circumstances. "What do you plan, Sir Samuel?"

"They are building a ram and they will break through the first gate. I intend to brace the gate and when they use the ram to pour hot coals upon them and burn it."

My archers nodded enthusiastically but Sir Ranulf shook his head, "They will have soaked the roof of the ram and it will be hard to burn. If you succeed then you risk burning the gatehouse."

"And if that happens we pull back to the inner ward and the Tower. We are outnumbered, Sir Ranulf. We have too few men to do as I would wish and face them blade to blade. Until Earl Mandeville or my father arrives we fight defensively."

"Your father? He is in France!"

"And my grandfather has sent for him. He will come!" I could see that he was far from convinced. I did not even attempt to try to. "I would have you and your knights at the tower by the river gate and on the inner wall. If you are right and we lose the gate then you will have to be ready to cover us."

"You are as brave and reckless as the rest of your family. We will hold the wall and the towers for you." He looked around as my men began to drag the timber into the gatehouse. "You use just your own men?"

I nodded, "There are none better and I am comfortable fighting alongside such warriors." I saw the pride in the eyes of my men as they heard my words.

Sir Ranulf and his knights left. We used hammers to force the timber so that it was braced between the cobbles and the gate. "That is all the timber used up, lord. All that is left are small branches which would not hold anything."

"Then make them into faggots and we will feed the flames of the fire which we will start." We re-entered the castle and slammed the gates shut. I said to the two men who stood there. "We need no gatekeepers this day. Go and collect as many darts and spears as you can. I want the wall between the Gate Tower and the south-west bastion tower with plenty of missiles."

"Aye lord."

When I reached the gate tower I saw that Aelric and six of his archers occupied the turret which was attached to the north side of the Gate Tower. They had a good vantage point. Atheling had half of the archers in the south-west bastion tower and the rest were busy feeding the three braziers on the fighting platform. John of Oxbridge had fetched tools from the smithy to help the men to lift the braziers and throw them over.

"Aelric, how goes the ram?"

"They have almost finished it, lord. They have four strong wheels on each side and the top is covered in hides. It will not be easy to burn."

I waved my hand in acknowledgement. "John of Oxbridge I would have you here with me. Sir Richard is at the south-west bastion tower. We will use the stones before we use the fire. If we can break the hides or tear them then the fire will spread quicker."

"There is some pig fat too, lord. It is not enough to heat and use that way but if we pour it when the skins are broken it will accelerate the fire. We can mix it with tallow."

"Make it so."

John of Oxbridge had a younger brother, James. He stayed with me and William in case I needed a runner. He was young. He had no mail. I recognised his helmet as the pot one John of Oxbridge had used for many years. His jerkin was a hide one studded with odd pieces of metal. They had been hand sewn. His sword was also a cast off from John and his shield was a small round one. In his belt was a dagger along with a hatchet. A leather satchel hung across his back. He was, compared with the men at arms who served Sir Ranulf, poorly dressed. He also had much less experience but I knew that unlike Sir Ranulf's men I could rely on my men.

"James, what are your hopes?"

"Hopes, my lord?"

"Your brother is now a sergeant at arms. He could become a captain or even a squire and then a knight. Do you have such aspirations?"

He smiled, "Lord I have seen barely seventeen summers. I am no fool. I hope to survive. If I do that then I can think of my next objective, I will try to kill someone with mail, a good sword and coins. Once I am dressed like my brother I can plan further but my brother has told me of many warriors who planned too much. They died young. I would rather not plan and live long."

I saw William nodding. This was what kings and lords like Sir Ranulf did not understand. What made their men fight for them. It was more than just the coin for if that was all there was then they would soon be fighting alone. My grandfather and father understood what lords called the common man. There was more to them than that. Sir Wulfric had been like John of Oxbridge and he had become one of the greatest knights in the land. That was due to the Earl Marshal who had treated him like a friend and helped him to become a knight. I now saw what I needed to do. This journey with the Earl Marshal was meant to be. I was discovering my future.

"Lord they have finished the ram and are pouring water on the hide roof."

"When they move it into range see if you can slow it up."

"Aye lord."

The men with the faggots and kindling arrived. We had enough to make a good fire. I saw that we had twenty stones. Most were from the Roman wall. Sir Richard had done well. I wondered just how much sleep he had had. William handed me my helmet and my shield. I took off my cloak and hung the shield over my back. If I needed it I could easily swing it around. My coif hung on my shoulders and I wore just my arming cap. I let my men choose how they would face the enemy. These were our men and they needed no instructions.

John of Oxbridge brought the jug of fat and he placed it between two braziers to keep it warm. I watched him as he checked that his younger brother had tied his helmet properly. "You have a good edge to your sword?"

"Good enough to shave with."

Davy of Ingleby bantered, "If you did shave. I am guessing that the cat can still lick off the fuzz you have!"

The others laughed but James just smiled, "If you mean I am a young warrior with better reactions than an old greybeard like you then you are right, Davy of Ingleby. I did not know that you rated me so highly!"

They all laughed even louder. They would do.

A horn sounded and the postern gate opened. Men began to file out. Our archers had taught them discretion and they each held long shields before them. I could not identify them for their shields bore no devices. I heard the rumble of wheels as the ram was pushed towards the bridge which led over the ditch to the gate. They would have to turn it at right angles when they neared the ditch. The archers near me were already selecting their arrows. None would be wasted. The men at arms hefted the throwing spears and darts. Each one would choose one which felt right in their hands. This was like a battle ritual. Every man prepared differently. I saw some head for the garderobe where they would make water. This was not a privy such as we had inside the castle. It was a hole which led to the moat. I watched one man pull down his breeks and sit. If there were not men coming to attack he would have been reprimanded by the captain of the guard, now John of Oxbridge nodded approvingly. Anything which made the ground and bridge slippery was a good thing.

We could do nothing more until they were within the range of our arrows. The archers also needed a target. The men pushing the ram were inside the war machine but there were others behind pushing. They held shields in their left arms. The men inside the ram were chanting to help keep their rhythm. I did not recognise it. There were no mounted men. All were on foot. They had no standards and that was strange for there was no rallying point. I knew that the slits in the city walls would bristle with crossbows. We could do little about them. We had shields and the archers were elevated.

I knew when the ram was in range for Aelric shouted, "Nock!"

There was no command to draw and release. They would each have a target in mind. Seven arrows flew. I heard shouts and screams. The men pushing had shields but my archers aimed at legs and feet. The wounded men dropped and cowered behind shields. The ram slowed. The men inside would have to push harder. The harder they worked the longer it would take to break down the gate. Time was an ally! It was then that they began to send crossbow bolts in our direction. Fortunately for us, they tried to aim at our archers. The ones in the turret above us were safe and Atheling and the others just stepped back a little. The bolts were wasted as they cracked into the stone walls of the gate and turret. The ram was nearing the point at which it would have to turn. The eight wheels helped it move in a straight line but made turning harder. Seven men were wounded as they tried to heave it around into position.

They paused. They were now less than a hundred paces from the ditch. They were giving the men pushing the opportunity to catch their breath whilst forming up the men at arms and knights behind. Our archers had done all that they could and now they took the opportunity of putting a new bowstring on their bows. Each archer had a leather pouch under their cap or helmet. A new string gave them a little extra power. Once the knights and mailed men at arms closed with the walls then they would learn that the bodkin arrows sent at a range of less than fifty paces would be deadly. Now that the bows had stopped the sound which dominated was the creak of the ram and the sound of its wheels on the cobbles. The ground was perfectly flat. The wheels rolled steadily and the men at arms behind the ram now added their weight to it.

"Ready the stones." I did not shout the command. I did not need to. Half of my men picked up a stone each while a shield brother held a shield before them both. When they stood to drop the rocks on to the ram they would be exposed.

I turned around to make certain that my grandfather hadn't joined us. He had not and for that I was grateful. I knew that we would lose the gatehouse. It might not be this day but it would fall. We had too few men to defend it. I had only chosen this course of action for I knew we could make them bleed. We had more chance of holding them with the smaller perimeter of the inner ward. The advancing men began to shout. It was partly to give them heart and partly to help them try to run.

I shouted, "Horn!" The horn sounded twice and my men rose and began to hurl rocks at the ram. Some hit the ground before the ram and that helped for they would hurt those inside and might turn the wheels off course. Others crashed and cracked into the roof. The roof was made from the hull of a boat. It was not intended to take such blows. Still, it lumbered towards the gate and the cheers from our enemies grew. One particularly large stone tore a hole in the hide and then landed so close to the wheel and the parapet of the bridge that the ram struck. James of

Oxbridge took a spear and hurled it at the warrior who tried to remove the stone. He sent it into the man's shoulder.

"Push it! We are almost there!" The voice from the rear of the ram was obviously a leader and the wheel lurched over the stone.

The ram was now just two paces from the gate. It was time. "John, now!" First, one of the braziers was lifted and then hurled over the side. A crossbow bolt sliced across his cheek. He did not stop and he and Harold Strongarm used the borrowed tools to deposit the burning brazier over the top. John's brother joined in with the others as they hurled kindling and faggots on to the fire.

Holding my shield before me I peered over the side of the battlements. The coals were glowing and the kindling ignited but the dampened hide refused to burn.

John and Harold picked up the next brazier. Our archers were ready this time and they sent arrows towards the arrow slits. The odds on hitting anything were minimal but it takes a brave man to keep your face close to one when you know that a barbed arrow is heading for you. This time the brazier almost exploded as it hit the smouldering ram. More kindling followed. This time the kindling flamed so much that they almost singed me.

John shouted, "Hold the last one!" He picked up the jug of tallow and pig fat and dropped it on to the inferno.

I was in the best position to see what was happening. The fire had begun to burn the hide. The tears and rips had allowed the flames to set fire to the ship's timbers. The fat and tallow seeped down finding gaps. It began to heat up and then suddenly it burst into flames. As more kindling and faggots caught fire so the whole of the ram began to burn.

"One more push!"

With a superhuman effort, the ram was pushed next to the gate. Then men began to scream. Some were on fire as they hurled themselves from the ram, over the parapet to plunge into the murky waters of the ditch. They hissed as they hit the water. Others burst from the doomed war machine and my archers, from their vantage points on three towers, took full advantage and the brave men who had forced the ram close enough to the gate, perished.

An enemy horn sounded and they pulled back behind the city walls of London. Now we were the ones who would suffer for the fire was out of control and the gate was burning. "William get men to make a chain of buckets from the river. Wet the inside of the gate. I will stay here with the archers."

He nodded, "Come, men of Stockton. You have shown us you can light a fire. Can you extinguish one!"

Harold Strongarm shouted, "Give me enough ale sir and I will piss it out for you!" Their laughter told me that they were in good spirits. We had wounded men but none had died and the men of Stockton had saved the castle... for now.

Chapter 14

The fire burnt itself out an hour before dark. A pall of smoke blew towards the city walls. In the dark and from the postern gate it would appear that the gate was still intact but it was an illusion. I had been down to examine it and the integrity of the wood had gone. There was nothing we could do. A determined attack by men with shields would break it and once they were close to the second gate they could attack it with impunity. We would not be able to touch them. By the time noon came, they would have taken the gatehouse. I had bought us but one more day.

Leaving Sir William in command I headed for the Tower and a meeting with Sir Ranulf and my grandfather. They were both in the great hall and there was warm bread with ale and cheese on the table. Once the gatehouse fell then we would lose the bakehouse. I would make the most of the bread whilst it stood and we could bake. I had forgotten what it was like to eat. I smelled of smoke and sweat and I was weary beyond words.

Sir Ranulf nodded, "Well done, Sir Samuel. I did not think that so few men could hold the gate. You did not need us."

"But when they attack tomorrow the gate will not hold and we will lose the gate."

My grandfather nodded, "And then we fall back to this wall. Now that you have cleared those trees our archers will decimate them."

I continued to devour the food and slake my thirst. "Sir Ranulf my men will need rest. Would you be so good as to set the watch for us?"

"Aye but I fear that unless help comes soon then we will succumb. They are a determined enemy."

I nodded, "And from what you and Davy said the danger may not be limited to the city of London. I wonder where Walter and the Earl of Essex are?"

"I would not be worried yet. The Earl's manor is to the north and east of London. Your man was on foot and it would take him up to a day longer to reach the Earl and then he would have to return west. Give them another day and then worry."

"I will go and set the watch." He left us and my grandfather and I were alone.

When we were alone my grandfather asked, "Did we lose any men?"

I shook my head and pushed away the empty platter, "We had wounds. John of Oxbridge had his cheek torn by a bolt. There were burns and other minor wounds but we kept them from the gate. Tomorrow it will be harder for we will have to flee across open ground. I fear that we will lose men."

"And that has always been hard for me. When I came to England I had none who followed me. Harold and Dick were the first and they lived long lives. There were others who did not. I have sat here, while the medicine took effect, and thought of them. I find it hard to remember what happened yesterday but I can remember their names, "Edward, Wilfred, Edgar, Gurt, Roger of Lincoln, William the Tall, Alan the Saxon. Will's son, Alan of York. The list is seemingly endless: Sir Hugh of Hexham, Richard of Yarm, Erre. All good men and true. Men will die before you return to Stockton and you will remember them. You are of our blood."

"And was it worth it?"

He laughed, "A good question and a hard one to answer. If you were to ask me would I change anything then I would say aye but that is looking back in time and knowing where I went wrong. There were men I trusted I should not and decisions I made which were not the best but I would not change my purpose. I fought for the Empress, her family, England and the Tees." I saw his eyes mist.

"And which of these was the most important?"

It was as though he shut a visor over his face and he shook his head. I could not read him. "There are hard questions and there are impossible questions. All I will say is that each strand of my life is woven tightly with all the others. Cut one and the whole fabric dissolves." He stood, "Now rest. I have had a day to sit and contemplate. I have taken the medicine and feel better. I need some action. I will walk the walls and I will speak with our men. You despair but, in my experience, you take each day as it comes. You celebrate the victory and wash away any defeat with ale or wine. Today was a victory. Tomorrow could bring either. Until the blade takes your life you fight on for that is what men do."

He patted my shoulder as he left. I would never be the man my grandfather was. He had been made of sterner stuff than I. William was already in our chamber. He had eaten in the kitchen with the other squires. The cooks looked after the squires. He had his mail laid on a sack.

"Lord, let me take off your mail. You have worn it for days."

I nodded, "And we will need to clean it but not this night. When we have defeated this foe, we will cleanse ourselves for there is no honour in this. We fight mercenaries whose motives are venal."

I slept but my dreams were haunted by my grandfather's face and all those I had seen die in battle. Arne, Jean the others all flashed before my eyes. There was burning and there was death and when I woke I was not refreshed.

It was still dark and no light came into the chamber. I did not relish visiting the dead once more and so I rose. I left my mail on the floor and draped my cloak about my shoulders. I went down to the Great Hall. By the glow from the fire, I saw my grandfather, asleep. He had a fur covering his body and there was wine on the table. He was barely breathing and not for the first time I wondered if he was dead. I held my breath and when he stirred I breathed again. I filled a goblet with wine. Here we had goblets and not beakers. It was a good wine. I did not wish to disturb him and when I had drunk I went to the garderobe and made water.

By the time I reached my chamber a candle was burning and William was awake and was donning his mail. "Lord you should have woken me."

"You need to sleep too. Come help me into my mail and we will walk the walls before we eat."

William carried our shields and helmets. When I reached the gatehouse, there was a hint of dawn in the east. Sir Ranulf had retired and Matthew, his Captain of the Guard was there.

"How goes the night?"

"Quiet lord but we heard scurrying beyond the city walls. They are roused."

I nodded, "Then we will be too. Sound the stand to!"

The horn's strident notes rang out. For those like Sir Ranulf who might have been abed for bare hours, it would seem like moments. Men would rise, make water, don mail. If they had the chance they would grab some bread and swallow some ale. The one thing they would all do would be to get to their posts. Dawn was the most dangerous time. The enemy had more men and there could be fresh warriors waiting to fall upon us.

I looked along the fighting platform of the gatehouse. There were still a few stones we had not thrown. Five darts and six spears were there. I hoped that, as there was an armoury here we had more missiles we could use. The longer we could keep the enemy at bay the better chance we had of surviving. Winning was not even an option.

Suddenly a bolt flew from the city walls and a careless sentry found his left arm pinned to his body. "Shields!" Even as I shouted the command I knew that Captain Matthew had not done his job. He should have impressed on his men the need for constant vigilance. We were now one man down. We had too few to waste. "Get him to a healer and the rest of you be alert!"

A few more speculative bolts headed for us but they struck shields or the walls. Crossbows were mechanical and prone to breaking down. They could waste their bolts on our walls. As my men arrived so Sir Ranulf's left. When John of Oxbridge came I saw the angry scar on his cheek. "John I would have you and your brother take charge of the south-west bastion tower. When they break into here you and the archers can cover us while we run back to the inner curtain. You have the fighting platform as an escape route and you can wade around the stakes and enter by the watergate. Ask Sir Richard and his squire join me here. See if there are any more darts and throwing spears in the armoury. I would have them here."

"Aye lord. Do you think the gatehouse will fall?"

"It may take the morning but they will reduce it. We both know that." He nodded, glumly, "With a few more men lord…"

"I know but as my grandfather will tell you it is impossible to have all that you wish. You make do with what you have and we have done that up to now. We trust to God and Sir James. He will have reached my father and he will not let us down."

I saw the smile on John's face and optimism returned to the grizzled warrior's scarred face.

By the time dawn broke Sir Richard had joined me and we waited with eight men at arms and ten archers. The rest were on the inner curtain wall, under the command of Harry of Norton. Leaving William, protected by a shield to watch the postern gate, I gathered the tiny garrison on the east side of the gate. "We hold them here as long as we can. Sweyn I want you and Brian by the inner gate. When you hear axes on the gate then call me. At that point, the archers will head for the inner wall and the rest of you will join me while we fight those who break through. Our aim is to slow them and not to die. When I give the order to run then be as deer fleeing the wolf. We run to the inner wall."

Harry asked, "Will they not use a ram again, lord?"

"The night watch did not hear them building one. They will use axes. We need to kill as many as we can while they are within range. Once they are beneath us then we can do nothing."

We returned to watch. A flurry of bolts heralded the postern gate being opened. Men appeared from the Aldgate. The attack was about to start. This time I donned my helmet. They were using bolts and my archers would have to thin the hordes which would descend from the city. I did not draw a sword. I picked up a throwing spear which John's men had sent.

The enemy formed up next to the wall. My archers sent arrows to catch any who were careless enough not to have their shields held before them. I saw that they had axes. They had examined the gate and knew how fragile it was. Even though they were careful my archers, although few in number, were skilled. They hit men. None were killed but when they were taken back within the walls then I knew that we were hurting them.

"They seem desperate to get inside the Tower lord."

"There is a treasure room there. The royal regalia are to be found in chests. This is the safest place in England. These are swords for hire. They do not rely entirely on the money their lord, de Mamers, pays them. They seek rewards. De Mamers will use that greed to get at my grandfather. For him, this is not about coin it is about vengeance and power."

Banging their shields, the men began to filter down to the bridge. Those who had come from the Aldgate joined the others. The column would be eight men wide when it reached us. As they tramped across the bridge a hail of missiles was sent in their direction. Stones were dropped from the battlements; darts and spears were thrown. The stones crushed heads even though they were encased in metal. Darts and spears found gaps in the mail for they were plunging vertically. When men fell that allowed our archers to send arrows to pierce mail. The column was thinned. Men fell over the parapet to land in the ditch breaking limbs or worse.

We heard the hammering of shields and axes on the burned gate. We used that time as well as we could. Six more men fell before we heard a crash and then a cheer as the charred remains of the gate crumbled. In their eagerness to get into the shelter of the gatehouse men lowered shields or raised their heads in triumph. They were hit and then I heard Sweyn shout, "They are here my lord."

"Aelric, you know what to do!"

As we descended the stairs the archers ran across the fighting platform towards the south-west bastion tower. They would join Atheling and his archers. When the enemy broke through they would have a killing ground to cross. Our bowmen would make them pay dearly for their gain.

Sir Richard and I stood at the fore. I drew my sword. Sweyn and Brian flanked us. Our squires stood behind and the other handful of men fanned out to protect our flanks. We would not hold them long but the more we killed the longer we would survive. Although this gate was not braced it was stronger than the outer gate for its face had not been weathered. The archers at the south-west bastion were still reaping a fine harvest. I watched as John of Oxbridge led his men back to the ditch with the embedded stakes. They would be safe. The dead would come from the men I had chosen to lead. As the axes crashed into the gate I said, "When they begin to overwhelm us then hurry back to the walls. Sir Richard and I have the best mail. Do not tarry for us." There was silence. "This is not a request, it is a command and you will all obey."

I had put steel in my voice and they chorused, "Aye lord."

The cries from the other side of the gate told me that my archers were still able to find flesh. The sun was rising and the day was passing. Would this be the day when the Earl arrived? My father? Speculation was idle. We would fight until we could fight no more. At least we would be able to have a greater concentration of men on our walls!

I saw the first crack in the gate appear. The enemy renewed their efforts and soon I saw a gap. Sweyn and Brian still had throwing spears they had not used and when Sweyn saw the bare head of a bearded man at arms he hurled it. The man saw the missile at the last minute and it struck him in the face. He fell backwards and as a second man picked up the axe he was struck by Brian. There was a delay while others donned helmets and began to hack at the gate. It would be a matter of time.

"On my command, we run at the men coming through. Cause as much harm as you can and wait for my order to fall back."

The gate fell suddenly. Two axe men hacked so hard that they fell sprawling to the ground.

"Now!"

We charged them. The two men who had fallen pushed themselves to their feet only to be struck down by Richard and me. Brian and Sweyn took two other axemen by surprise. Their shields were around their backs and my two men at arms used the tried and trusted method of smashing them in the face with their shields and then slicing across their necks. The narrow gateway helped us. Six of us were able to block it. We were facing men at arms and I saw knights trying to reach us. I swung my sword backhand and hit a man at arms below the rim of his kettle helmet. Richard lunged and used his point to stab at the throat of a second. Sweyn and Brian along with Dick Tom's son were enjoying success too as men who had been using weapons two handed now had to swing shields around. Sweyn was roaring in his own language and seemed to bear a charmed life.

The tall knight five rows from the front lifted his visor to shout, "Hold! Fetch spears!"

They were going to use a shield wall and it was time to leave. "Fall back! Now"

Sweyn was a Frisian. They were related to Norse and Danes. I think at that moment he went berserk. While Brian and Dick obeyed me Sweyn hurled himself into the heart of the enemy at the gates. As we were falling back I saw that his attack had taken them by surprise and two men fell to his sword. Then a spear was rammed through his leg. Even though he was badly wounded he continued to fight. He used his shield as a weapon. Hacking his sword at a squire who tried to stab him Sweyn was speared a second time. I saw the bloody spearhead come through his back. He was still fighting. He was dying but they would have to take his head to stop him. The tall knight did just that. He brought his sword around and decapitated my brave Frisian.

By the time Sweyn fell we had covered half of the distance to the gate in the curtain wall. Richard and I were with Brian and Dick. The others had reached its safety already. We walked quickly backwards. The men in the gateway freed and unconstrained hurtled after us. I heard a voice shout something but the words were lost. I guessed the tall knight was ordering them into line. Some obeyed but my archers, now moving parallel to us on the fighting platform of the river wall were sending arrows into them. Two men reached us. "The rest get back!" The squire who brought his sword across my shield had the right technique but he lacked the strength he would need. The blow made his arm shiver more than mine. Instead of going for his shield, I swung from on high. He brought his shield up and instead of doing as I had done and angling his shield he held it flat. I heard his arm break. I smashed him in the face with my shield and he fell unconscious. The knight whom Richard was fighting was gaining the upper hand. I had spared the squire. I would not spare the knight and I brought my sword backhand across his back. As his back arced Richard hacked him across his thigh. He dropped to the ground.

Sir Ranulf shouted, "Sir Samuel, run the rest are safe!"

I saw that there were just archers left on the fighting platform. When we were safe they would cross the stake filled ditch. Slipping my shield over my back we ran. I saw that the walls were thickly lined with knights, men at arms and archers. When we were just forty paces from the wall I saw goose fletched arrows soaring over our heads. The gate slammed shut and we were safe.

Sir Richard looked at me and shook his head, "Why did Sweyn do that?"

"Ralph of Bowness and Erre once spoke to me of warriors who had the madness of battle upon them. They said a man did not choose that end. It chose him. Who knows? Whatever the reason he saved us. We now have a chance. They may have the gate but our archers can make the outer ward into a killing ground. They will have to attack the north wall or the east wall. We have a chance."

We hurried up to the fighting platform. The Earl Marshal awaited us, "That was bravely done by all." He pointed at the piles of bodies which lay between us and the gatehouse. I counted at least thirteen dead men and others, the squire and knight included, were being helped back. Shading my eyes, I saw that the sun was almost at its zenith.

"Sir Samuel take your men. Have wounds healed and take sustenance. We will watch. We have set them a conundrum. There are many ways of taking this Tower. Which one will they choose?" My grandfather seemed remarkably calm. It was like a game of chess to him and he was seeing which move our foe would make so that we could counter it.

William and Harry had not escaped unscathed. While Sir Richard and I had helmets with visors we could lower they just had a helmet with a nasal. The squire I had fought had even less protection for his face. He had just had a round pot helmet. Both the mail of the two squires had been damaged and both had cuts upon their faces. None would be disfiguring but they had both had a valuable lesson. Most of our men at arms had such marks of honour. As we headed to the Great Hall I said, "Head for the dispensary and see the healer. Such wounds can go bad. We will save food and ale for you."

As we ate Sir Richard gave me a strange look. "My father would be alive but for the treacherous Abbot. We were surprised. Even though we have been outnumbered since then we have not lost men. The Abbot will pay."

"I understand your murderous thoughts and I agree that he should pay but think on this Richard. He may have fled already. What if he seeks sanctuary in a church? Would you risk losing your spurs for such as he?"

"Would you let your father go unavenged?"

"In truth, I know not but if I had a friend then I would hope he would give me counsel and guidance." He nodded. "Let us first defeat this enemy and seek to bring to justice all those who deserve it. We have three butchered men who need vengeance. Do not forget them. They deserve as much as your father."

"You are right." Just then our squires arrived. We smelled them before we saw them for the healers had applied strong-smelling salves.

William said before he had even sat, "I would have a better helmet and mail, lord."

"I fear you will have to wait until you win your spurs."

He poured himself some wine."

"And when will that be, lord. I have served for some time."

"You are right and I should have thought on this earlier. You can play the rote?"

"I can get a tune from it but my singing voice is so dire that it matters not."

I smiled. "I know you have languages and that your sword and horse skills are of the best. I would say that when we return home and I have the opportunity of seeing if my pages are ready to begin training as squire then I will ask my father to knight you."

He beamed.

Sir Richard knew the question on Harry's lips and he forestalled it. "Harry, you will have to wait some time. Ethelred and Walter were about to be knighted and you would have followed soon after. I know I was lucky to have your services as well as Walter. I have a young brother at home and we need to train him to become a squire first. He was to have been my father's but... I fear he will resent being my squire. I will fight one battle at a time."

Harry was a pleasant lad, "I understand lord and I have much to learn. I need languages and the skill to play the rote and to sing."

I said, more to change the subject than anything else, "Duke Richard of Aquitaine is said to have not only a sweet and melodious voice but he has composed many songs. When next we meet we should ask him to teach you if he is able."

"Did he not revolt against his father, lord?"

"He did Harry but if the King can forgive him then so can I."

We ate in silence until Harry asked, "How will we hold them off a second time, lord?"

I sighed for I had thought all of this through. I had put myself in the enemy's position. How would I take the Tower? "They can now attack at two places. The Tower has solid walls but there are just arrow slits low down and they cannot be used to defend the last gate. If they concentrate in the south, by the river then we just have the wall and river gate tower that we can use. They will demolish the buildings by the gatehouse and build another ram. There is neither ditch nor bridge near to the gate. It will fall. At the same time, they can keep up the pressure on the north wall, perhaps even the east wall. We have three walls to defend during the daylight."

Sir Richard glanced up at me, "And night time?"

"Nighttime means we need men on the river wall and gate. They can attack there too. I will use John of Oxbridge to watch the river. He has proved himself to be resourceful and invaluable. Had we more knights then I would have used one there. Sir Ranulf and his knights can defend the north wall and we will take the inner curtain wall. Richard I would have you and the garrison defend the east wall."

"That is the least likely to involve danger."

"True but the garrison has been badly mauled. Captain Robert and his men will be with you. It is the best plan that I can think of. If they build a ram on the east side of the wall then we are in trouble for our archers are stretched thin enough as it is."

"I am sorry, Samuel, you are right. It is just that I will be further away from the Abbot there."

"I think our clerical friend will be as far away from danger as it is possible."

When I had finished eating I went to tell the others where they would be stationed. Aelric nodded when I told him. "We are running short of arrows, lord, and we have only enough for two more days. It might be possible to stretch that to three but I am not sure."

"Do your best. We have to pray for help."

"Your father will come."

The Earl Marshal came from his room where he had been resting. He looked to have a little more colour about him. He must have heard my words for he said, "You are right Samuel." He tapped his chest. "I can feel it here. He will come!" I smiled. "I will stand with you on the inner wall."

By the ninth hour of the day, we were all in position. The enemy had moved his men up so that they were beyond bow range but ready to advance. I saw that they had either been reinforced or they had finally committed all of their men. I had twelve archers on my wall. Half that number were on the north wall and the rest were in the tower. Atheling was in command and he would shift them between rooms to use the arrow slits. We had throwing spears and the last of darts. The armoury was now empty.

A horn sounded and the enemy began to advance. As I had anticipated they headed for the river side of the outer ward. They were helped by the fact that they held their shields on their left arms. Aelric shook his head at my unspoken question. "We would be wasting arrows, lord. Better wait until they are at the gate."

I nodded. I had Brian and four other men with rocks and stones at the gate which led into the inner ward. They had no ram but I saw axe men and they also had huge shields to protect them. One of Sir Ranulf's pages ran to me, "Lord they have begun to attack the north wall."

"Thank you." I turned to William, "If they come to the east wall then we are lost."

My grandfather said, "We have held them off before. If you were the enemy would you relish attacking us? We have beaten off all of their attacks and they have lost many more men than we. This is bravado. We fight for every inch of this castle. Make them bleed, Samuel! Make them bleed!"

I hefted a throwing spear as the line of men drew closer to the wall below me. Behind the ones with shields were others with ladders. They were simple ones. The flooded ditch which led from the river could be waded by men. Equally, they could, if the had to, use the shields.

Just at that moment, I heard another horn. This time it was from the east gate. "Well, lord, it looks like they have decided to attack from three sides."

I nodded and then shouted, "Remember men, we sell our lives dearly!"

"That is the spirit, Samuel." My grandfather drew his sword. "The Earl Marshal of England fights with you men! We stand or fall together!"

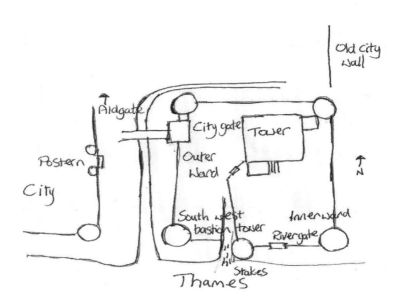

Chapter 15

The horn seemed to give the enemy heart and they surged forward. Arrows flew towards them but my men were so spread out that it was not the deadly shower we usually used. Even so, men fell and their charge slowed as they moved more cautiously. The enemy warriors were shouting and cheering. It was what men did to give themselves courage. Some of them made the mistake of heading for what they perceived as the shallow part of the flooded ditch. It was shallower but it was also in the range of the Tower. Six men fell and the others changed direction and came further south. The archers aimed at the men carrying the ladders. They had shields and wore mail. They had not repeated their error of using lightly armoured men. When the first ladder was pressed against the wall I leaned over. I had my shield over my head and a bolt smacked into it. The force was such that the tip came through. I looked down and saw a shield below me. It was advancing towards me. Had I had a stone then I might have hurt him but our last stones were with Brian by the gate.

Dick Tom's son hurled a dart from the side. I know not if luck guided his hand or he was particularly skilled but the outcome was that he struck the sergeant in the left leg. I heard a grunt. Emboldened, Dick picked up small stones. They would not kill but they would annoy. Still, the shield came up as stones rattled off the sergeant's mail. The sergeant was only human and when he was three paces from the battlements he began to lower his shield in preparation for pulling himself over the crenulations. It also afforded him some protection from Dick's stones. I seized my opportunity and I hurled the spear. I threw it with great force and it entered his shoulder between his head and his arm. Blood spurted. He tried to pull his shield over his head again but merely succeeded in losing his balance. He tumbled backwards. His trailing leg brought down a second man.

Just then I heard a cry from behind me, "Open the gate!"

What was Richard thinking? The Earl Marshal sheathed his sword, "I will go and see what is happening. Fear not you are winning."

He was right for we had held their ladders. Axes rang on the gate but it was studded with metal and the axes would be blunted. Brian and his men had thrown stones to stun or kill four of the attackers but the attack on the west wall was a disaster. Here we were holding them. The gate tower had a good line of sight and they were sending arrows into the sides of the men who climbed. They could only hold their shields over their heads. Some of the men were brave and struggled up even though they had arrows in their mail. I drew my sword for three men had managed to reach the battlements. "With me William!"

I saw that the two men who had been defending that section had been struck by crossbow bolts. They were using the south-west bastion tower. There we could not touch them. I had to deal with the problem at hand; the men before me. This time I held my sword above the crenulations and I roared as I ran. Once again, the enemy leaders were using sergeants and men at arms to bear the brunt of the fighting.

"Stay on my left, William, and look for an opportunity to strike." The fighting platform could accommodate three men but not with shields. As I rammed my shield towards the three men I swung my sword. I saw the points of three swords aimed at me but I ignored them. Unlike the three men I fought, I had a visored helmet. They were so focussed on hitting me and my shield that the man on my right failed to see the sword as it came towards his coif. One sword hit my coif, another my mail and the third found an eye hole in my visor. Alf had made it well and the tip did not penetrate. My sword, in contrast, hacked through the coif of the first man and into his neck. The blood sprayed the other two as my shield hit them. William had listened to me and he knelt to swing a backhanded blow at the knee of the man closest to the fighting platform. As the two struck by our swords fell to the cobbles below the last one was knocked from his feet. William lifted his sword and drove it into the chest of the sergeant who died.

"Get his feet!" William picked up his feet and I, his head. We went to the battlements. As crossbow bolts flew at us we dropped the body over and it smashed through the ladder. The three men on it fell into the ditch. We both managed to lift our shields as bolts cracked into them.

I peered over and saw that we had broken this attack but the open gate to the east spelt the end for us. Just then my grandfather ran towards me, "We are saved. It is the Earl of Essex."

I looked down and saw the Earl. Walter Wulfestun was with him but I could see less than thirty men. Where were the rest of his men? We had had more than that wounded in this attack.

The Earl of Essex raised his visor, "If your men open the gate we will see if we can clear the ward for you, Earl Marshal."

My grandfather waved his hand, "Brian, open the gate!"

I said, "William go and fetch our men at arms. We will join them!"

"Aye lord."

"Atheling, clear the ladders! We have reinforcements!"

"Aye, lord!"

I ran down the fighting platform to the gate. Even as I reached it Brian and Dick had opened it and the Earl and his men galloped through. It was the one thing the attackers were not expecting. Those that were neither speared nor trampled, fled. They suddenly became easy targets for our archers. From the city walls came the sound of a horn. The attack was being halted. I ran amongst the horsemen as they jostled in the gate. I ran towards the south-west bastion tower. I saw John of Oxbridge leading men across the flooded ditch. Behind me, a half dozen of my men at arms followed me. The Earl would use the gate but there were crossbows in the south-west bastion tower. Despite my fatigue, the arrival of help gave me energy I did not think I possessed. I ran into the door at the base of the tower and up the ladder. I discarded my shield. Using my left hand, I pushed on the trapdoor and then leapt up. There were eight crossbowmen and I was alone. I grabbed my dagger and swung at the nearest two men. A crossbow is less than useless at such close range and they drew their short swords. James of Oxbridge appeared next to me and we both slashed and stabbed at the eight men. My sword hacked through muscle and then bone. My dagger tore across one man's throat. I felt the blows from the short swords but I had a good helmet and the best of mail. I would be battered and bruised but I would live. When William my squire appeared, it was all over. There were eight butchered bodies.

"Come let us get to the gatehouse. I would have our enemies know that we are still alive!"

By the time we reached the gatehouse, the Earl had driven the enemy back into the city and he and his men had withdrawn back through the gatehouse. The enemy had sent stones, bolts and arrows at them. We had pushed our luck enough.

"David, take charge here. John, take your men back to the river gate. We have not yet won but we have not been defeated. God smiles on us."

"Aye lord."

"William, let us go and speak with the Earl. There is a tale here."

"A tale, lord?"

"He came but why the delay and why with so few men. We sent for help days since and I would have expected us to be reinforced now so that we were in a position to retake the city. We cannot do that yet. Why so few men?"

The Earl and his men were stabling the horses as we entered the gate to the inner ward. Walter Wulfstan was speaking with Brian and Davy of Ingleby. My grandfather stood close by. When he saw me, Walter dropped to one knee, "I am sorry I could not bring help quicker, lord I..."

My grandfather raised him up. "You have told me all, Walter and have no cause to berate yourself. Go to the warrior hall there is ale and food. Speak with your shield brothers. I will talk with my grandson."

They turned and left.

"I would not have chastised him, Earl Marshal."

He nodded and led William and me towards the stone steps which led into the White Tower. "I know Samuel but from what he has told me you need to hear this from the lips of the Earl for there is a greater threat than you can imagine."

"Greater than losing London?"

He nodded, "This is an attempt to take the crown. These mercenaries do the work of another. You and I have spoken of this and had our suspicions. Now I think we have confirmation but better to hear it from the Earl's lips."

Sir Ranulf was in the Great Hall already. His surcoat was bespattered with blood. "It is good that the Earl came when he did, Earl Marshal. I lost two knights and some men at arms. Had the horn not recalled the attackers then they would have had the outer wall."

My grandfather waved an arm around the hall, "King William built well. This Tower would have lasted months."

We heard the buzz of noise as the Earl of Essex and his household knights strode in. As was right and proper the Earl addressed my grandfather. "Earl Marshal we came as soon as we were summoned..."

"First take ale and second let me thank you for your timely arrival. We might have lost the outer wall but for you and your men and so we are eternally grateful."

Servants had poured ale and the Earl nodded and drank deeply, "Thank you. I needed this. When your message came I summoned my knights and the men of Hervey de Walter, Lord of Parham and Sir Richard of Peckham. I know that delayed my march but it turned out to be fortuitous. You have good men, Earl Marshal. This Walter of Wulfestun forced his way into my counsel of war." He laughed. "Had he served another then I would have had him whipped but my father always held you and your men in the highest regard and so I allowed the impertinent intrusion."

"Your father fought well for the Empress."

He nodded, "Your man said that he had been delayed in reaching me as there was an army gathering at Tilbury." My grandfather caught my eye. This was the news he had spoken of. "That changed my plans. I dared not come to your aid with an army so close. My lands would not have been safe. Walter of Wulfestun told me that the land twixt mine and the Tower was ringed with men. The safest way seemed to be along the river. Yesterday we met with the enemy and we fought a battle. It was hard fought for these were veterans and mercenaries." He shook his head. "They broke the fyrd that we had summoned. We fought all day and only the coming of the night ended the slaughter. When we awoke this morning the last of the enemy had fled. Lord Hervey of Parham and Sir Richard of Peckham led their men to hunt them down for I did not think that you would wish them abroad and causing mischief. I sent my son, Richard to help them. Those are the reasons I came so late and with so few men. If I did wrong then I apologize."

The Earl Marshal walked over and clasped the Earl's arm, "William, you did well. You made the right decision. We cannot have our enemy rampaging through the land. Now we need to make plans to recapture the city."

I sat back to listen. My grandfather had taken charge and that was right. He had been granted a little more time by God. I knew that I had learned much already but it was not enough. I had no idea how we would retake the city with the men we had.

Sir Ranulf had been confined to the Tower too long. I knew him to be a man of action. He was a horseman who liked to be on the offensive and squatting behind stone walls did not sit well with him. "Earl Marshal, we have more knights. Let us ride forth in the morning and bring these men to battle."

My grandfather spoke softly but there was the weight of years behind them, "Ranulf, we have less than thirty knights. Our men at arms and archers have fought hard and we are short of arrows. We fight a cunning and determined enemy. Until Earl William arrived we thought the attack on the city was the only danger. What of the land to the west? We need to know the enemy plans. My son is coming. He may not be here for a week or more but we can spend that time making the Tower defensible once more."

The Earl of Essex, "Who is behind this, Earl Marshal? We had some men we captured. They were badly wounded and died but we questioned them first. Some knew not whom they followed. They said that were summoned by the promise of gold and manors. From their bodies, some were from the east but there were others, knights from Livonia and Estonia, Germans and Lombards. All seem to have been drawn as though by magic."

The Earl Marshal took out the letter which Sir Leofric had sent. He held it up and then read part of it.

Thus disguised we were in an inn on the road to Angers when I spied a device I recognised. It was the de Mamers three golden orbs on a red background. It has been many years since I saw it. There were four men and two of them wore the surcoat. I might have just passed that off as a coincidence and left but I heard your name. When they said, 'Earl Marshal'. I pricked up my ears. We were in a darkened corner and I think they thought they were alone. They spoke quietly but I could hear them.

They were being sent to England. They are the men who would be your killers, lord. They had been hired by someone, I could not discover who, but one of them, he was called Hubert said that he would do it for nothing. It was a matter of honour. They were about to divulge more when some Gascons came in. There was an altercation. I know not how or why it began. In the mêlée which ensued, Jean, my squire and I, were thrown to the ground and a Gascon's body fell upon us. By the time we had regained our feet two more Gascons had been killed and we were held, albeit briefly, on suspicion of complicity in their deaths. Had it not been for the innkeeper we might have been imprisoned.

By the time we reached the outside, they were long gone. When we spoke with the Gascons we discovered that the four men were being sought for murder. A certain Geoffrey de la Cheppe and his family were slaughtered in

their home. Was there not one of the Knights of the Empress with the same name? I heard names but I am not sure what they meant. They could have been other conspirators or potential victims. D'Oilli, Guiscard, and de Mamers were the ones I heard but there were others.
One of the other men was a Templar. I recognised his sign.

"This was the stone which set off this avalanche. Hubert de Mamers is here in London. I recognised his surcoat." He turned to me. "He was the tall knight who led the attack the first day. I may not have been on the gate but the tower affords a good view and I have seen him each day. While you fought, Samuel, I watched." He smiled, "The Warlord of the North may not be a warrior who can fight with his sword but he still has a mind. That, Earl William, is the enemy. De Mamers seeks to take London and the Tower so that the crown will go to his master."

"Young King Henry."

"Young King Henry indeed. It is the only thing which makes sense. That and the fact that many of those in this conspiracy, D'Oilli, de Mamers, seek vengeance against me. That may be the mistake they make which saves the kingdom."

The Earl had spent less time with my grandfather than the rest of us, "How so?"

"De Mamers has lost focus. His task was to take control of the Kingdom. He had us bottled up here and he should have just contained us while he tightened his grip on this part of England. He had an army at Tilbury. If he had joined them then, from what you said, Earl, you would have lost."

He nodded, "Aye it was a hard-fought battle and hung in the balance. If those besieging you had joined then we might well have lost."

"And with your forces out of the way, the way would have been clear to bring Young King Henry from France. He has been crowned already. No, Hubert de Mamers wished to hurt me first and foremost and that may have saved the crown. So, has anyone else a view they wish to express?"

Sir Ranulf smiled, "Earl Marshal, I see now that I have much to learn. Let us benefit from your wisdom and experience. What is it that you wish?"

"We spend this day healing the men and the walls. The enemy has been hurt and de Mamers will now be wondering where are the men from Tilbury? The priority is to repair the city gate. The hall by the gatehouse has been damaged. Let us use the wood from there. We gather the rocks and arrows from without the walls. We take the weapons from their dead and their ladders. Tomorrow you can ride forth Sir Ranulf. I will come with you and we will take knights to ride around London and see what mischief they have caused."

I was suddenly alert, "You are making yourself bait!"

"De Mamers wants me. By showing myself, I blind him to his real purpose. He will see that I am still alive."

"You are gambling that you will be able to outrun him."

"See Samuel, you have learned. Aye, we ride back and hope that we can lead him into the range of our archers. Aelric and the others could end this by taking the head of the snake. The Earl of Essex has given us a chance. One army is destroyed and we just have one to dismay." His eyes told me to be silent and I nodded. "Good then let us set to. We have much to do."

All of us joined in. We left a skeletal watch on the walls but every man, archer, knight and squire, kept their arms close by. We did not burn the enemy bodies which lay to the north and west of our walls. They would begin to stink but the sight of their increasingly bloated bodies, ravaged by carrion would be a reminder to the rest of the enemy of their failure. Our archers concentrated upon recovering and making arrows. The Earl of Essex had few archers. We were still reliant on those that my grandfather had brought. The bodies inside the castle were piled together and, as the wind was from the east, we burned them. The smell of burning flesh filled the air and covered the city.

My grandfather was the only one not working and when Atheling told me that he had not seen him since the counsel of war I left the wall to seek him. I found him on the floor of his chamber. He was still. I summoned a doctor while I lifted him to his bed. I found his empty medicine jug on the floor. The doctor came and examined him. I showed him the medicine. He sent me out of the chamber so that he could examine him thoroughly. After a while, he called me back in. "I do not have this medicine here. I do not have the means to make it. The Earl Marshal told me of his complaint." He shook his head, "I am sorry, lord, I cannot heal him."

"But can you make the time he has left less painful?"

"I can give him a draught which will numb the pain but he said that he needed his mind sharp until this was over."

"Make the draught! He has suffered enough." He nodded. "Until my father comes I command."

174

By the time evening came, we had a gate in place. We had enough men at the gatehouse and in the south-west bastion tower to deter any attackers. The archers had managed to make enough arrows to fill a quiver each. Dislodged stones had been replaced. The stones we had used were salvaged along with darts and spears pulled from the bodies of the dead. The danger now lay in hunger. The extra mouths meant that we would be reliant on bread and water for the ale and wine were almost gone.

More of the Earl's men reached us just before dark and I forbade the entry of any more until dawn. I did not trust the enemy. Any who arrived later could camp outside of the walls by the east gate. We now had sufficient men to make four watches. I stood the watch for the first few hours after dusk. I had a suspicion that the enemy might try something but I had an uneventful watch and then I retired.

I was woken by Davy of Ingleby. "Lord, John of Oxbridge says a boat is approaching from the south bank. One of Sir Ranulf's men commands the watch but John asked me to fetch you."

"And he did right." William was already awake and with a sword in hand, we hurried across to the river gate. I saw that the gate was opened and I frowned. Had John decided to take on the mysterious visitors? I heard voices and they were not raised but were laughing. Then their faces turned towards me and I saw my father, his squires and Sir James. Help had come. I did not wonder why there was but a handful of men. I was just pleased that my father had arrived before the Earl Marshal had died.

My father beamed as he hugged me, "John has told us of the battles you have fought I am sorry that we took so long getting here." I looked beyond him. There were no more boats and he had a handful of men. "Fear not, by noon the rest of our men and Duke Richard's will be at London Bridge."

Now I recognised the knight who waited impatiently behind my father. "Your arrival is timely, father." I lowered my voice. "Your father is dying."

If I had hit him with a blacksmith's hammer I could not have had a great effect. "John did not say that he had been wounded."

I took his arm and led him across the inner ward, "There was a wound in his arm but that is not the one which threatens his life. This is a wound he received in our battles against the Scots. Brother Peter gave him months to live and those months have elapsed."

My father stopped and turned, "Then perhaps the warrior priest was wrong. He may recover."

I shook my head, "So I thought but the Warlord is a master at deception. He is asleep now but when you see him he will appear dead. You have arrived just in time. This rising in the city is nothing. The Earl Marshal is passing and that is like the crack of doom."

"Amen to that my son. At least he has had you with him. I should have been at his side and not wasting my time in France fighting petty wars for inconsequential pieces of soil! I shall not leave England again!"

The arrival of my father and Duke Richard roused Sir Ranulf and the Earl. Sir Richard hurried to greet him too. Sir James said, "Is your father still asleep, Sir Richard?"

"My father sleeps with the angels, Sir James as does my brother. They both fell when we were betrayed by the Abbot of the Augustine Friars."

Poor Sir James looked distraught. "I am sorry for my words. I would cut my tongue out. I did not know."

Sir Richard gave a weak smile, "I am only just becoming accustomed to the loss of my father. We have had many battles since then. It seems a lifetime ago and yet it was not."

We entered the Tower and Duke Richard growled, "There are many men who will pay for this treachery! When do we begin?"

"Sir Ranulf, would you and the Earl explain the situation to the Duke. I will take my father to the Earl Marshal's quarters."

As we ascended the stairs my father said, "You have grown, Samuel. You give commands like a seasoned warrior."

"It was forced upon me for the Earl Marshal, whilst willing, has been unwell."

We entered the chamber and my grandfather was waving away the doctor, "My son is here and I must greet him, leech!"

"You need your rest."

My father said, "Heed the doctor, father. That is a command from me!"

The Earl Marshal sat on the bed and laughed, "I must be getting old. My son and grandson order me about as though I am a doddery old codger!" He nodded and I saw the pain it caused him. "I am pleased that you are here William." He glanced at me. "From your face, I see that your son has given you the news."

I felt briefly guilty then said, "You did not say I could not tell my father."

"True. You are not foresworn. You are forgiven." He patted the bed. "Doctor, you may leave us. My son has some news. You may send a servant with some ale if you would."

"Medicine would be of more use."

"Medicine cannot save me and ale will ease the pain as well as your draughts. Tell me all my son."

My father waited until the ale arrived and we were alone before he began his tale. Occasionally my grandfather would interrupt to add some knowledge and information he thought to be relevant. I said nothing. I was learning and I had the best two teachers in the world.

The Earl Marshal leaned back, "So King Henry will deal with his son. I pray that the Earl of Pembroke is not involved in this conspiracy."

My father said, "From what I learned from Sir Leofric this Hubert de Mamers is of an age with the young King Henry. I suspect they met when enjoying competing in the tourney. Both have reasons to be bitter. Young Henry feels he should have more control of his own finances and de Mamers wishes the land his grandsire lost. It strikes me that they would be drawn together."

My grandfather frowned. It was a sure sign that the pain in his head had returned. "That is not our concern. London and this gathering of men at Windsor is the immediate danger. Now I see why the mayor fled west. I had thought he sought to escape trouble. It is obvious now that he was part of it. When Earl William's men return from scouring the land we will have more men. The ones who will follow you and Duke Richard should swell our numbers. We need to attack tomorrow morning. They will not expect that. Send Sir James south of the river to meet with Roger of Bath, our men and the Duke's knights. If they can attack across London Bridge then we can attack here at the postern gate. Duke Richard is keen?"

"He is desperate to avenge the knights he lost."

"Then he can lead the Earl of Essex's men, Sir Ranulf's and all but the garrison and Captain Robert."

I spoke for the first time. I had seen how the garrison had been battered. I wondered if they would stand. "That is a gamble!"

"Perhaps but think about this, Samuel. All that we have done is defend. They know not about the men to the east of the Tower. Our men south of the river are also a secret. Even the arrival of a prince of the blood is a secret. They will expect us to do the same as we did today and sit behind our walls. Use our men at arms. They are keen to avenge those who were butchered. They can slip across the wall during the hours of darkness and when we attack, at dawn, they can let us in at the postern gate. With Duke Richard parading before the north wall then all of their attention will be on him. Bringing the King's son was an act of genius William, well done."

My father shrugged, "It was an accident."

The Earl Marshal rubbed his head again. "I leave the rest of the planning to you. I have planted the seed, you can water it, watch it grow and harvest it. I will rest."

We bade farewell. In the corridor, my father leaned against the wall. "He is so old and ill. How did I not see it?"

"Because he hid it. I now know the signs but that is because I have not been out of his company for some time. Each time I leave him I fear it will be for the last time."

We headed down the corridor, "There is little justice in this world. For what he did for England he should have been feted and honoured. Instead, he is holed up in this tower and fighting for his life." He looked at me. "It is up to you and me, Samuel. We have to end this petty war and take him home. If he is to die then it should be in Stockton."

I said nothing. The Earl Marshal would die in London; of that, I was convinced.

Chapter 16

My father told the others of the plan. It was interesting for he never asked, he commanded. There was a Duke of Aquitaine present but none questioned the orders. I realised that part of that was down to the fact that most of the risks would be taken by our people. Duke Richard just had to parade knights and mounted men at arms before the Moorgate.

"We send a small group of men to take the postern gate in the city. Our archers and the rest of our men at arms will hold the gate. At the same time, Sir James will lead our men who are south of the river and they will attack the river wall. Duke Richard and all of the knights will draw the attention of the defenders to the north wall and they will assault the gates when we have drawn enough men from the north wall and people flee."

It was the Duke who showed he had a good mind for such things by asking pertinent questions.

"How do we coordinate our movements?"

My father pointed to Sir James, "Sir James will leave now." We had kept the wherry on our side of the river. "After gathering our men, he will wait until you are in position on the north side. You, my lord, will sound your horn three times and our men will make their way across the bridge. My son will speak with the men who are to sneak into the city. When they hear the horn, they will unlock the postern gate and Samuel and I will lead the rest of our men to attack."

The Duke frowned, "We do nothing but parade?"

"When you sound the horn, lord, you begin to prepare three lines as though you intend to charge the walls."

He snorted, "Only a fool would do that!"

"Then let him think that you are a fool, lord. We know you are not. When the people flee from the gates then you attack."

"There is much upon your shoulders." I heard the respect in the Duke's voice.

"My family has always had the weight of the country upon its shoulders. When my father dies then it will fall upon mine and then Samuel's. When Samuel is no longer with us then it will be Thomas, his son." He left much unsaid. He did not mention the revolt by the princes nor the race for land and riches which drove many others. Instead, he allowed them to reflect on the unselfish legacy my grandfather, the Earl Marshal had left. "If there are no further questions then my son and Sir James have tasks to perform." He turned to me, "Samuel impress upon the men that they must succeed. If they fail then Sir James will lose many men in his attack."

"I will, father."

I felt honoured that I would be the one to brief our men. It demonstrated the trust my father had in me. I went to the warrior hall. At the door, I parted from Sir James, "Take care, Sir James."

"I have the easiest of tasks. I lead the men of the Earl Marshal and Duke Richard's knights. Your men at arms have to enter the lair of the fox. I hope that they are well prepared."

I had sent William to bring the men at arms we had chosen to make the attack from the walls. There were fewer of them now. We had chosen the ones who were known for their skills. We needed men who could sneak in the dark and think on their feet. We had more archers than men at arms. The bulk of the men my father had brought would be waiting at London Bridge. Ralph, Tomas and Henry Warbow had rejoined the other archers. They listened as I spoke with the six men at arms who would have to get into the city. Even as I briefed them I knew that there were not enough of them. William and I would have to go with them. In truth, I had decided it earlier. It was not an attempt at gaining glory. It was calculated and it was reasoned.

"The six of you, led by me and accompanied by my squire William, will enter the city within the next hour. We will hide there until we hear the horn sounded three times. Then we take the postern gate and hold it until Sir Richard, my father and our archers can enter. We then get to London Bridge to ensure that Roger of Bath and the rest of our men can enter."

The men at arms nodded but Ralph asked, "Why you, lord? We archers have good knife skills."

"And I have not?"

"I did not mean that, lord, but you are too valuable to be risked."

"Did the Earl Marshal hide from danger, Ralph?"

"No, lord. He led from the front."

"As shall I. Besides, I know our enemies. I know the city. Do you?" He shook his head. "You will be called upon to use your war bows to great effect. We will be outnumbered until Duke Richard can enter the city. We may be a handful but we are a band of brothers who can cause more harm to an enemy than five times our number."

James of Oxbridge grinned and said, "Aye, lord, you are right there!"

His brother cuffed him, "Silence whelp! You are honoured that Sir Samuel leads us. Forgive him, lord. Has fought a couple of skirmishes and thinks he is a hero! He will learn."

Ralph was like a dog with a bone. "Lord the Falconer's Glove has sympathetic folk inside. The innkeeper fled south with his family but his whores and his tapster stayed in the inn. They are loyal and can be trusted. Why not use the inn as a place to hide?"

I was not certain. "This might bring harm to the folk therein."

"The whores are quick-thinking, lord and as I have learned to my cost can simulate most realistically." The bawdy laughter of the others gave his words a meaning I had not grasped. "What I am saying lord is that if this fails, and I do not think that it will, then they will say you forced yourselves upon them. They will tear their clothes and they will weep. But lord, we will not fail. You will not fail."

"Good, then prepare yourselves."

Henry Warbow said, quietly, "Lord you cannot wear mail nor your spurs. They will make a noise. You must go as the others do in leather jerkin and boots." I suddenly felt out of my depth and I nodded. "Tomas, go fetch suitable war gear for his lordship and young William."

Even as they began to strip my mail from me John of Oxbridge wiped his hands with soot from the chimney and smeared it on my hands and face. "You will need to be as a blackamoor. White shows at night. If you close your eyes then none can see." I opened my mouth to ask the most obvious of questions and he smiled, "Use your ears and nose. At night time they are more valuable than sight anyway."

There was neither mirror nor polished dish to view my reflection but when I saw William smile I knew how I looked. I nodded, "Let us go."

John of Oxbridge said, "Lord if I might suggest?" I waved a hand. "Let us not use the gatehouse. They will be watching it and it will make a noise. I have watched from the river gate. We can slip around the outer wall and walk between it and the river. There is no moon this night. We might have to wade the ditch near to the gatehouse, perhaps even swim, but we wear no mail. If we scramble up the bank we will be unseen by all."

Aelric nodded, "It is a good plan, lord."

"Then I will follow. Lead on John of Oxbridge."

We left the gate quietly. The sentries were not my men and thought nothing of allowing us through. My father would be angry. I knew that. Once we were through we headed to the west side of the stake filled ditch and waded through the shallows until we were on the mud. It sucked at us for a short time. The tide had gone out. The archers waved a silent farewell and we were alone. I walked behind John of Oxbridge and his brother brought up the rear. That was his punishment for interrupting me. When we reached the ditch, I caught the smell of the fire from the brazier in the gatehouse. I heard the murmur of conversation. It showed that we had not been seen. I was in John of Oxbridge's hands. He suddenly waved his hand and we headed up the east side of the now tidal ditch. The sound of the sentries became louder. We reached the bridge into the castle and John led us silently across. It was knee-deep and we moved slowly to avoid splashes. Once on the other side we walked down the west side.

We reached the river and he stopped. He held up his hand and disappeared. A few moments later he returned and waved me towards him. We were on the river side and the bank was not as steep as it was by the bridge. We began to climb. There were sentries above. I could hear them but not see them. That boded well for, if we did not make a noise then we would be invisible too. The walls were just three paces high. I wondered how we would ascend them. Normally we used shields. We had not brought shields. When we reached the wall we all stood with our backs to it. John was, effectively, in command. I saw him listening. We seemed to wait for an age. I knew what he was doing. He was working out the routine of their patrol.

He waved his brother and Davy of Ingleby forward. He and Brian stood with their backs to the wall and they cupped their hands. John pointed to James and his brother ran fearlessly at the two men and planted his feet in their hands. They boosted him. His hands grabbed the crenulations and he used the degraded mortar between the stones to climb. John and Brian moved down the wall and Davy of Ingleby emulated them.

I pointed to myself and I stepped down the slope. They moved to their right this time. I ran and put first one foot and then another into their cupped hands. As I was lifted it felt as though I was flying and I grasped the crenulations. My feet scrambled for the cracks in the mortar. It was not as easy as the other two had made it look but I managed to gain a foothold and pull myself halfway up. Davy and James helped to pull me up and over. They pointed and I saw that the two sentries were at the turret by the south-east corner of the city walls. I heard the rattle of dice. The careless sentries had given us a chance. Leaning over the wall the three of us helped the others over the top.

I knew where we were and I led them away from the sentries towards the ladder which led down to the Billing's Gate. There were two towers over the gate but there were stairs which descended close to the turret. I gambled that they would think the river side was safe. We stepped quietly down the stairs to the ground. As we reached the cobbled surface I could smell a mixture of fish and beer. Once we had reached the cobbles of the street the hardest part of our task was over. We leaned against the wall, beneath the fighting platform. We could have just hidden there but there was always the risk that we might be seen and so I headed for the Falconer's Glove. I vaguely remembered where it was. I nearly went wrong and took the wrong turning in the narrow maze that was the busy streets of London. John tapped my shoulder and pointed left. I saw the glove hanging from the metal hook. It was a crude but effective sign.

John went to the door and tapped three times, gently, stopped and then repeated it. He waited. Instead of the door opening a wooden shutter was lifted. John slid along the wall and I heard whispers. Then he came back and the door opened. The interior was smoky. It had been lit with tallow candles and brands. One still flared and it gave the room an orange glow. There was a musky smell mixed with the odour of stale ale and sweat. I had rarely been in such an inn. Four girls stood with cloaks draped around them. The tapster was a huge man. His job, when the innkeeper was present, was to bring up new barrels and tap them.

One of the girls laughed when she saw our faces, "Harold, how much do we charge blackamoors? I have heard their manhood is bigger than that of Englishmen."

Harold turned and snapped, "Keep a civil tongue in your head, Mary Soft Breast! This is Sir Samuel. He is the grandson of the Earl Marshal."

The girl looked contrite and she tried to bob a curtsy. She failed and her cloak slipped revealing a naked form beneath. As she pulled up her cloak she said, "Sorry, my lord."

I smiled, "We can wash this off now and you will see that we are Englishmen. As for our manhood? That will have to remain our secret." The girls giggled.

"Fetch ale and dress yourselves." He turned to John of Oxbridge. "Is the master still alive then? We feared for him when he fled. The wherry was heavily laden. He has many children."

"He is fine and he has done great service. He will be rewarded."

"Just get rid of the scum who have invaded our town. One of the girls, Alice the Virgin was beaten by one of them yesterday night."

"Why?"

He looked at me, "He had lost men in the battle and he had drunk too much. He said that Alice was not a virgin and he beat her. I would have stopped him but he had three men with him."

"Why is she called the Virgin then?"

"She looks young yet she has seen seventeen summers. The men who use the inn and pay the girls know that. It is a name. We have two Marys and two Mauds. Men like to have the same girl."

The four girls reappeared with both ale and river water. We would not need to be blacked up any longer. Mary Soft Breast came to me and she gently began to wash the soot from me. The girls must have washed in rosemary water for she smelled sweet. I found myself becoming aroused. She giggled, "I have never had a lord before."

I shook my head. I knew that, despite my years I was blushing, "I am sorry, Mary but I am married and have a son."

She shrugged as she began to dry me with a piece of drying cloth. "If the men who used us were all single then we would have no business at all. It is the married men with the coin in their pockets who can pay us. The single ones just look."

Another girl brought some ale for me. To take my mind off the aptly named Mary I said, "Tapster, is there a way for us to get to the wall unseen?"

He nodded. "We have a wharf where we land the barrels. This a labyrinth of buildings and paths. Our inn goes east behind other shops. They are only occupied during the day. Anne sells her pies next door and beyond that is Sal Shellfish. They do not live above their shops. Those are the rooms my master uses for guests. They are empty now. There is a path which leads to the city wall. It emerges between the turret and the postern gate. The women will come before dawn but by then you will be at the gate, I am thinking."

I nodded, "The wharf is inside the walls?"

"Aye lord, the Billing's Gate is opened at daylight to allow boats in. The bridge is often crowded and our gate is used by small fishing boats to land their catches. When daylight comes then the shops will be busy for people like Anne's pies. She uses spice in them. You had best be gone an hour before dawn."

I was about to ask when that would be when John of Oxbridge said, "By my reckoning, lord, that would be soon. Men who come from a night watch relax and do not look beneath their feet. We can wait beneath the fighting platform."

I nodded, "Then lead on tapster and I thank you, ladies. When this is over you shall be rewarded."

"Thank you, my lord, and God speed." Mary Soft Breast threw her arms around me and kissed me hard on the lips. She said huskily, "I could give you a night, lord, such as you would remember your whole life."

I gave her a weak smile and stroked her cheek, "That I doubt not but I am married and I am not like those who use this inn."

She looked sad, "Then I will have to imagine the pleasure we would have enjoyed. It would have been a change to lie with a man who shaved and did not stink of fish. A man who spoke gently and had a soft caress. I will think of you Sir Samuel of Stockton." Her hand stroked mine as I left.

I followed John of Oxbridge and we descended some stairs. The ceiling was low. I did not know how the tapster avoided cracking his head. The passage twisted and turned. There were openings to the left and right. The different smells in each chamber indicated a different purpose. The passage. I realised, was wide enough for a barrel to be rolled. Then we began to climb and the floor became earth and compacted. The tapster pulled back a bolt. I had expected it to creak but it was greased. John stepped out and waved us through. I clasped the arm of the tapster. I swore to myself that when this was over I would return for these people had risked all for us and deserved a reward.

The darkness of the passage had prepared our eyes for the night. John led us swiftly to the wall. Above us, I could hear the watch as they prepared for the day. The men in the turret walked down the platform towards the postern gate. The two small turrets over the gate also contained men and I heard the five of them above us as they had a conversation. If they had looked down between the cracks then they would have seen us. I know not what we would have done but we had luck or God on our side and they did not look down.

"Someone said the men we were expecting from Tilbury are not coming."

"That is a rumour, Frederick! Do not spread them! The men who came from the east yesterday were a handful is all! The rest will be here soon." The voice had a Scottish burr I knew so well.

"Aye, the captain is right. We expected the ones in the Tower to be reinforced. We took the gate once and it will be weaker now. We can take it again. With the west subdued his lordship can bring the men from Windsor."

"Still, they have held out longer than we thought!"

"You are right Sven. It is that damned Warlord, the Earl Marshal! He must have made a pact with the devil! My father and grandfather fought him in Anjou before I was born."

The one they had called Frederick said, "I have heard that he cannot be killed. He has a sword which is magic. Some say the sword was touched by Merlin."

"And that is nonsense. He is a man and any man can be killed. If he comes close enough to me then my war hammer will end his life."

"Aye Captain, you Scots like your war hammers."

Just then we heard feet climbing the stairs. The Scottish captain said, "All quiet, my lord. we saw a wherry on the river but it looked to be manned by but two men."

"Did you not send for his lordship?"

"There was no need. It was not going to the Tower it was heading for the south of the river."

"Then you should have told someone. It could have been going for help."

"I am sorry, my lord. We were told that we would only have to hold the walls for a couple of days. Fighting each day and watching each night makes a man's judgement flawed. Next time I will disturb his lordship's rest."

The feet above us shuffled and tramped and then, as the night watch descended the stairs there was silence. The sky began to lighten. From the shellfish and pie shop, we heard the sound of shutters being opened and the murmur of voices as the women and the children who worked them prepared for trade. I had not done this before but I knew that this was the crucial time. Once the streets were busy we would be able to move more easily. Until then the eight of us, armed with swords, would stand out. We huddled under the wooden platform with fingers on the hilts of our swords. We waited for the sound of the horns which would make every man on the walls alert and then we would strike. A stone pillar hid the postern gate from us but we knew that on the other side was a wooden stair leading to the fighting platform and a gate manned by two or three men. We had to kill the men and those on the gatehouse and then hold until Aelric and his men arrived. I prayed to God that we were good enough.

Chapter 17

Dawn had still to break fully but I could hear the city coming to life. I moved away from the wall and headed to the stone pillar. John of Oxbridge had done the leading up to now. I was the knight and I would take over. William followed me. He would watch my back. John nodded as I passed him. It was an accolade for it showed that he trusted me. I drew my sword and my dagger. We had to be ruthless. Hesitation would be fatal. From what the girls had told us the men we were fighting were less than men. They were mercenaries. The longer they stayed in England the more harm that they would do. The gate would not be opened until dawn at the earliest and so far we had seen that the only time they opened it was when they were about to attack. I was hidden by the stone and I was in its shadow. I peered out when I heard the murmur of conversation and heard the tramp of feet. I saw six crossbowmen heading from the direction of the East Cheap. They would man the arrow slits in the towers. Time seemed to drag as we waited. I hoped Duke Richard, whom I did not know at all, would do as my father had ordered. The whole plan hinged on his initial action. Even if Roger of Bath and our men had not reached the bridge by dawn they would not be far away. The sky had lightened enough for me to see the supports under the fighting platform above me. It was almost time.

When I heard the three notes I felt like cheering. The effect was instantaneous. I heard the captain of the watch above us shout down. "Watch through the slit in the door lads. These are sneaky bastards and may try to come up from the ditch. They are attacking to the north and there is a chance they might try to take the postern."

There were two small slits in the postern door. It allowed those who were inside to inspect any visitors. This was our chance. William and I leapt out. Two men had their heads pressed against the slits. The third turned as he sensed our movement. Even as he opened his mouth to shout the alarm I whipped my sword backhanded across his throat. The blow stopped any call of alarm. William stabbed the other two, one with his sword and one with his dagger. John of Oxbridge led the rest of our men up the steps to the fighting platform. All those above us had their attention fixed upon the Tower. I heard a scream and a crash as one was hurled to the ground on the other side of the wall. Then there was the sound of deadly combat. My men had the advantage that they had come upon the sentries from behind and I knew that John of Oxbridge would have sought the captain of the watch first.

"William, get the gate open."

I stood facing Tower Street and the road which led to the East Cheap. The crossbowmen had come from there and it stood to reason that there would be other men heading down to the fighting platform in response to the alarm. Above me was the sound of steel on steel but my men had the advantage. They knew the numbers of the opposition and the defenders did not. The men with crossbows could not use their weapons for fear of hitting their own men. To the north and west of us, I heard the noise of men shouting and running to face the threat that was Duke Richard. My grandfather's plan was working. All attention was on the north and we had a small chance now to gain entry to the city.

A pair of men at arms appeared just a hundred paces from me, "Hurry William!" I heard bolts sliding back. The two men conferred and then ran. I heard them shouting the alarm. De Mamers had not made many mistakes thus far. We had beaten him because my grandfather was cleverer. Would he see our threat as the very real one? Men screamed above us. The captain of the watch fell to the ground just two paces from me. His entrails lay on his stomach like an untidy nest of worms and snakes. The bar on the gate was thrown down and it creaked open. Aelric and Atheling were through before it had swung fully open. They each had an arrow nocked and the two of them turned and sent their arrows into two crossbowmen. They raced up the stairs to the fighting platform. As Henry Warbow and the others entered they took to the fighting platform. Our archers could keep us covered whilst clearing the walls towards the Aldgate and Bishopsgate. Our men at arms raced in. Peter Pig Man shouted, "Your father has gone with Duke Richard, lord. He said to take the bridge gate and hold."

I nodded, "Prepare shields."

We waited. John of Oxbridge led the men at arms to join me. Captain Robert and his four men also entered through the gate. I looked at him questioningly, "It is my city, lord. I helped to lose it. Let us take it back

189

for you." I nodded. "The Earl Marshal said you might need us. He has a sharp mind that one!"

I nodded. "We stay together. They have been warned that we are here. We wear no mail and have no helmets. Let us use our skill and our unity to aid us. Peter have your men with mail before us. John and James, flank William and I. We will head towards East Cheap and then try to help Roger of Bath."

I knew that Ralph and five archers would be racing along the fighting platform towards the London Bridge gate. They would reach there quicker than we. We marched down the street. There was a mixture of workshops and houses. The closer we came to East Cheap the more dilapidated were the dwellings. We managed to cover two hundred paces unopposed before we ran into trouble. I had just sent Peter the Pig Man and the men with mail down a side alley to see if it led to the gate. A handful of sergeants appeared from the road which led to the Cornmill. They came without any order and that aided us. They ran at us for without helmets and mail they did not see us as a threat. Perhaps they thought that the city had risen against them. I know not. A sergeant with a crusader shield and round helmet ran at me. He pulled his sword back and I saw him preparing to punch with his shield. His comrades were a couple of paces behind. It was not much but it was enough. William swung his sword to smash against the shield of the sergeant. At the same time, James of Oxbridge swung at the sergeant's sword. He had to block the blow and my left hand darted forward to pierce his throat. He fell gurgling blood from a mortal wound.

The next men saw the danger and one, an older man shouted. "Shields!" They presented five shields and the other four stood behind them.

The ancient city was a labyrinth of alleys and tiny streets. None knew them better than Captain Robert. "Captain, use the streets and get behind them."

"Aye, my lord!"

As the mercenaries advanced Dick, Brian and the others poked their swords over our shoulders. This would be bloody. Just then an arrow flew between my head and William's. A surprised man at arms suddenly found that an arrow had sprouted from his chest. He slid to the ground. I did not look around but I knew that some of our archers had been left to watch our backs. I took advantage of the shock. The other four raised their shields over their faces and I blocked one sword which flailed blindly and then rammed my dagger up under the sword arm of the sergeant facing me. I saw the tip emerge from his shoulder and he screamed. John of Oxbridge brought his sword from on high to hit his opponent on the helmet. He fell, stunned. I knew what the enemy did not. Our archers could no longer help us for we were too close. Three men lay dead and John and I stepped forward as William and James tried to manoeuvre their daggers into the unprotected parts of the enemies' bodies. I saw more men joining the enemy. Where was Captain Robert and where was Peter and our men at arms?

The men behind were watching us and a sword came straight for my face. I blocked it with my dagger but the edge sawed across my cheek. I saw the joy on the man at arms' face as he drew first blood. It did him little good for I punched him with the hilt and crosspiece of my own sword and I took out an eye. A man can fight with just one eye but it takes training and this man brought his hands up for protection. My dagger tore up under his surcoat and I gutted him. He fell writhing to the ground.

There was a shout as Captain Robert led his men into the back of the remaining men. At the same time, Peter brought my men at arms from the other side. They showed them no mercy. Even as we were recovering there was a shout from behind us and I saw the tapster from the Falconer's Glove and other local men from the area. They had clubs and axes and they roared as they charged towards us. Had I not spoken with the tapster I might have feared treachery but I knew they were friends.

As they neared us I shouted, "Take the weapons from the dead men and follow us! I command!"

The tapster shouted, "Aye Sir Samuel! We are your men!"

Now that we had more men and before the enemy could realise that there were so few of us I changed our plans. "We make straight for the gate!"

William said, "And what if Roger of Bath and the others are not there with Sir James."

"Oh, ye of little faith! He will be there and we will help him to gain entry. Peter Pig Man, take us to the gate!"

"Aye lord. We are not far!"

We turned left and headed down the road which led to the river. We passed St Mary's church. Our sudden move south took us away from the main thoroughfares. I could hear the noise from the bridge gate as Sir James led our men at arms to try to break through. Their feet thundered on the o old wooden bridge and there was the sound of shouts and cries. It would not be easy although the archers he had with him and Duke Richard's knights would help. As we neared the church of St Magnus I glimpsed Henry Warbow and Ralph on the fighting platform as they sent their arrows towards an unseen enemy. There was a narrow passage between what looked and smelled like a fishmonger's stall and a money lender. Ahead I saw some of the mercenaries running to brace the gate. We had to strike quickly before they knew what we were about. Our numbers had been swollen by loyal Londoners. The enemy would not know that.

"The Earl Marshal!" We shouted as we burst from the gloom of the alley into the light of Watling Street.

I brought my sword down across the back of a knight who was just ahead of me. He tumbled to the ground and Captain Robert used his own axe to great effect. It was a crowded and confused mêlée. It was hard to see who we were fighting. As I blocked a sergeant's strike with my sword I said, "William and James, get to the gate and open it."

"Aye, lord!" They turned and slipped back through the ranks of Londoners eager to butcher the mercenaries. There was an incentive. Mercenaries had money and they carried it with them. I knew that some of the ones who followed us would waste time searching and stripping bodies. It could not be helped. So long as they helped us to get the gates open and secure this side of the wall then I was happy.

I could hear axes hammering on the gate. Men fell from the fighting platform as our archers picked off men who were sending missiles at Sir James and our reinforcements. "John, Peter, we must turn them and drive a wedge between the gate and the men. James and William need help." James of Oxbridge and William were trying to get to the gate and open it. We had to turn the attention of the men who guarded it towards us.

"Aye, lord!" He bent to pick up a fallen shield and he held it before us. Peter and the other mailed men at arms stood with him. "Brian, Dick, the rest of you, push!"

The men at arms then put their weight behind John, Peter and the others. John swung his sword above his head. We had the advantage that our enemies were trying to get to the gate and we were hitting their side. When first one and then a second man at arms fell I stamped and stabbed on their bodies. The attack of our men at arms made a knight order his men to turn to face the threat. It created a gap which I exploited.

I had no mail and I could move quickly. I had fast hands and two sharp weapons. Although the men I faced were mailed their faces were not and I stabbed, slashed and hacked as I used the dead bodies to spring into the air. I ducked beneath a swinging axe and, as I rose, drove my dagger into the groin of the sergeant at arms. I used his body to fend off a blow from a squire's sword and I rammed my dagger into his knee. He fell. I saw that James of Oxbridge was trying to manhandle the bar which held the gates. William was fighting three men and he was losing. I saw that men's backs were to me. There were just four men between me and William. Three were fighting William. As the fourth raised a poleaxe to strike over his comrades' heads I ran up to him and slit his throat from behind. His spurting blood alerted one of William's attackers who tried to turn. My sword rammed into his back and came out of this front. It was almost too late for William as one of the sergeants at arms headbutted him. The raised sword never reached William who was falling to the ground. My sword took his arm at the elbow and the last man who turned to face the new threat fell with two arrows in him.

William would have to wait. I sheathed my sword and helped James to lift the heavy bar. As we started to pull the gates open I saw Sir James and Roger of Bath. They were leading Duke Richard's knights.

"James of Oxbridge help me pull William to safety." The two of us manhandled the unconscious squire to the stairs which led to the fighting platform. "Stay with him."

"Aye lord."

I turned and hurried after Harry Lightfoot. He swung his war axe one handed and smote a man at arms' skull in twain. He pulled it out as I reached him. He frowned, "You should be wearing iron, lord! It is not safe for a lord to fight like that. Stay behind me! You have one wound already."

I had forgotten the cut. I could taste the salty blood, "Fear not Harry, I will use my speed and I promise that I will not tangle with knights." I pointed my sword. "Head up this road. Duke Richard is attacking towards the Moorgate."

"We know, lord, Sir James told us and the Duke's oathsworn are keen to protect their lord."

John, his brother James, Brian, Davy, Dick, Peter Pigman and the other men at arms all joined me as we followed the wall of metal as we headed towards the Moorgate. I saw that the Londoners were exploiting the dead. Mail was being stripped from bodies and their purses searched.

I did not blame them. As Mary Soft Breast had told us the ones who had remained had suffered at their hands. Our archers followed behind taking their chances as they came. I heard horses ahead.

Sir James shouted, "Shields!" The street was narrow but Hubert de Mamers and four other knights led a conroi to charge with couched lances at Sir James and Duke Richard's household knights. It was a vain attempt to dislodge us for they locked shields and braced themselves against the wall. Lances shattered and horses screamed as they were hacked. I heard a voice shout, "Fall back!" De Mamers, his squire, standard-bearer and eight others escaped the wrath of Duke Richard's knights. They fled north-west along Watling Street and in their haste not only trampled some of the own men onto the cobbles but also created a gap into which Sir James ran.

I heard Roger of Bath's voice, "Sir Samuel, open the Moorgate!"

"Stockton, on me!" There were fewer men before us and no knights. In fact, it seemed to me that the best of the men who were left had fled with Sir Mormaer. Unless Duke Richard could reach them in time then they would escape to Windsor through the Newgate and we would have to winkle them out of there. My visage, with its bloody scar, must have terrified some of those we came across. They did not know I was a knight and so they did not surrender but there was little honour in their defeat and death. The last men did us a favour for they opened the gates and attempted to flee. They were ridden down and lanced by Duke William and my father.

I pointed west, "De Mamers is heading west."

My father shouted, "Men at arms, follow my son! Keep him safe! The rest, we ride to Windsor."

There were just eight men at arms who joined us but, with the archers and Sir James and his men we had enough.

"John, secure the gates."

"Aye lord."

The eight men assigned by my father dismounted. I knew what I had to do. "Come with me. James of Oxbridge, help Sir James scour the city."

"Where do you go, lord?"

"I go rat-catching!"

We strode to the Augustine Priory. It lay close to the Moorgate. The door was open and we strode inside. It was deserted. Someone had left in a hurry. I headed to the church. The door was closed.

194

"Open the door in the name of the Earl Marshal! Hurry for my patience wears thin." I heard a whispered conversation within and then bolts were pulled back. When the doors swung open I saw the friars prostrating themselves. "The Abbot has fled lord! Do not harm us, we beg of you! We are just simple friars!"

I sheathed my sword, "You will forgive me if I do not believe you. The last time we were here then betrayal was in the air and men whom I loved died." I turned to the men I had brought with me. "Search the priory and leave no stone unturned. If that snake is hiding here then I would know of it."

I went into the open air. The smell of incense in the church turned my stomach. William, his head bandaged and guarded by Henry Warbow and Ralph arrived. "Sir James sent me, lord. The city is back in our hands. Those who surrendered have been stripped of weapons and valuables. They have been taken to the tower to wait for the judgement of your father."

I nodded and I waited for my men. They returned shaking their heads. "He is not here, lord, nor is the treasure of the priory. Four friars rode with him. They left yesterday and headed west."

"Then I know where they will be! If there is food in here bring that. The friars can enjoy a fast to teach them to be loyal."

We left and headed for St. Paul's and the Cheap. Sir James, Roger of Bath and the knights of Duke Richard were there. The mercenaries had used it as their camp. They had billeted themselves in the church and their stink was everywhere.

As we passed the merchant's hall I saw a sight which turned my stomach. Alan of Hauxley and the other guards had been crucified against the wall of the hall. He had been loyal to the end and paid the price for that loyalty. "Cut those men down! They were brave warriors!"

"Aye, lord!"

Alone I strode on to meet with Sir James. I had black thoughts in my mind.

Sir James came over to me. He looked at my face, "A healer!"

"It is fine!" I was still distracted and thinking of Alan of Hauxley.

"It is not and we have good doctors. I would not have you disfigured for your lovely wife." He laughed and shook his head. "I am guessing that your father did not give you permission to accompany John of Oxbridge."

I smiled, "He did not tell me not to. I assumed he would want a knight with them."

"Then you have been lucky! Do not push your luck. A knight only has so much luck and I fear you have used your stock! The wound to your face could have been fatal!"

The healer who came took one look at my wound and said, "Lord, you need the doctor in the castle. I would make a mess of this. It will need careful and delicate stitches."

Sir James said, "William needs the doctor too. Go and I will take command here." He smiled and gave me a mock bow, "With your permission, of course, my lord."

I nodded. I knew when I was beaten. "Of course."

My grandfather was watching me as William and I walked across the outer ward. Archers surrounded the twenty or so men who had surrendered. They were seated in the area we had felled the trees.

When he saw me the Earl Marshal shook his head, "Your father is not a happy man, Samuel. He did not wish you to be put in such danger."

"And you, grandfather? What of you?"

He laughed, "I knew he could not stop you and I trusted that you would not come to harm. I was half right. Doctor if you leave him as handsome as he is now there is a purse of gold for you."

"Fear not Earl Marshal, you can keep your gold. It will be an honour to tend such a hero."

My grandfather listened while I was stitched and I told him of the battle as I had seen it. He shook his head, "Poor Alan of Hauxley. He fought with us and that makes him a shield brother. I will pray for his soul. Those battles are the hardest to fight, Samuel. I always prefer a battle where I am mounted. Is it over do you think?"

I realised he was still in the dark about the escape of the Abbot and Hubert der Mamers. "They have fled to Windsor. I am uncertain if we have enough men to deal with the problem."

"We have enough men. I have written the order this day and raised the fyrd. London alone can supply a thousand men. From what you say they are roused already and they will wish to hurt these folk who made their lives a misery. Duke Richard's presence is vital. We will win but I hope we lose no more men."

My father and Duke Richard arrived back just before dark. The Duke of Aquitaine was angry. He raged and he ranted. Sir Richard told me why. "He was ambushed as we rode through the deer park. Two of his favourite knights were killed."

I nodded. "And the Abbot is also within Windsor. We will have more battles to fight."

The Duke turned and pointed. He roared, "And those men outside will hang! I want them strung up and hanged. Then their heads can be displayed on the walls of London!"

My father tried to remonstrate with him, "Duke, reflect on this. We may turn their capture to our advantage." I knew that, as prisoners, we could gain valuable information and one never knew what else their capture might yield. Death was permanent!

"I care not for advantage. Their deaths will lessen the pain for my lost knights!" This was ever his way. He was often ruthless. He rewarded loyalty well but woe betide any who betrayed him.

The Duke's wishes were honoured and his knights and squires went outside and using whatever ropes they could the men at arms and sergeants had a noose placed around their necks and then they were thrown over the outer walls. They struggled and they kicked but eventually, their jerking ceased and they were dead.

When the last man had finished jerking the Duke nodded and turned back towards the Tower, "And tomorrow we ride to Windsor and end this. I will lead the men."

My grandfather shook his head, "Let me remind you, Duke Richard, that your father left me in command of this land in his absence. I am not yet in the ground and I will command." My grandfather wanted no repetition of the hanged men at arms.

I thought the Duke would argue but he merely nodded. He had been brought up in the shadow of the Warlord and it was understandable that he would acquiesce. My father, on the other hand, was ready for an argument. "And you are still ill, father. You cannot ride abroad. You must stay here and rest."

Only the three of us knew that my grandfather did not have long to live but all in the room knew that he had been wounded and my father's words must have sounded reasonable.

"Rest?" He shook his head, "Rest will not cure me and you know that, William. I would be with my son and grandson. I can ride and I do not have to raise a sword. I still have a mind and I can use that." He held up the seal which hung around his neck. "And I have this authority. I will lead."

Silence hung like a pall of smoke until my father, reluctantly, nodded. "But I will have two men riding with you. It would be unseemly if the Earl Marshal was to fall from his horse at a crucial moment."

"Indeed. And there is another reason I need to go. Hubert de Mamers. He wants vengeance and my presence on a tired old palfrey might encourage him to come forth and do battle." I saw Duke Richard frown. The Earl Marshal was patient. He was always ready to explain his actions. Sadly, Duke Richard never learned that lesson, "Apart from the Earl of Essex's knights and those of Sir Ranulf, we do not ride warhorses. We ride to Windsor on the sad and sorry beasts you brought from Southampton. We hide our archers amongst the fyrd. I lead the column. I want de Mamers to fight us outside the walls of Windsor. It is not my wish to make men bleed to take the King's own castle. We fight with the deer park to our backs. There the archers can rain death upon them and the fyrd will be protected and safe. It is we who will bear the brunt of the fighting and it is we who will face them sword to sword."

This would be my grandfather's last battle. My father and I would ensure that, in the short time he had left, he would never have to fight again. After we had taken him to his chamber my father took me to one side. "Thank you for watching and protecting him, Samuel, but tomorrow we have to ensure that he does nothing reckless."

"Reckless?"

"Remember how feeble Wulfric became at the end?" I nodded. "My father told me it was better to go out with a sword in your hand. Despite his words, I can see how he might choose tomorrow to die. Let us prevent it eh?"

Chapter 18

The next morning as we rode to Windsor the heads of the dead were displayed on spears along the walls of the city. It was a sombre sight. We crossed the bridge and headed south and west along the river. We had over twenty miles to go. Even though we had left at dawn we would not be there before noon. Harry Lightfoot and Peter Strongarm rode behind the Earl Marshal who rode White Star. I was pleased that he was on the old familiar horse. Peter Strongarm carried the standard of the Earl Marshal and Harry Lightfoot that of Cleveland. Masood had been sent off in the night to discover the dispositions of the enemy. He would also spot any ambush. Duke Richard had lost men because he had not availed himself of the services of a scout! My father and I flanked the Earl Marshal. The Duke rode with Sir Ranulf and the Earl of Essex. He had commandeered a warhorse for himself. Despite the words of the Earl Marshal Duke Richard would ride forth as a prince of the realm. He rode ahead of us for he wanted all to see him as the leader. We knew he was not.

The Earl Marshal chuckled and shook his head, "Even when I was a babe in Constantinopolis I was not so closely watched as this. Do you fear I will fall from my horse and embarrass you?"

"None would be embarrassed, father, but we would not wish you hurt."

"But I am hurt already. Each morning when I wake I know it might be my last. I have a priest with us so that before we fight I might be shriven." He put his hand on my father's. "I am just happy that, in the end, I shall have my son and grandson with me. Through our veins runs the blood of the housecarl, Ridley. Our heads are filled with the knowledge of war and our hearts pulsate with the love of this land, England. As Erre might have said, *'This is a good day to die.'*"

I said, firmly, "But you will not."

"What will be will be. However, I am convinced that this day will see us end this threat to King Henry's crown."

My father nodded, "On that, we agree but do not tempt fate. She can be willful!"

"Remember, my son, when the Earl Marshal is no more it will be incumbent upon you two to see that Richard is protected."

I turned and stared at my grandfather, "But his elder brother has been anointed."

"And so was Stephen the Usurper but I still fought him. Young Henry has disappointed both me and his father. Richard is wild it is true but his heart is English. He has shown courage already. As he grows older he may become less reckless. William, he respects you. Use that. I did so with Geoffrey of Anjou and King Henry was made because of the changes I wrought in him. I cannot see young Henry ruling England."

"Are you a seer, grandfather? Can you see through the mists of time that which will be and will not?"

"I have lived longer than any man I know. I might have become feeble but the knowledge I have in my head and the people I have met tell me that Henry will never sit upon England's throne." In the event he was right but by then my grandfather was long since buried.

We had over a hundred knights for, as we passed through the manors south of the river, the Earl Marshal summoned other knights. Each town we passed sent men to follow us. We grew. We raised the fyrd so that we had almost two thousand men behind us. They would not be of much use in the battle but they would give us numbers and might intimidate our foe. The three of us knew that our strength lay in the fifty archers we had with us. The majority of them were ours and we knew their worth. It was the same with the forty men at arms who rode behind us. They had been trained by the Warlord and his son. They were the legacy of the Earl Marshal. None other used ordinary and base-born men at arms and archers so well as my grandfather. The affection they shared was something which was quite remarkable. Even those who had come from the Holy Land with my father fell under his sway. We would not see his like again.

Masood met us at Egham. "Earl Marshal, they occupy the castle but they have a mighty camp before it too."

My grandfather punched his right fist into his left palm. "Then we have him! He has to fight us. How many knights?"

Duke Richard reined his horse in next to my father. Masood looked at him and then returned his gaze to the Earl Marshal, "I counted more than two hundred banners. They have crossbows in the castle and I counted enough horses to mount five hundred men."

Duke Richard said, "Then we outnumber him!"

It was his lack of experience which spoke. Even I saw the nonsense of his words. The Earl Marshal gave a pointed look to my father who explained, "Not in the key area. They have two hundred knights and three hundred sergeants at arms. These are all veterans and they are mounted on good horses. They scoured the land to get them. In addition, these have fought the Seljuk Turk. They will not be easy to beat. We have one hundred knights and barely fifty men at arms. Will the fyrd stand against heavy cavalry?"

Realisation dawned and I saw the young prince subside in his saddle, "Then how do we defeat them!"

My grandfather gave him a sad smile, "We use me as bait. There is a deer park to the north of the castle. The river is beyond it. We put the fyrd and archers in the park and array our men before it. De Mamers will attack us."

"We fight defensively?"

"If we wish to win then aye."

"But if the river is so close might not the fyrd flee?"

"They might but would you wish them to die just so that we can charge?"

"They are my father's subjects. They should be honoured to do so."

"And your father is in France. These are the people who have to grub a living despite harsh winters, hot summers and overbearing taxes. I brought them to hide our archers. I would not wish one of them to die this day. It is we who are the warriors and not they. Today the battle will be decided by warriors. Daylight is wasting. We ride."

Our men at arms and archers were no fools and they knew that my grandfather was ill. They rode close together and there was none of the normal banter which accompanied our men. The mood was reflective. My father kept glancing over to the Earl Marshal. I knew what he was thinking. It was all the undone years. He was thinking of the time when there had been a split between them. My father admitted that it was his fault but you could not go back and change events. You lived with them and they haunted your dreams. Ever since then the duty both men owed to their King and country had meant they had not seen as much of each other as they might have wished. I felt blessed. Of late I had not left my grandfather's side. I had cherished each moment. Every word and each conversation was etched into my mind for when he was gone I would have just a memory. I determined that as soon as he was old enough I would tell Thomas of his great grandfather. He would be the warlord of the future. That mantle would pass to my father and thence to me. My family understood duty and loyalty better than most men. It had cost us dear.

We kept close to the river as we headed west. Masood had already told us that their camp lay between the castle and the town. Our arrival would be seen but it would take them time to move men around to face us. My father was worried about Duke Richard. He told me that when in France the Duke had seemed happy to obey my father's commands but since he had arrived in England he appeared to be more intent upon building his own reputation. The plan of the Earl Marshal relied upon drawing our enemy to us and letting our archers thin them while our men at arms held them at bay.

When we reached the castle, we saw that the standard which flew was that of Hubert de Mamers. He had not yet declared for his true master. Perhaps our victories had weakened his resolve. If we could win this day then that threat would be gone. The fyrdmen were marched into the eaves of the wood which was the royal hunting park. The archers had left their horses just five miles from the park. The fyrd were strung out for miles along the road. The fact that they would be arriving when the battle was joined did not worry us. The reinforcements would bolster the ones who had arrived first. What we were doing was disguising our archers. The whole land knew of the skill of the archers of the north. The enemy would look for them but they would be hidden in plain sight amongst the fyrd. We took our place in the centre of the line. Duke Richard and his knights lined up on the right. Sir Ranulf, the Earl of Essex and the rest line up on the left. The men at arms dismounted and tethered their horses in the woods. They then took their spears and formed a double line before us. We had too few for three lines. To aid them we had brought caltrops from the armoury of the tower. The men at arms surreptitiously seeded the ground before them. They would break up the first assault. The knights we had brought from home, Sir James, Sir Padraig, Sir Morgan, Sir Gilles, Sir Richard: all of them flanked the Earl Marshal. They would protect him during the battle.

We heard horns. Our battle plan relied on de Mamers wishing to fight us. If he retired to the castle then we were in trouble for it was a mighty castle. The Earl Marshal was calmness personified. He looked around him and smiled at all that he saw. He spoke to the men at arms using their names and recalling the warriors they had known. He spoke of battles past in which they had fought. He laughed and he joked. He stroked White Star often. Mostly, however, he looked over to me and then to my father.

"One day your son Thomas will ride behind you, Samuel. He will go to war. His mother may not like that but for you, it will be a proud day. I remember when I went to war with your father clinging to a palfrey. Aye, we drubbed the Scots that day."

My father smiled at the memory, "Much as my son rode behind me against the Scots too."

The Earl Marshal nodded, "We are at peace with the Scots now but I know in my heart that it will not last. I have fought them for the last time but you, my son, will have to put them in their place again for they are ever desperate to claim that which has never been theirs. Stephen gave it away once and they seem to think it was a gift for life!"

Just then Brian shouted, "Warlord. They come!"

The gates to the castle opened as men began to filter around from the east and west. They were all mounted. My grandfather seemed pleased, "They have taken the bait and, so far as these old eyes can see, there are no crossbows." He turned, "Go and tell Aelric to get into position."

With the men at arms before us and our line of fifteen horsemen, Aelric and his archers would be able to move and stand behind us. They would be hidden from view. Before they were moved into their final position then the enemy would have to commit to the charge. I wheeled my palfrey from the line. The woods were a sea of faces. I had yet to don my helmet and my coif hung over my shoulders. I saw Aelric and Atheling speaking with those of the fyrd who had bows.

"The Earl says to move into position."

Aelric nodded, "Lord there are another fifty archers in the fyrd. Some serve with your father and grandfather. I would have them fight alongside us. It will double our attack."

I nodded, "Make it so!" I wheeled and rode back to the standards. "Aelric is using the archers from the fyrd."

"That is good." My grandfather smiled at me, "That is the result of good training and trust. Keep those in mind and you will do well, Samuel."

"I have learned much from you and I would that I could continue to learn."

"As would I but…"

Just then we heard another horn and saw the enemy dividing into three battles. The centre one was the smallest and made up of the knights and their squires. The other two were larger and made up of sergeants at arms. I heard my grandfather chuckle. "He comes for me then."

"Do not worry, grandfather. We will protect you."

He turned suddenly, "You will do no such thing. I do not wish to die today but if this is meant to be then I will die fighting. The alternative is for me to return to my chamber, close my eyes and then one day never to wake up. Wulfric did not enjoy that end and nor will I."

I knew then that this was my grandfather's choice. He had chuckled for he saw an opportunity to die as he had lived, on his terms. Death was another enemy and he would defeat him just as he had defeated all the others. Would I be able to face death as stoically?

A horn sounded and the three battles moved forward. One disadvantage of our position was that the battlefield was wide and suited the enemy. The two battles of men at arms moved east and west respectively so that they could charge our knights. The enemy knights came at a slower pace.

My father shouted, "Now Aelric. They are committed."

The archers filtered through our horses and took up a position behind the men at arms. The fyrd archers did not have bodkin arrows but their hunting arrows would do damage to horses. As they took up their positions I saw that Aelric had divided the fyrd into two and they flanked the Stockton archers. Atheling commanded one band of fyrd and Henry Warbow the other. I felt the ground shake as the horses increased their speed. Our knights would wait until the last moment to counter charge. I was confident that they would see off the sergeants at arms. The danger lay in the knights. They outnumbered our men at arms and despite the caltrops and the archers, I knew that many would penetrate our lines and when they did that gap could be exploited.

I donned my helmet and swung my shield around. The Earl Marshal, although he was not going to fight, did the same. After fifty years it was hard to lose old habits. We would not be using spears. The enemy lances would be shattered by the time they reached us; if they reached us. I heard Roger of Bath shout, "Lock shields and brace!" The spear butt would be pressed against their right foot and the spear supported by the shield arm. I had faced knights on foot before now and knew that it took a special kind of courage. Our men had that.

Aelric shouted, "Nock!" Even as he nocked his own arrow he looked down the line. "Draw!" The noise of the double line of bows being pulled back was audible. It was as though the bows were alive. When the arrows were released it would be a satisfied sigh we all heard. I had witnessed this often enough to anticipate the sounds. Then there would be the sight of a hundred goose fletched missiles heading up into the air before descending to wreak havoc on the advancing men. "Release!" Almost as soon as the arrows were in the air I heard him shout, "Nock!" This was for the benefit of the fyrd. They were being given a master class in archery. When the battle was over their shoulders and arms would burn for they were fighting alongside the elite.

The fyrd's arrows did not travel as far as our archers but Aelric had compensated for that and given the order when the enemy warriors were closer than they would normally be. I saw horses struck. Only one horse actually fell. The wounded ones, however, twisted and turned as they tried to rid themselves of the barbed irritant. Two squires tumbled from their saddles. I saw other arrows embed themselves into the mail of knights. Some would have struck flesh but the riders were ignoring the irritation.

As I glanced to my right I saw and heard the clash as Duke Richard led his men to charge into the sergeants at arms. Our knights had lances and they used them well. They shattered and they shook the enemy. Sergeants fell from their saddles. Horses were impaled. Some reared and some fell. There was a similar picture to the left. Then my attention was drawn to the centre where the first horses discovered the caltrops. Their riders spurred them. They were warhorses. Two reared and threw their riders but the rest continued on their way.

I saw knights rise in their saddles to pull back their arms and to punch with their spears. It was what I had been trained to do. There was a crack like thunder as wood met wood. Inevitably there were casualties on both sides. Knights fell, horses were speared, men at arms died. Henry son of Watt fell as did Richard of Ely. They were to the left of Roger of Bath and there was suddenly a gap in our front rank. The second rank were not made up of our men. They too died but I did not know their names.

Roger of Bath roared, "Reform! Hold them!"

The Earl Marshal suddenly said, "Fool!" I looked to where he gazed. Duke Richard had broken the enemy. Instead of coming to our aid, he and his knights were pursuing the survivors as they raced back to the castle. Even worse a large contingent of the fyrd had followed and were streaming across the flat ground to ransack the dead. What might have been a victory was suddenly taking on the aspect of a defeat.

On the other side, Sir Ranulf and the Earl of Essex had obeyed orders. They were still fighting against the men at arms but they were also applying pressure to the right-hand side of the enemy knights. The battle hung in the balance. We were helpless to intervene.

My father shouted, "There, I see the standard of de Mamers and that of D'Oilli. They have made a wedge."

Others had broken our line of men at arms and the enemy leadership exploited it. Roger of Bath had only managed to strengthen the side closest to Sir Ranulf. Duke Richard's reckless charge had exposed the other men at arms and I watched in horror as Tom the Badger was cut down by Hubert de Mamers. Our archers were doing their best but the knights neared the archers of the fyrd. It was too much to expect them to stand against charging knights. Henry Warbow tried to rally them but when he was speared by D'Oilli's squire they bolted. Suddenly holes appeared all the way along our lines. Sir Padraig and Sir Morgan rode to fill one hole. Sir Gilles and Sir Richard a second. Wherever a hole appeared a knight of the valley and his squire rode to plug it.

De Mamers shouted, "Now I shall have vengeance old man!"

He and another three knights, including D'Oilli rode at my grandfather. I only had a palfrey but it mattered not. I spurred the animal and he leapt forward. I swung my sword and it rang against Hubert de Mamers' just as he was about to strike the Earl Marshal.

"You shall not occupy me long, pup!"

I saw, through my eyehole, that my father was fighting D'Oilli and that William and Thomas had placed themselves next to my grandfather. I swung my palfrey's head around and blocked the next strike from de Mamers. I had also placed my horse and myself between the rogue knight and the Earl Marshal. To get to my grandfather he would have to go through me!

De Mamers had a superior horse and it snapped and bit at my poor palfrey. I was finding it hard to control the animal. My only advantage was that I had the higher ground. I stood in my stirrups and brought my sword over as hard as I could. De Mamers had quick hands and he brought his sword around backhanded to smash into my side. The breath went from me as my ribs were broken. My sword connected with his helmet and I saw that I had not only dented it but that it was cracked. The blow had made him turn slightly.

The rest of the battlefield disappeared and all that I saw was the distance from my hand to the tip of my sword. De Mamers sought to exploit my wound and he turned his horse to swing at my damaged ribs. I wheeled my palfrey and blocked the blow with my shield. At the same time, I spurred my horse so that I was closer to the knight. If the battle continued like this then I would lose. I kicked my left leg free from my stirrup and then I launched myself over my cantle at the surprised Hubert de Mamers. He was not expecting me to do that. Miraculously I pulled my right foot from the stirrup and we crashed heavily to the ground. The traitor was unable to get his right leg from his stirrup and his horse fell upon his leg. I heard the knight grunt in pain. The fall made me roll over the horse's rump.

My ribs were hurting but I forced myself to struggle to my feet. De Mamers had the luck of the devil. Even as he pulled his foot free his horse rose and galloped off. De Mamers damaged helmet had also fallen. He saw my grandfather and lunged at him. William was in the way of the blow and I saw blood spurt as his chausse was torn. I screamed in rage and brought my sword down on to de Mamers' sword. It struck the ground and I backhanded my sword towards his chest. I hit him and, with a weakened right leg he could not keep his balance. He fell.

I ran to him and raised my sword to end the life of this traitor.

He must have recognised my intent for he shouted, "I yield!"

I heard his words but I was so angry that my sword continued its arc. My grandfather's voice made it halt. "Samuel, he has surrendered. You cannot continue the strike."

I was panting and I was angry but this was the Earl Marshal who commanded me. I took off my helmet so that he could see the anger in my eyes. "Then drop your sword!" His fingers released his sword. I picked it up and handed it to my grandfather. "You are lucky you snake! The Earl Marshal has just saved your life."

I looked up as there was a cry and D'Oilli fell backwards from his horse. My father had slain him. It was the end of the battle. Our men at arms took the surrender of many knights. Even more fled and this time they were pursued by Sir Ranulf, the Earl of Essex and the fyrd. Our archers and men at arms had paid a terrible price protecting the Earl Marshal and none of them were in a position to do anything other than regain their breath.

My grandfather handed the sword to Thomas. After taking off his helmet he started to dismount. I saw that William was being tended to by a healer. My father dismounted. He took off his helmet. I lowered my coif. The air felt cool. The Earl Marshal looked in pain although he had not been wounded. He saw my look and said, "The pain came again but I saw the future, Samuel. You are the knight who will save England long after your father and I are dead. Men will speak your name and when they do their words will be filled with awe."

I shook my head, "I just did that which you taught me."

"Then I did it well."

I looked at the healer, "How is my squire?"

"He will live. The blow missed anything vital. He will limp for a while and it will itch but that is all."

One of the captured knights helped Hubert de Mamers to his feet. I saw that one leg had been hurt by the falling horse. I heard hooves and, looking up saw Duke Richard. He had taken off his helmet and he was grinning, "A great victory, Earl Marshal!"

My grandfather shook his head, "And would have been even greater had you not disobeyed my orders." He pointed to the dead bodies of Aelric, Roger of Bath and Atheling who had fallen in the last mêlée. "These brave men would be alive if you had done as I commanded."

"I am the son of the King! I do not answer to any."

"And I am the Earl Marshal of England and I do command! Shame on you sir!"

All eyes were on my grandfather and the red-faced Duke. I sensed it but did not see it as Hubert de Mamers suddenly launched himself at my grandfather. His dagger entered the back of the Earl Marshal.

"No!" I still had my sword in my hand and in one blow I took the head of the treacherous knight. Almost instinctively I swung to my right as the other knight who had surrendered pulled a dagger from his belt. I took his head too and then throwing my sword to the ground I knelt by my grandfather. My father rushed to his side too.

"Healer!"

I rolled my grandfather over and he looked at me. He held my left hand with his right one, "Tell your father it is too late." The healer grabbed a cloth and held it to the wound to stem the bleeding. "I am dying. It will not be the sleep which lasts forever which takes me. I died in battle. Thank you, Samuel. You behaved with honour. It was de Mamers who showed his true colours. William, you have been the best of sons and Samuel is the best of grandsons."

I smiled, "I am the only one!"

He looked over my shoulder and said, "Perhaps." He closed his eyes and I thought him dead. Then he opened them again. "I do not like to be a bother but I would be buried with my wife in Stockton. Dick, Wulfric and Edward will be there. I shall be in good company." I noticed his voice was getting weaker. The healer shook his head.

My father said, "I am sorry for the times I let you down, father."

"You did not. You made the mistakes all young men make. I did the same. Samuel, it seems does not make mistakes. He is the perfect knight."

I found myself crying. I was unmanned, "Do not go, grandfather! I still have much to learn."

He sighed, "Then you must learn it without me for I have comrades to meet." He looked to the skies. "I come, my love I…"

His eyes closed and the Earl Marshal of England, Alfred, Knight of the Empress and Warlord of the North died. He would never be replaced. All over the battlefield men from both sides dropped to their knees as the word was spread. This was the end of someone who had changed England for all time. He had made kings and princes and been laid low by a treacherous knight. A legend had fallen and I looked to the skies for I expected some sign from heaven.

My father eventually pulled me to my feet. "Come, my son. We have one more task to perform. The Earl Marshal gave us a command." He glared at Duke Richard, "And we will obey that command. We will take our sire home to Stockton and do him the honour which he deserves." He pointed to the dead men at arms and archers. "And we will take those back too. Healers, I wish these bodies preserved. We have a long journey home."

I thought that they might object for it would involve much work but one look at my father's face made them reconsider. It was dark by the time we were ready to leave. Duke Richard and the other knights could deal with the aftermath of the battle. We were done with all of that. We had a hero to bury.

Epilogue

The day we buried the Earl Marshal and the others who had fallen at the battle of Windsor was a cold one. A blue sky seemed to echo the surcoat of my grandfather and the cold wind seemed appropriate for we were at the edge of England. It was hard men who lived here and none had been harder than my grandfather. The Archbishop of York came to speak over him and to see all was done well. The tiny church my grandfather had built was packed but it was just family and those, like Alice, Alf and William, Aiden, Edgar and Edward who gathered within. The outside of the church was a sea of mourners: the folk from the town and every manor within twenty miles had come to pay their respects. The men at arms and archers, the knights of the valley, their family and their squires, all were gathered for it was such a momentous occasion that it was as though a king had died. I saw Alice weeping uncontrollably as she was comforted by William the old steward.

The journey home had been a long and tortuous one and all my tears were shed before we reached the Tees. We had spent a few hours in London. It allowed me to thank Mary Soft Breast and the tapster for all that they had done. They asked me if they would be allowed to call their inn the Earl Marshal and I readily agreed. I knew that my grandfather would have approved. The people I had met made me reassess my view of Londoners. Most were venal but there were enough decent folk left to give us hope. It was while we were resting in London and having wagons found to take back our bodies that news of the Abbot of the Augustine Friars was sent to us. Duke Richard had found him cowering in the wine cellar of the castle at Windsor. He had convened a trial and the Abbot was condemned for his treachery. His head joined the mercenaries on the walls of the city. Duke Richard, Sir Ranulf and the Earl of Essex had continued to hunt down the hired swords. After Hubert de Mamers' treacherous act none were given the opportunity to surrender.

On the journey up the Great North Road, my father had told me that he was done with warring for the King. He would protect the north from the ravages of the Scots but he would not leave England again. I did not think that I would either. I was wrong but unlike the Earl Marshal, I could not see into the future. That page had yet to be writ. Riders had travelled ahead to warn the families that we were bringing home the dead and that the Warlord was coming home for the last time. From York north, the road was lined with those who wished to witness the passing of the Warlord. Most had never even seen my grandfather but all knew his story. Everyone understood the part he had played in saving England. I was touched. I knew that he would have not wished the accolades but I was proud to ride behind the wagon with his body. I was part of a dynasty. I knew then that I had to ensure that my son, Thomas, learned to live up to the high standards set by the Earl Marshal.

My sister was on one side of me in the church and my son Thomas between me and my wife. I had my arm around his shoulders and I felt his body shake as he wept. My grandfather had spent as much time as he could with my son but it was still not enough. Thomas had seen just two years but his grandfather had been a major part of that time. A lifetime would not have been enough. The Archbishop's words seemed to come in waves. I heard some of them but I could not take my eyes from his body. Mailed and with his sword, he lay in the stone coffin. When the lid was placed on the top I would never see him again. I want to etch every detail into my memory.

My father tapped my shoulder. I was suddenly aware that the Archbishop had finished and was gesturing for us to go closer. Sir James, Sir John, Sir Morgan and Sir Padraig joined me as we went to the carved stone lid. The stonemason, old Leofric's grandson, had not finished yet but he would continue to work on the inscription and decoration while my grandfather slept. We all gripped the stone lid and my father nodded. We strained and lifted. It was heavy. Carefully we walked to the coffin and I saw the peaceful smiling face of my grandfather. He had been smiling when he had died. He must have seen my grandmother for he had said, *'I come, my love'*. It gave me comfort that they would be together in heaven. He had been shriven before the battle and he died with God's grace. I wondered if he would meet his old comrades, his father, his mentor Wulfstan, the ones who had helped to make him. I knew that if they did meet then the honour would be theirs for the greatest Englishman had done his duty and died as he had lived, fighting for his king and for England.

I said, quietly, as the lid was slid into place, "Farewell grandfather. If I can be a quarter of the man you were I shall be pleased."

The others, my father included just said, "Amen to that."

The Earl Marshal was laid to rest and England was not quite the place it had been when he had lived.The End

Glossary

Aldeneby - Alston (Cumbria)

Al-Andalus- Spain

Angevin- the people of Anjou, especially the ruling family

Arthuret -Longtown in Cumbria (This is the Brythionic name)

Bannau Brycheiniog – Brecon Beacons

Battle- a formation in war (a modern battalion)

Booth Castle – Bewcastle north of Hadrian's Wall

Bachelor knight- an unattached knight

Banneret- a single knight

Burn- stream (Scottish)

Butts- targets for archers

Cadge- the frame upon which hunting birds are carried (by a codger-hence the phrase old codger being the old man who carries the frame)

Caerdyf- Cardiff

Caparison- a surcoat for a horse; often padded for protection

Captain- a leader of archers

Chausses - mail leggings. (They were separate- imagine lady's stockings rather than tights!)

Cheap- Anglo Saxon market- hence Cheapside

Chevauchée- a raid by mounted men

Coningestun- Coniston

Conroi- A group of knights fighting together. The smallest unit of the period

Corebricg – Corbridge

Cuneceastra- Chester-Le-Street

Demesne- estate

Destrier- warhorse

Doxy- prostitute

Dyflin- Dublin

Dùn Èideann- Edinburgh

Fissebourne- Fishburn County Durham

Farenberg-Farnborough

Fess- a horizontal line in heraldry

Galloglass- Irish mercenaries

Gambeson- a padded tunic worn underneath mail. When worn by an archer they came to the waist. It was more of a quilted jacket but I have used the term freely

Gonfanon- A standard used in medieval times (Also known as a Gonfalon in Italy)

Hartness- the manor which became Hartlepool

Hautwesel- Haltwhistle

Hovel- a temporary shelter used by knights and men at arms on campaign

Hulle- Rhyl (North Wales)

Kingeston- Kingston upon Thames

Liedeberge- Ledbury

Lusitania- Portugal

Mansio- staging houses along Roman Roads

Mare anglicum – English Channel

Maredudd ap Bleddyn- King of Powys

Martinmas- 11th November

Mêlée- a medieval fight between knights

Mohald -Mold (Flintshire)

Morthpath- Morpeth (Northumbria)

Moravians- the men of Moray

Mormaer- A Scottish lord and leader

Mummer- an actor from a medieval tableau

Musselmen- Muslims

Nithing- A man without honour (Saxon)

Nomismata- a gold coin equivalent to an aureus

Novo Burgus -Newport (Gwent)

Outremer- the kingdoms of the Holy Land

Owain ap Gruffudd- Son of Gruffudd ap Cynan and King of Gwynedd from 1137

Palfrey- a riding horse

Poitevin- the language of Aquitaine

Prestetone- Prestatyn- North Wales

Pyx- a box containing a holy relic (Shakespeare's Pax from Henry V)

Refuge- a safe area for squires and captives (tournaments)

Sauve qui peut – Every man for himself (French)

Serengford- Shellingford Oxfordshire

Sergeant-a leader of a company of men at arms

Striguil- Chepstow (Gwent)

Sudweca -Southwark

Surcoat- a tunic worn over mail or armour

Sumpter- packhorse

Theophany- the feast which is on the 6th of January
Ventail – a piece of mail which covered the neck and the lower face
Veðrafjǫrðr -Waterford (Ireland)
Veisafjǫrðr- Wexford (Ireland)
Witenestaple- Whitstable (Kent)
Wulfestun- Wolviston (Durham)

Background to the novel

This is almost the end of the series that began with English Knight. It is a work of fiction set against a historically, generally, background. For those who have read all of the books in the series, thank you for travelling this road. As you can see I have taken out the end section. It had grown too much and can now be found on my website under background to the anarchy novels.

If you have enjoyed this saga and wish to see what happens next then Thomas, Sir Samuel's son is the hero of my Border Knight series which begins with Sword for Hire.

Books used in the research:

- Chronicles of the age of chivalry- Elizabeth Hallam
- The Varangian Guard- 988-1453 Raffael D'Amato
- Saxon Viking and Norman- Terence Wise
- The Walls of Constantinople AD 324-1453-Stephen Turnbull
- Byzantine Armies- 886-1118- Ian Heath
- The Age of Charlemagne-David Nicolle
- The Normans- David Nicolle
- Norman Knight AD 950-1204- Christopher Gravett
- The Norman Conquest of the North- William A Kappelle
- The Knight in History- Francis Gies
- The Norman Achievement- Richard F Cassady
- Knights- Constance Brittain Bouchard
- Knight Templar 1120-1312 -Helen Nicholson
- Feudal England: Historical Studies on the Eleventh and Twelfth Centuries- J. H. Round
- Armies of the Crusades- Helen Nicholson
- Knight of Outremer 1187- 1344 - David Nicholle
- Crusader Castles in the Holy Land- David Nicholle
- The Crusades- David Nicholle
- Bamburgh Castle Heritage group
- Warkworth Castle- English Heritage Guide
- The Times Atlas of World History
- Old Series Ordnance Survey Maps #93 Middlesbrough
- Old Series Ordnance Survey Maps #81 Alnwick and Morpeth

- Old Series Ordnance Survey Maps #92 Barnard Castle

For those who like authentic maps, the last two maps are part of a series now available. They are the first Government produced maps of the British Isles. Great Britain, apart from the larger conurbations, was the same as it had been 800 years earlier.

I also discovered a good website http://orbis.stanford.edu/. This allows a reader to plot any two places in the Roman world and if you input the mode of transport you wish to use and the time of year it will calculate how long it would take you to travel the route. I have used it for all of my books up to the eighteenth century as the transportation system was roughly the same. The Romans would have been quicker! I used it in this book and according to Orbis the journey from London to Rouen would have taken 2.7 days! In summer it would have been 3.1! it is an impressive resource. It explains why Henry gets to and from Normandy so quickly.

Griff Hosker
July 2018

Other books by Griff Hosker

If you enjoyed reading this book, then why not read another one by the author?

Ancient History

The Sword of Cartimandua Series
(Germania and Britannia 50 A.D. – 128 A.D.)
Ulpius Felix- Roman Warrior (prequel)
The Sword of Cartimandua
The Horse Warriors
Invasion Caledonia
Roman Retreat
Revolt of the Red Witch
Druid's Gold
Trajan's Hunters
The Last Frontier
Hero of Rome
Roman Hawk
Roman Treachery
Roman Wall
Roman Courage

The Wolf Warrior series
(Britain in the late 6th Century)
Saxon Dawn
Saxon Revenge
Saxon England
Saxon Blood
Saxon Slayer
Saxon Slaughter
Saxon Bane
Saxon Fall: Rise of the Warlord

Saxon Throne
Saxon Sword

Medieval History

The Dragon Heart Series
Viking Slave
Viking Warrior
Viking Jarl
Viking Kingdom
Viking Wolf
Viking War
Viking Sword
Viking Wrath
Viking Raid
Viking Legend
Viking Vengeance
Viking Dragon
Viking Treasure
Viking Enemy
Viking Witch
Viking Blood
Viking Weregeld
Viking Storm
Viking Warband
Viking Shadow
Viking Legacy
Viking Clan
Viking Bravery

The Norman Genesis Series
Hrolf the Viking
Horseman
The Battle for a Home
Revenge of the Franks
The Land of the Northmen

Earl Marsha

Ragnvald Hrolfsson
Brothers in Blood
Lord of Rouen
Drekar in the Seine
Duke of Normandy
The Duke and the King

Danelaw
(England and Denmark in the 11th Century)
Dragon Sword
Oathsword (October 2021)

New World Series
Blood on the Blade
Across the Seas
The Savage Wilderness
The Bear and the Wolf
Erik The Navigator

The Vengeance Trail

The Reconquista Chronicles
Castilian Knight
El Campeador
The Lord of Valencia

The Aelfraed Series
(Britain and Byzantium 1050 A.D. - 1085 A.D.)
Housecarl
Outlaw
Varangian

**The Anarchy Series England
1120-1180**
English Knight
Knight of the Empress

Earl Marsha

Northern Knight
Baron of the North
Earl
King Henry's Champion
The King is Dead
Warlord of the North
Enemy at the Gate
The Fallen Crown
Warlord's War
Kingmaker
Henry II
Crusader
The Welsh Marches
Irish War
Poisonous Plots
The Princes' Revolt
Earl Marshal

Border Knight
1182-1300
Sword for Hire
Return of the Knight
Baron's War
Magna Carta
Welsh Wars
Henry III
The Bloody Border
Baron's Crusade
Sentinel of the North
War in the West
Debt of Honour

Sir John Hawkwood Series
France and Italy 1339- 1387
Crécy: The Age of the Archer
Man At Arms

The White Company

Lord Edward's Archer
Lord Edward's Archer
King in Waiting
An Archer's Crusade
Targets of Treachery (August 2021)

Struggle for a Crown
1360- 1485
Blood on the Crown
To Murder A King
The Throne
King Henry IV
The Road to Agincourt
St Crispin's Day

Tales from the Sword I (Short stories from the Medieval
period)

Conquistador
England and America in the 16th Century
Conquistador (November 2021)

Modern History

The Napoleonic Horseman Series
Chasseur à Cheval
Napoleon's Guard
British Light Dragoon
Soldier Spy
1808: The Road to Coruña
Talavera
The Lines of Torres Vedras
Bloody Badajoz
The Road to France

Earl Marsha

Waterloo

The Lucky Jack American Civil War series
Rebel Raiders
Confederate Rangers
The Road to Gettysburg

The British Ace Series
1914
1915 Fokker Scourge
1916 Angels over the Somme
1917 Eagles Fall
1918 We will remember them
From Arctic Snow to Desert Sand
Wings over Persia

Combined Operations series
1940-1945
Commando
Raider
Behind Enemy Lines
Dieppe
Toehold in Europe
Sword Beach
Breakout
The Battle for Antwerp
King Tiger
Beyond the Rhine
Korea
Korean Winter

Tales from the Sword II (Short storis from the Modern period)

Other Books
Great Granny's Ghost (Aimed at 9-14-year-old young people)

For more information on all of the books then please visit the author's website at www.griffhosker.com where there is a link to contact him or visit his Facebook page: GriffHosker at Sword Books

Printed in Great Britain
by Amazon